Beginn

co

THE DOUBLE-SPIRAL WAR

In the long centuries following man's dispersal into space, humanity divided into two mighty powers destined to meet in a vast and tragic confrontation. *Midway Between* chronicles the first decisive battle of that total war, when one small star system became a pawn in an interstellar game of life and death . . .

On a vast and bloody battlefield of stars, a handful of players fought for the fate of a galaxy. . . .

FRYE CHARLTOS: U.C.S.'s most brilliant military strategist, turned by tragedy into a ruthless killer.

MARSHALL JUDOFF: Leader of a band of mercenary irregulars, driven by pride to betray Charltos's battleplan.

CAPT. BENJAMIN "LUCKY" TEEMAN: Smuggler, pirate and outlaw forced by fate, and his own conscience, to choose sides in the war.

MARSHA YEDNOSHPFA: Lucky's friend and lover, torn from his side by ties of blood and honor.

AYNE WALLEN: Gifted physicist seeking the key to the ultimate weapon—to sell to the highest bidder.

A few courageous souls—men and women, human and alien—who gambled with billions of lives:

ADM. JOSIAH GILBERT: Sondak's ablest commander, and Charltos's oldest opponent, willing to wage a brutal battle to avert an all-out war.

CAPT. MICA GILBERT: Assigned by her father to seek out a spy, torn between emotions of loyalty—and love.

HEW ROCHMON: Head of Sondak's military intelligence unit, disturbed by the threat of treason, and his unwanted feelings toward Mica.

LERI GISH GERIL: Decadent Proctor of the resource-rich alien world of Cloise.

EXETER: The Castorian diplomat who dared to oppose Leri and side with Sondak.

DELIGHTFUL CHILDE: An Oinaise space merchant pledged to neutrality, drawn to aid humanity by his code of ethics.

"Unlike so much science fiction, [*Midway Between*] conveys a sense of a future and of other worlds that are different from anything we know here and now. The nonhuman characters are indeed nonhuman—and the human ones are indeed human."
—*Poul Anderson*

"Tackling with ease a story that most writers only dream about, Norwood has managed to bring humanity and understanding to a vast array of sentient alien intellects, while at the same time showing us the horror and futility that is war. There are no good guys and bad guys in *Midway Between*; there is only the struggle to survive, only the anguished cries of souls caught in something beyond their control."
—*Mike McQuay*

MIDWAY BETWEEN

by
Warren
Norwood

BANTAM BOOKS
TORONTO • NEW YORK • LONDON • SYDNEY • AUCKLAND

MIDWAY BETWEEN

A Bantam Book / October 1984

Caricature of Warren Norwood by Mel White.
Maps by Robert J. Sabuda.
All rights reserved.
Copyright © 1984 by Warren Norwood.
Cover art copyright © 1984 by Frank Morris.
This book may not be reproduced in whole or in part, by mimeograph or any other means, without permission.
For information address: Bantam Books, Inc.

ISBN 0-553- 24440-X

Published simultaneously in the United States and Canada

Bantam Books are published by Bantam Books, Inc. Its trademark, consisting of the words "Bantam Books" and the portrayal of a rooster, is Registered in U.S. Patent and Trademark Office and in other countries. Marca Registrada. Bantam Books, Inc, 666 Fifth Avenue, New York, New York 10103.

PRINTED IN THE UNITED STATES OF AMERICA

0   0 9 8 7 6 5 4 3 2 1

For Margot,
who helped me through the beginning.

THE DOUBLE SPIRAL WAR:
MATTHEW'S SYSTEM

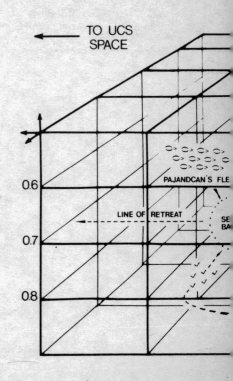

← TO UCS
SPACE

0.6

PAJANDCAN'S FLE

LINE OF RETREAT

SE
BA

0.7

0.8

UCS ATTACK
LINES ■ ■ ■

SONDAK
ATTACK
LINES

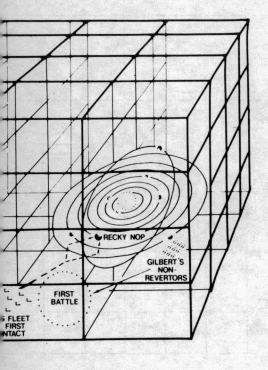

RECKY NOP

GILBERT'S
NON-
REVERTORS

FIRST
BATTLE

FLEET
FIRST
NTACT

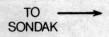

TO ——→
SONDAK

STYLIZED VIEW OF CAVENESS GALAXY FROM
THE SOUTHERN POLAR PERSPECTIVE

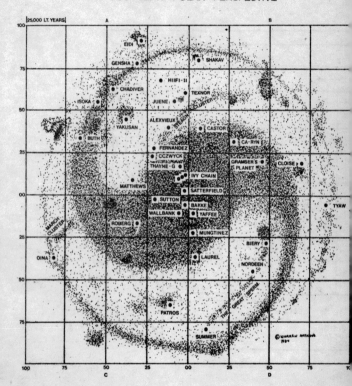

CHRONOLOGY

Ninety-two years after the signing of the treaty that officially ended the Unification Wars, Earth sent forth the first two-generation ships to seek new homes for mankind in the stars.

The *Bohr* and the *Heisenberg* together carried a total of three thousand seven hundred eighty-three pioneers and crew members. Each ship was powered by ten linked Hugh drives that eventually pushed them to a speed of one-point-four times the speed of light relative to Earth. At that speed their Benjamin drives took over and they crossed Einstein's Curve where relative speed could no longer be measured.

Two hundred forty-one ship years later the descendants of those first pioneers celebrated the thirtieth anniversary of their landing on the planet they named Biery after the woman who led their forebears from Earth. Much to their mixed surprise and fear, that celebration was interrupted by the landing of an alien ship containing a race called the Oinaise. To everyone's relief—including the Oinaise's—the contact was peaceful.

Nine years later the Kobler calendar was established and set the date of the first landing as New Year 2500. The following chronology gives a brief listing of major events dated according to that calendar.

2530—First contact with the Oinaise.

2575—First pioneers arrive on Nordeen, the most Earth-like of any planet ever discovered in the galaxy.

2599—Approximate date the last generation ship left Earth, carrying fourteen thousand new-human pioneers, genetically altered people known as *homo communis*, whose major difference from *homo sapiens* was a greatly extended longevity.

2648—The anti-intellectualist riots.

2657—Beginning of the early expansionist movement seeking other planets and stars systems suitable for human settlement.

2664—Last known message from Earth indicating war, famine, and increasing chaos.

2681—A group of Nordeen's brightest people call themselves *homo electus* and leave aboard the *Mensch* in search of what they hope will be a better home for the intellectually elite.

2723—The Gouldrive tested and proven. Marks the beginning of the Great Expansionist Movement, the settling of many independent systems, and the establishment of true interstellar trade. The phrase, "a planet for every clan," became popular at this time. During the whole movement scientific research and technological progress were extremely limited.

2774—News reaches Nordeen from the so-called *homo electus*'s first contact with the alien Verfen, a reclusive race inhabiting a cluster of star systems near the galaxy's center.

2784—First contact with the crab-like, methane breathing Castorians.

2846—Discovery of Cloise.

2862—Foundation of Sondak, a loose federation of fifty-eight sparsely inhabited planetary systems. *Homo electus* demanded and received recognition as a separate human race as the price of joining the federation.

2893—Foundation of the United Central Systems, twenty-seven planetary systems inhabited mostly by *homo communis*. The establishment of the U.C.S. marked the end of the Great Expansionist Movement.

3021—The first galactic war between Sondak and the U.C.S.

3024—The U.C.S., unable to match Sondak's capacity for producing the tools of war, sued for peace. After extended negotiations during which the fighting continued, the U.C.S. promised to pay heavy economic reparations to Sondak and the independent systems, and also agreed not to produce new war materials for one hundred years. Neither promise was kept.

3029—Seemingly spontaneous civil disorder broke out on several planets populated mostly by the fair skinned, racially distinct, politically fractious Pikeans. Although called by some the Pikean Civil War, the dissidents had neither the numbers nor the equipment to fight a true war, and consequently were forced to leave their home planets. Many of them chose to go to systems controlled by the U.C.S. where they quickly aligned themselves with the political factions that supported a new war with Sondak.

3033—The Cczwyck Skirmish occurred when U.C.S. Admiral Nance made an officially unauthorized attempt to take control of that independent system just as a Sondak border squadron was making a courtesy visit. There was no serious fighting, but the political repercussions caused the U.C.S. to accelerate its secret rearmament program; caused Sondak to increase its economic pressures on the U.C.S. and also on the independent systems that refused to join the confederation; and caused Cczwyck to become more isolationist.

3034-3042—Sporadic raids on U.C.S. chartered freighters by unknown agents are blamed on Sondak despite fierce diplomatic denials and a total lack of evidence.

3038—Long range plans begin in the U.C.S. for a new war against Sondak.

3046—The war begins.

MIDWAY BETWEEN

1

Frye Charltos read the battle reports with harshly conflicting emotions. So far the surprise attacks had worked almost exactly as he had planned them. He should have been pleased. Yesterday he would have been. Yesterday Doctor Nise had not called him with the final news. Yesterday there was still hope that Vinita might be cured of her disease. Yesterday was gone.

Today the combined task force of the United Central Systems had attacked six of Sondak's most outlying planets and destroyed most of their peripheral fleet. Today war had started between the two spirals of the galaxy, a war which Frye Charltos had been advocating and planning for years. Today was the beginning of freedom for the U.C.S.

Today was the beginning of the end for Vinita.

Frye shut off the microspooler. Leaning back in his chair, he closed his eyes and folded his long, pliant hands in his lap. As he thought about Vinita, he unconsciously clenched his fingers until they were locked in a rigid hammer of tan flesh which pounded softly against his thighs.

Vinita had tried to prepare him for this. She had known in some deep, interior way that she was dying. With that knowledge had come a peace that angered him almost as much as her disease did. To Frye it seemed as though she were giving up, refusing to fight this tragedy any longer. But Vinita had countered by saying it was better to live with the truth than to hide from it.

Frye smiled slightly, and his hands relaxed for a moment. She had thrown his own words back at him. "Live with the truth," he had told her when she finally understood after twenty years of marriage that he was first and foremost a soldier. "Live with the truth," she had said before she went to Nise-Kim Center for the last-chance tests.

The truth. The truth was that Frye had never loved anyone in his whole life like he loved Vinita. The truth was that he had promised to help her avoid the suffering she faced if these test results confirmed all the previous ones. The truth was that he had promised to kill his wife, and Frye Charltos did not want to live with the truth.

The microspooler's tiny bell binged rapidly; another set of battle reports had been received. Reluctantly Frye opened his eyes. One by one he blocked his emotions off from the immediate present in a way he had done so many times before. This was a great day for the U.C.S., and that was a larger truth than any personal tragedy he would ever face.

The eyes that read his microspooler were calm and professional. The brain that sorted and analyzed the reports concentrated solely on the task at hand. The voice that gave orders into the lapelcom he wore was the stern, controlled voice of Joint Force Commander Frye ed'Laitin Charltos. But deep beneath the conscious levels of his mind, a husband cried for his wife in the dry tears of despair.

*   *   *

Frenzy ruled in the Situation Room at Sondak's military headquarters on Nordeen. Scattered reports and pieces of information were coming in from bases on planets in six systems, each report, each fragment of description seemingly worse than the one which preceded it.

"Who's in charge here?" a harsh voice bellowed above the noise.

The sound level subsided like a landslide slowly coming to a halt. Suddenly a young captain looked up and saw General Mari standing just inside the door. "I am, sir," she said firmly with a salute from half-way across the room.

Other heads looked up, but when they saw Captain Gilbert turn away from the general, they went back to what they had been doing. The information flow did not stop just because a general walked into the room.

Trailed by two aides, General Mari strode quickly through the crowded room. Despite what appeared to be pandemonium when he had first entered the room, he could see little wasted effort as he made his way to the captain who had answered him. For the moment he would bite his tongue and find out what the hell was going on. Then he would chew that captain's ass up one side and down the other.

"Sorry, sir," Captain Gilbert said when the general was less than two steps away, "but I had to relay some information to BORFLEET Command before we lost our com-window."

"How bad is it?" Mari asked.

"If all this is true, sir, and I can only assume it is, then it's worse than bad. From the reports we have so far, I estimate that we have lost close to seventy-five percent of the Border Fleet either heavily damaged or totally destroyed."

"The Ukes?"

"Four confirmed reports say yes. Half-a-set of others still to be confirmed suggest the same."

"Damn. Damn, damn, damn. Who all have you notified?"

"Every major command and commander we could reach. We won't have a com-window for Polar Fleet for another two days, so we sent their message through Mungtinez Relay. Should have their acknowledgement in six hours or so."

"What makes you think they haven't been hit also?"

Captain Gilbert barely blinked. "I haven't had time for speculation, sir," she lied. "I can barely deal with the information I've got rolling in on me."

A com-tech demanded the captain's attention, and while she was dealing with the problem, Mari took another look around the room. The total shock of what had happened still had not reached him. He had been one of the leading voices arguing that the U.C.S. would never risk going to war with Sondak. The Ukes were still too dependent on Sondak resources and technology, he had said. They were also too bound by their traditions and culture to enter another war without a long period of loud diplomatic protests and internal rationalizations.

That's what Mari had argued, because that's what he believed. Now all his beliefs were being proved wrong in the worst possible way.

As that thought struck home, the shock of understanding struck with it. Mari was galvanized by anger. "Captain," he said just as Gilbert turned back to him, "I'll be in the Command Center. You will update all information as soon as you receive it, and send it there."

"I'm already doing that, sir. Admiral Stonefield has been in the Command Center for the past hour."

Mari was furious. "Why was he notified first?"

"Because he was in the building, sir."

Without a word General Mari turned and left the Situation Room. Captain Mica Gilbert watched him go without regret. All she needed was more top brass giving her orders and slowing down the work her understaffed crew was trying to get done. Moments later she was back in the middle of it, sorting through the new reports, giving new sets of instructions, and waiting for the one report that wasn't due for another six hours. Her father, Admiral Josiah Gilbert, was the commander of Polar Fleet.

                              *   *   *

Lucky Teeman stared in disbelief at the sight on his screens when his ship emerged from behind Ivan's Sun. What he should have seen was a set of navigational signals forming a grid he could follow to Roberg. Instead, his navscreens showed wavy lines and his lightspeed communications receiver was clanging on four frequencies.

It didn't make any sense, but Lucky had not come by his nickname casually. Luck, he had learned early in life, was making the best of every situation. He immediately reduced *Graycloud*'s speed and opened the first lightspeed communications channel. All he got was coded junk, so he switched to the second one. More of the same. The third channel yielded a voice babbling in a language Lucky didn't recognize. What he heard on the fourth channel chilled him to the core of his trader's heart.

It had finally happened. U.C.S. had finally declared war on Sondak. But of all places to do it, why Roberg? Almost as soon as he asked himself that question, he knew the answer. Roberg had a fleet repair base. It was so far off limits from everything Lucky was interested in on Roberg that he never really thought about its presence. Now it was important, very important.

The fleeties would be watching every incoming ship with sights trained on them. And when they let him land—if they let him land—they would be very interested in his cargo.

For a brief moment Lucky thought about spacing the two hundred crates of laser rifles now secured in *Graycloud*'s hold and letting them fall into Ivan's Sun. He immediately discarded that idea. Sure, they were U.C.S. laser rifles, but he had bought them on the open market. They were legitimate cargo, if you stretched the rules a little. And now that Sondak and U.C.S. were at war, he might have a better customer for the whole lot of them than he could ever have found on his own.

Sondak would need lots of new weapons, and in a hurry. Lucky would be the last person in the galaxy to be opposed to a little war-time profiteering. Best to contact the fleeties and tell them he was bringing help.

Four hours later he got through on an open channel. "I said this is the space trader *Graycloud*. I'm carrying a cargo—"

"From where?"

"From half-a-set of systems . . . sir," he added as an afterthought. "I think your commander will be interested in what I have to sell."

"You'll be lucky if he doesn't lock you up and swallow the key, the mood he's in," the voice responded. "What navbeacons are you receiving?"

"Seventeen, thirty-three, thirty-nine, and forty are coming in strong. The rest of it is garbage."

"Tough. Follow thirty-nine until you get an alpha signal. Brake and hold within a thousand kilometers of that spot. Don't deviate off your course, and don't move after you've stopped. We've got all our remaining pipe jockies on patrol, and they'd like nothing better than to blast something out of space. You got that?"

"I've got it. Now when—"

"Out." The receiver went dead for a moment, then the voice started giving instructions to some fancy passenger liner, and Lucky knew there was no use trying to get any more information.

He locked *Graycloud* on beacon thirty-nine and went back to the galley to get something to eat. No sense in waking Marsha, he decided. She had stood the long watch coming around Ivan's Sun. Besides, there was nothing so pressing that couldn't wait until she woke up.

Just as he finished cleaning up the galley after his meal, the alpha signal went off. It was much sooner than he expected, and by the time he got back to the cockpit, *Graycloud* was well on its way to violating the thousand kilometer limit.

He braked hard, but the dampers refused to absorb all the inertial energy. Moments after they came to a stop, Marsha was screaming at him from the companionway.

"What in the name of all that's holy are you trying to do, kill me?"

He looked up with a smile on his face, but she didn't give him a chance to answer.

"Sometimes I think you lived too damn long by yourself before I came along," she said as she crossed the cabin in her easy stride and sat in the chair next to him. "You better have a zimbo of an answer for that stupid maneuver."

"Sondak and U.C.S. just went to war."

"Don't give me that kind of—"

"Truth, Marsha. Look at the screens."

"Just because the screens are putting out garbage, you want me to believe that there's a war going on?"

"It's the truth, I'm telling you. The Ukes hit Roberg like they really meant it. The fleeties told us to park here and wait for further instructions, or . . . get blown to space dust. Thought I'd just park it like they said."

"You're serious, aren't you?" Her face wrinkled with sudden concern. "The Ukes really did it?"

"That's what the fleeties said. Who else would be crazy enough to attack them?"

Marsha waited a long moment before she said anything. "Lucky, do you trust me?"

"Lady, if you don't know the answer to that after five years of spacing together, I can't give you one now."

"We have to get out of here."

"What are you talking about?"

"We have to get out of here. We have to get back to U.C.S.-controlled space. Believe me, Lucky, it's important. It's our lives."

Now the concern was on both their faces. "What's so important to risk getting shot here as we head for Uke space and risk getting blasted there?"

"I can't tell you."

"The hell you can't. You want me to trust you on this, but you won't trust me? What kind of deal is that?"

"It's the only deal we can make. Please, Lucky, I made a promise, a promise I have to keep. As soon as I've kept it, I can tell you everything, but until then, you'll. . . ."

"I know. I'll just have to trust you." He looked at her, knew he loved her, and knew what he was about to do made no more sense than the garbage on the navscreens. "All right. I'll turn us around nice and easy. Then I'll blast us back toward Ivan's Sun at full throttle. You pray that those pipe jockeys out there aren't paying too much attention to us, and I'll pray that *Graycloud* holds together under the strain." He turned away from her and cut off the next thought in his mind.

"Thanks, Lucky."

"Don't thank me until we're safe. Then the only thanks I want will be in the form of information."

*   *   *

Frye saw the look on her face the moment he walked in the door and knew that she had talked to Doctor Nise. She waited until he was almost to her before she stood up. Vinita always greeted him standing up. It was one of those traditions which started early in their marriage and had stuck for twenty-five years. Now, even though standing was difficult, she insisted on maintaining the tradition. It made him love her all the more.

An observer watching them wrap themselves in each other's arms and kiss might have thought them newlyweds except there was no wasted motion, no frantic necessity in their embrace. It was a practiced passion that each of them cherished.

"Today was the day, wasn't it?" Vinita asked as Frye released her.

"Today was a monster," he said wearily.

"Not for me."

He looked at her with surprise as she sat down and the chair adjusted to her frail body.

"Don't look so shocked, darling. I've known about this for a long time. So have you. But I believed it. Now you must, too. What else made it a monster?"

"We attacked Sondak today," he said flatly.

Her eyes lit up. "Revenge? Revenge at last? That's wonderful, Frye! But how could you keep it a secret from me?"

"I don't know. It's the only secret I think I've ever been able to keep from you. I wanted it to be a surprise." He sat down beside her and took her hands in his. "When did you talk to Doctor Nise?"

"Before he called you."

"Oh." He heard the disappointment in his voice and wished he had known. "He didn't tell me he had talked to you."

"I told him not to."

"Did you tell him anything else?"

"Yes. I told him I wanted the special prescription. He sent it over, and it's—"

"We can talk about that later," Frye said as he released her hands and stood up. A huge chasm had opened inside him, and he was afraid that any moment he might fall in.

"I don't want to put it off much longer, Frye," she said quietly. "I don't want to go on like this. Today . . . today I had to write your name down because the first time I called Doctor Nise I couldn't remember it." She looked straight at him with anger burning in her eyes. "Do you understand that, Frye? I couldn't remember your name. I had to *write it down!*"

Suddenly she was crying, and he was beside her again, holding her in his arms. Never had he faced a more difficult decision nor one so impossible to come to terms with. This most precious of all women was deteriorating before his eyes. She wanted the only escape open to her from the madness that was eating away at her body and her mind, and he had agreed to help her with that escape.

When she finally stopped crying, she looked at him with an expression that he had to turn away from. "You promised me, Frye. You promised to help me before . . . before . . ."

"I know," he said softly as he rocked her gently in his arms. "I'll do what I said. Don't worry. I'll take care of you. I promise."

Dinner was quiet and intimate despite the fact that Vinita kept asking questions about the attack on Sondak. After dinner he told her all he could about the war, and she rejoiced that the U.C.S. was finally going to have revenge—the revenge it deserved for all that Sondak had done to the U.C.S.

Frye opened the vacuum bottle of liquor he had been saving for a special occasion. As they sipped the sweet liquor, their conversation gradually changed into reminiscence. Then from reminiscence it settled into the quiet, unspoken pleasure they had always enjoyed in each other's presence.

"Lisa Cay will be coming home now," Vinita said. "She'll be coming home to help you, Frye. You can count on her."

"I know," Frye responded with a tiny catch in his voice. "I've been thinking about that." As he refilled Vinita's glass with the last drops from the bottle, Frye added the contents of the small capsule Doctor Nise had sent to her.

"To victory," Vinita said after he handed her the glass.

"To love," Frye answered.

Later he carried her to bed as usual. Then he lay awake all night, holding his dead wife in his arms and crying until he had no tears left for anyone in the whole universe.

"That's what our cryptographers believe he said, sir," Rochmon said quietly.

"But you are not sure?"

"Nothing's positive in this business, General. All I can tell you is that we made a major breakthrough in the Ukes code about ten months ago."

"What kind of breakthrough?"

"We discovered they're using a cycling key in their routine subspace transmissions."

"A cycling key?"

Rochmon suppressed a sigh. He hated having to explain cryptography to staff officers. "That means they use a cycle of standard keys to encode their messages. Not very sophisticated, but difficult to break because the key changes at random times during the message. Anyway, since then we've been piecing lots of fragments together."

"How accurate is that?"

Rochmon bit off his response and took a frustrated breath. "Well, sir, we feel it is pretty yanqui accurate. What you have in your hands has been part of half a dump of messages to high ranking commanders in the past several cycles. The fact that it was repeated in so many interceptions was what led us three days ago to the second major break—one of the cycle keys."

General Mari frowned, then read the message aloud. "In the first year of the war . . . run wild over their systems. Victory will follow victory . . . build a stellar barrier which . . . be indestructible . . . no promise of success . . . not fully prepared for Sondak's counter attack. Then we will fight a battle of wills testing . . . willing to make the sacrifices necessary to defeat us, and whether we are . . . necessary to hold what we have gained.'"

General Mari placed the message carefully in front of him on the neat desk and loudly cleared his throat several times. "What about all the missing parts?"

"Key changes, sir. But I think what we have gives us a fairly good representation of their intent."

"Yes, I guess it does. How determined are we? And how determined are they? I guess Charltos asked two good questions, didn't he, Commander?"

"I'd say he did, sir. Charltos isn't the type to make threats lightly—not promises either."

"You talk like you know him."

Rochmon smiled slightly. "Not really, sir. I did meet him once, very formally when he visited Drahcir and I was the senior cryptographer there. But, well, General, I guess studying Commander Charltos has become a kind of hobby of mine. Seems like an interesting enemy to me. He's smart, and not just book smart, if you know what I mean."

"So what is your military assessment of him?"

For all that he disliked General Mari, Rochmon admired him as a soldier. There were few men among Sondak's military leadership who had General Mari's skill and understanding. Yet somewhere deep in his heart Rochmon knew that Mari was not equal to the opposition presented by Commander Frye Charltos.

"Well, sir, if you want my honest opinion, I'd say that not only are we up against the best strategist the Ukes have to offer, but we're also up against a man who understands the tactics of interstellar warfare better than anyone before him."

"You're discounting a great number of people when you say that, Commander."

Rochmon heard the quiet censorship in Mari's voice, but chose to ignore it. "I know that, sir, but you asked for my assessment. I've been following Charltos's career for the better part of fifteen years, and it seems to me that the only thing we have going for us at the moment is that he has a respect for life that may prove to be his weak point."

General Mari frowned. "Be specific, Rochmon."

"That's hard to do, General. It's just that from all that I've learned about him, I'd be willing to bet on the design of his overall strategy."

"Meaning what?"

"Meaning, General, that he will not risk any more lives on the Ukes' side than is absolutely necessary to obtain the victory he's promised them. That's the way he is. He'll fight for that victory—fight as hard and as well as any military commander we know about—but at the lowest possible cost in lives."

"I suppose you have a suggestion of how we can take advantage of that weakness?"

Rochmon didn't like the tone of Mari's voice, but that wasn't going to stop him from giving his opinion. "I do, sir, but I doubt if anyone is going to like it."

"Don't second-guess my reaction," Mari snapped. "Just tell me what you would do if you were in charge of overall strategy against Charltos."

"I'd back him into a corner every chance I got, sir. I'd raise the cost in lives as high as possible every time we faced the Ukes—in space or planetside."

"And you think he would back away?"

"Not necessarily, sir. But I think it would make him more cautious. The more cautious he becomes, the better our chances are of defeating the Ukes and whatever allies they pick up among the neutrals."

"So you are advocating a bloodbath."

"No, sir. Not at all. But I am saying we should make the Ukes pay in lives."

"As I said, a bloodbath. Thank you, Commander." General Mari turned and left the room.

Rochmon didn't like having his words twisted like that, but maybe the general was right. Yet when he thought of all the lives Sondak had lost already, he didn't care. Maybe he was advocating a bloodbath. But whatever anyone called it, Rochmon was sure it was the one tactic which gave Sondak a chance. He wasn't willing to bet on anything less.

*   *   *

Lucky Teeman stared at his viewscreens with the eyes of a man at once angry and confused. They had made good their escape from Roberg and dodged the fleeties through six warps. But now *Graycloud* was headed straight toward the most heavily fortified regions of Uke-controlled space.

And for what? That was the question which gnawed at Lucky's thoughts. Why was he doing this? Oh, sure, Marsha had asked him to, and that might have been reason enough for some other man. Marsha could charm the warp gyros off a fleety or intimidate the most arrogant bureaucrat if she wanted to.

No, there was more to it than the fact that she had almost begged him, and more than her promise of a future explanation. There was something deeper, something inside Lucky himself that he wasn't quite willing to admit out loud. But he knew what it was. He wanted the Ukes to win this war.

Lucky quickly shut down that thought and called Marsha on the vidcom. "We're entering Uke space," he said when her image appeared on the screen. "Want to give me some idea of what we're going to do next?"

"I'll be right there."

When she arrived in the flight cabin several minutes later she gave him a quick kiss before taking her seat beside him. Only then did Lucky notice the small star-map case in her hand. "What's that for?"

"The kiss? Or the case?"

Lucky snorted in mock amusement. "Both."

"The kiss is because I love you. The case holds the information we'll need to get where we're going."

"And do you think you can tell me where that is now?"

Marsha frowned ever so slightly and put one hand over his. "Not yet, Lucky, please? You'll just have to trust me a little longer. All right?"

"Tensheiss! No, it's not all right." Lucky reached out and slammed the emergency braking lever. The inertial dampers vibrated in protest.

"Lucky! Don't!"

"It's still my ship," he said calmly as he eased off on the braking lever, "and I'll do whatever I spacing well please until you give me some answers."

Marsha turned her chair so it faced him. "You won't like it," she said quietly.

He laughed. "I don't like it now!" Lucky glanced at the viewscreens and then at his summary instruments. When he looked back at her, he felt a small stirring of regret. "Look, Marsha, I'm sorry I yelled at you. But this is a partnership, remember? You have to trust me as much as I trust you."

"It is not a matter of trust," she said, looking down at the map case clutched in her hand.

"What is it then?"

"Loyalty. I was born on Chadiver. I was raised on a dozen planets, all a part of the United Central Systems. I'm a Uke, Lucky," she said looking him straight in the eyes.

"So? I guessed that a long time ago. What difference does that make?" As he looked at her, her gaze softened.

"Then . . . then you didn't believe what I told you about—"

"Not for a minute. Too many giveaways."

"And you took me on anyway?"

"That's pretty obvious," he said with a smile. "Why shouldn't I have taken you on? I was falling in love with you so fast I thought I was going to go spaceblind."

Marsha reached out and took his hand again. "I'm really sorry, Lucky."

"For what?"

"For not telling you earlier."

"So tell me the rest of it now."

She stared at him for a long, still moment. "All right," she said as she dropped her eyes. "But don't get angry at me."

"Promise," Lucky said, giving her hand a gentle squeeze. She kept her head lowered, and when she spoke, the emotional strain was clear in her voice.

"I made a promise, years ago, that if war ever broke out I would go home . . ."

"And?"

"And serve my father," she whispered.

"Come on, Mars, spit it out."

"In the military," she finished.

Lucky's stomach twisted and flopped. "You mean—"

"Yes. In the U.C. S. military." She looked up at him again. "I can't expect you to understand that, but you've got to know that I love you." Tears burned in the corners of her eyes.

"But, what about us?" Even as he asked his question, Lucky knew the answer. Their partnership, private and professional, was over. "And you don't have a choice?"

Marsha got up from her chair and moved to his lap. Her tears ran freely down her face. "No. I promised." She put her head on his shoulder. "Lucky, no one in the universe means more to me than you do. No one. Not even my father. But it's a promise I can't break. Please—" A quiet sob choked her words off in her throat.

"It's all right," he said as he pulled her tight and stroked her hair. "It's all right. So we go find your father. Maybe he'll take me, too."

She pulled back from him and snuffled. "You mean that?"

"Of course I do. Why wouldn't I?" He pulled a facecloth from his pocket and handed it to her.

After she blew her nose and wiped the tears from her eyes, she said, "He might not take you."

"Because I'm—"

"Yes. He hates Sondak."

Lucky felt a sudden stirring of concern, but he refused to let it build to something more. "I'll take my chances. What's the worst they can do to me?"

"I don't know. Father will protect you. But you might end up spending the duration of the war stuck on some planet."

The stirring of regret broke free from his restraints. "Marsha? Do you understand what you're saying to me? You're telling me I have to take you home. But you're also saying that might cost me my freedom."

She started crying again. "I know. I know. But better that than to have you disappearing into the void."

He held her close and let her cry it out. Yet all the time a voice was screaming defiance in his brain. Lose his freedom? Become a prisoner? Never! Never!

*　　*　　*

Frye Charltos stood unmoving throughout Vinita's cremation. Only one of the mourners had been inconsiderate enough to reach out and touch him, and he had glared at her with such ferocity that she shrank back.

Now as he watched the fire burn low on the other side of the thick crystal wall, he almost wished someone would touch him—would grab his arm and scream that it wasn't true, that Vinita was still alive. The military part of his mind scorned his weakness. Nothing could make him like reality. But no amount of self-pity could keep him from accepting it.

A vorian began playing softly in the background, sending a solemn tune like damp mist through the mourners. Frye had heard the tune all too many times before—the Kothhymn of the Dead. The last flame died away with the last strains of the song. The crystal wall went dark.

There was one more duty he had to perform, and then it would be over. Frye turned, straightened his shoulders, and acknowledged the mourners one by one as they came to share their grief. Only days later while sitting in his office did he realize that he had not spoken to a single one of them.

"Melliman," he said quietly into his lapelcom, "I want to see the latest reports."

"Yes, sir," her voice responded from his desk speaker.

Moments later his microspooler came to life. But before he had time to read half of the first report, Melliman's voice came over the speaker again. "Admiral Tuuneo here to see you, sir."

"Send him in," Frye said quietly. The last person he wanted to see at the moment was Tuuneo, but there was absolutely no way protocol would allow him to turn away a senior officer. He also realized that having Tuuneo come to see him was an honor directly connected with Vinita's death. He rose when the door opened. "Admiral," he said quietly.

"Sit down, Commander. Sit down," Tuuneo said as he crossed the room. "There is no need for formality with us."

Frye remained standing. "I am honored by your presence."

"Thank you, Commander. Now, please, sit down," he said with a wave of his hand as if the office were his own.

Frye took his seat behind the desk and looked Tuuneo squarely in the face. "What can I do for you, Admiral?"

"The question is whether or not I can do anything for you, Commander."

"I'm not sure what you mean, sir?" Frye thought he detected an odd tone in Tuuneo's voice, but couldn't classify it.

"Well, Commander, I understand how greatly you must feel the loss of your wife, but I certainly hope that has not blinded you to the, uh, shall we say, uh, political realities of the moment?"

Frye had some idea what Tuuneo was referring to, but waited for his senior to continue.

"It seems, Charltos, that several members of Bridgeforce are concerned about your performance."

Frye was not surprised. "The messages?"

"Not just those, although Decie knows they are not very happy about the messages either. No, this time they seem to be concerned about your judgment—that is, they wonder if you can continue directing our forces in your current mental state."

"Heller's fleet, sir! What is that supposed to mean?" Frye heard more anger in his voice than he felt.

Tuuneo shifted in his chair and looked squarely across the desk. "They are talking about a month's grief leave for you."

"Tell them to take their leave and. . . . I'm sorry, sir. I have no right to speak to you like that."

"'The wrath of bad news falls on the messenger.'"

Tuuneo's quotation from the Concordance only mixed Frye's emotions. But he sensed that something more important than Bridgeforce's concern was involved here. A brief flash of insight told him what. "Who else is after me, Admiral?"

"Judoff."

Frye laughed coldly. "I should have known. But surely, sir, the Bridgeforce wouldn't put that political rumpsuck in a position as critical as this one?"

"No," Tuuneo said with a faint smile as he smoothed the few silver hairs still left on his head, "not immediately, anyway. But Judoff knows that, too. She and her group have suggested that Commander Kuskuvyet could serve as acting commander until you, uh, recover."

In a steady voice which betrayed none of the hatred he felt whenever that name was mentioned, Frye said, "Kuskuvyet is a well-trained officer with a commendable record, but—"

"But everyone on the command staff knows he is no more than a mediocre tactician—and a worse strategist."

"It would be unfair of me to comment on that, sir."

"In Decie's name, Charltos! What's the matter with you? Don't you understand how serious this is?"

"Only too well," Frye said evenly.

"Then why—"

"Why am I not upset? Oh, but I am, Admiral. I am. But showing it isn't going to do any good. Pardon my interruption, but I believe you came here to tell me something you haven't gotten to yet. Until you tell me what that is, I would be well advised to control whatever emotions I feel."

"You seem pretty sure of yourself for a man who could be replaced at any time by an incompetent. If it weren't for the fact that the command staff has been supporting you, you would be gone already."

"So that's it. You almost sound like you regret that support,

Admiral." Frye had a perspective on the problem which let him see it now with cold detachment. If Bridgeforce wanted to replace him with an idiot, that was their problem. For the moment he was indifferent to their political concerns. His duty was to finish this campaign.

"Charltos, I'm trying to tell you that you're in trouble."

"But you are also telling me that the command staff will not let that trouble get out of hand. Isn't that right, sir?"

Tuuneo shook his head and pressed his lips together. "Yes," he said finally, "we will control Judoff—and Kuskuvyet, too, if necessary. But we need your cooperation."

Frye tensed slightly, then let the air escape slowly from his lungs. "I have the feeling you are about to get to the point of this whole visit, sir. I also have the feeling I'm not going to like it."

"Command doesn't give a finger in space whether you like it or not. We want you to put together a plan to capture and control the Matthews system."

With a grim smile of relief Frye said, "I've already begun working on it."

"You've what?"

"Begun working on it, sir. It seemed one of the next logical steps if our initial plans worked." Frye couldn't tell whether Admiral Tuuneo was angry or confused.

"Then why in Decie's name haven't you mentioned it to the command staff?"

"Because it was premature. It still is . . . unless, of course, it is politically expedient to . . ."

Silence hung between them for a long moment before Tuuneo looked carefully at Frye. "It is more than politically expedient, Commander. It is necessary if we want to continue leading and winning this war."

Frye finally understood what had brought them to this point. He was not the only one who had doubts about their ability to win the war. Admiral Tuuneo and some of the U.C.S. command staff must share at least some of those doubts. Suddenly he felt much better. A man who knew he could lose would be much better prepared to win. "How much time do we have?" he asked quietly.

Tuuneo smiled. "To announce the plan to Bridgeforce? A month, at best. After that, who knows?"

"Would you like to make the announcement, sir?" Frye

knew he did not have to make that offer, but since they were dealing with politics . . .

"No, Charltos. You make it. As soon as you're ready. That will be more effective against Judoff, I think." Tuuneo stood.

Frye stood with him. "Very well, sir."

The admiral narrowed his eyes, then spoke very quietly. "You keep me posted on this, Charltos. I'll need at least a day's notice before you make the announcement."

"Will do, sir," Frye said as he escorted Tuuneo to the door. "I'll let you know as soon as my staff and I are ready."

Once Tuuneo was gone, Frye returned to his desk and sat staring at his folded hands. He was making a mistake. Somewhere deep inside he had been harboring the notion that taking the Matthews system was the wrong thing to do. But he had no logical argument for that feeling.

The Matthews system was a sound military target, and once U.C.S. controlled it, Sondak would have a far more difficult time mounting a counteroffensive. It was midway between the two galactic powers, a strategic base without equal. Yet it was also a higher-risk target, one which Sondak would even now be preparing to defend.

Frye shrugged wearily and turned on his microspooler. There were many things which had to be done before he could concentrate on the new plan—things which involved life and death for their forces right now. But even as he reviewed new reports which showed fewer than expected losses in the surprise attacks, his uncertainty about the Matthews plan nagged at the back of his mind.

3

"There's an alternative," Marsha said quietly. "We could go to Alexvieux and—"

"That backspace system? They don't even have a real starport. You ever try landing a ship as big as *Graycloud* without even the crudest of beacons? Besides, why would you want to go to Alexvieux?"

Marsha curled tighter against him, comforted by the feel of his skin and the hardness of his body. "Chadiver has a scientific mission on Alexvieux Five. From there I could get home."

"What's the advantage?" he asked softly as she shifted one leg over his.

"You wouldn't have to face . . ."

"Your father? The Ukes? But I'd be stranding you there. Anyway, it's probably too late to change course." As Lucky said that, he realized the double meaning of his words, but he didn't care. A deep sense of melancholia had taken hold of him.

"I'm sorry," Marsha whispered. "I never meant for you to get caught up in this. I thought if it ever happened—the war, I mean—well, I thought I would have some warning. Then . . ." She let the implications hang, unhappy that there was no better way to express what she meant. "I really am sorry, Lucky," she repeated.

"I know, Mars. I know. Me, too."

"Are you worried?"

"More than that. I'm scared. Being locked up and tied down isn't my idea of a very happy life."

20

"But I told you, my father—"

"Don't. Don't make promises for your father. He might not be able to keep them." Suddenly Lucky tensed. "Wait a minute. You said there was a scientific mission on Alexvieux Five, right?"

"What's the matter?"

Lucky pulled away from her and climbed out of the bed. "Maybe it's not too late to change course," he said as he put on a baggy exercise suit. "Come on, Mars. You've gotta help."

By the time she entered the flight cabin a few minutes later, Lucky was tapping away at the navigation console. "Can we make the change?"

"We'll know pretty soon," he said as a series of red numbers started flashing across the green screen.

"Why did you change your mind?" she asked as she sat down beside him.

"Didn't, Mars," he said, giving her hand a quick pat before responding to a query on the screen. "Just figured another angle." He leaned back and looked at her when the numbers started flashing again. "If we go to Alexvieux, then we can communicate with your father from there—make a deal for me to take you wherever he wants you to go—and at the same time get him to guarantee that I can leave afterward."

Marsha smiled slightly. "You don't know my father." With a pause she thought of how little she really knew him, and how mixed her emotions about him were. "He doesn't like deals very much—unless they're his own."

"Then maybe we'll have to go with your idea. But at least this way we have a chance for something else."

The console buzzed. "There's your answer," Marsha said.

"Two short warps with course corrections in between," Lucky said as he checked the data, "then a long shot to Alexvieux."

"So what are you waiting for?"

He looked at her and an odd twitch tensed his chest muscles. "I don't know. Your approval, I guess."

She reached out and took his hand. For a long moment she cradled it in her own. Abruptly she raised it to her lips and gave it a quick kiss. "Any way you want to do it is more than fine with me."

"Thanks, Mars," he said softly, as he caressed her cheek. "I really mean that." Then he turned back to the console and started tapping in instructions. He felt better now than he had since before Roberg.

As she watched him, Marsha wondered, not for the first time, how she had been fortunate enough to become his partner. Her answer before had always been Fate, but now she wasn't so sure. Fate was too remote, too nebulous a concept to account for the intimacy of their relationship. It had to be something greater than that, something more personal—like God.

That idea surprised her. She had not had any strong religious feeling since childhood. Yet at this very moment she felt a sense of presence, a conviction that some loving power was watching over her and Lucky. A warm rush of assurance made her want to tell him what she felt, but she dared not. She knew his agnostic cynicism wouldn't accept it.

"There," he said happily as he turned away from the console. "You want to make this warp in bed?"

"Yes!"

The warm eagerness in her response and the glow on her face puzzled him a little, but only for a moment. Before he could get up, she was in his lap, her arms locked around his neck, her mouth feeding on his with hungry, searching kisses. Lucky didn't need any encouragement to return the heat of her passion.

When they finally paused for a brief moment, he freed an arm, reached out, and switched off the artificial gravity. With a gentle push from his feet, they floated up out of the chair.

"You devil," Marsha said with a grin as he guided them toward the companionway.

"Angel, you mean," he responded as they floated toward their cabin, holding each other with well-practiced grips.

"Both."

As they drifted through the cabin door they released each other with simultaneous giggles. Lucky did a slow tumble, and when he came out of it, he floated naked toward the bed and his empty athletic suit floated in the opposite direction in a comic parody of his actions. While Marsha finished getting her own suit off, Lucky released the zero-g net and pulled it down over the bed like a billowing tent. By the time he fastened it to the safety rail, she had wrapped her legs around his waist.

With a vigorous twist he set them spinning. Their bodies

sought contact at impossible angles that only zero-g allowed them. Even under the best of circumstances they were awkward lovers, but they always found a special joy in each other when they made love without gravity.

The slow-motion effects demanded a concentration which focused each of them on the other's most subtle movements. Their nerves seemed more highly tuned in weightlessness. Like dancers in some private, erotic ballet, they moved in a harmony all their own, turning, bending, spinning toward the center of their love. There they flew together in a tightening spiral of sensuous joy until first one and then the other was consumed in the white-hot blindness of release.

* * *

Captain Gilbert and General Mari walked down the long hall to the Command Center in a silence broken only by the soft sounds of their hyleather boots on the polished floors.

Mica Gilbert felt too good to be disturbed by General Mari's bad mood. Her father was safe. He and the Polar Fleet had escaped relatively unscathed. Apparently the Ukes didn't think the polar systems important enough to concentrate their energies there. The scattered attacks had seemed designed more to demoralize than to severely cripple the systems.

In that sense they had probably been effective. Already there were demands from Eresser, Hilldill, and Lindshaw for increases in the Polar Fleet and a doubling of the systems' garrisons. Those demands were part of the political uproar which now required General Mari's and Mica's presence in the Command Center.

"You don't have to take any rads from these people, Captain," General Mari said suddenly. "And if they try to pull you into the political argument with questions that don't apply to your area, you duck them. You understand?"

"Perfectly, sir. But what could they ask me that—"

"Don't you worry, Captain. They're liable to try to ask you anything. You just talk about facts and leave the rest of it to someone else."

"Yes, sir," Mica said quietly, as she suppressed the urge to ask more questions. She was all too aware of what politics could do to a military career. Her father had been shunted off to the Polar Fleet for what had been termed "unorthodox political values"—meaning that he had wanted an alliance with the aliens of the Castorian systems. None of the parties in power in

Sondak nor even the Castorians themselves had approved of his suggestions. So despite an outstanding military record, Admiral Josiah Gilbert had been given an insignificant command—insignificant until the Ukes had pulled their surprise attacks.

When they entered the Command Center auditorium, Mica was startled by the number of civilians present. She had expected a hundred or so of the leaders of government and the political parties. But the Center's auditorium seated close to a thousand people, and it was packed with civilians from the TriCameral and the Combined Committees, all wearing security collars locked tightly around their necks. The three tiers of seats facing the civilians were only sparsely filled by military personnel. Anyone who did not absolutely need to be there was performing double duty so that the others could attend.

"Stay close," Mari said over his shoulder as they made their way through the crowd.

Mica did as she was told, for once glad of Mari's presence and his rank. People cleared a way for them almost as though an invisible bodyguard was parting the crowd. Too many people had seen or heard stories about Mari's temper to want to slow him down. The scowl on his face did nothing to encourage those who did not know about his temper. But even with General Mari leading the way, Mica felt very much alone in the room until she spotted Commander Rochmon as they climbed the steps to the uppermost tier of seats.

"General. Captain," Rochmon said with a salute for Mari and a return salute for Mica Gilbert. "I think the civies are restless."

Mari snorted with a half-smile. "That is the understatement of the day, Rochmon. They're going to want blood before this meeting is over. You interested in donating?"

"Not me, General. I don't have any. Just ask my staff."

"Scuttlebutt says you grind them so hard they can't say anything," Mica said with a straight face.

General Mari snorted again. "She's got your I.D., Rochmon. Better never let her on your staff. She'll grind you right back."

"Might take my rough edges off," Rochmon said with a smile.

Mica had learned at the academy not to blush, but verbal interplay with Rochmon always gave her a warm feeling in the pit of her stomach. As one of her father's protégés, he had known her since she was in prep school and he was the handsome young staff officer who had delighted in making her blush. He was still handsome.

"Where's Admiral Stonefield?" General Mari asked.

"On his way, sir," Rochmon replied, "and madder than a crazed Castorian, according to his aide."

"Makes two of us," Mari said as he took his seat.

"Or a thousand," Rochmon offered with a smile and a slight nod of his head toward the politicians.

For the first time since she had joined General Mari for breakfast that morning, Mica saw him smile with pleasure. He's going to enjoy this confrontation, she thought. As they waited for the arrival of Admiral Stonefield, she wondered if that was a sign of strength in Mari or a sign of weakness.

* * *

Ayne Wallen looked up from the screen with a sigh. "No good. No good. No good," he said with a weariness that showed only in his voice.

"It's only the first stage," Sjean said from behind him. "You need to get some rest before you can evaluate those results with any degree of certainty."

"No happy morning wake-up can improve these numbers. We be telling you, Sjean, this is not good approach."

Sjean stepped up closer and looked over his shoulder at the screen. "What's wrong with those numbers?"

"Everything. They be showing complex variations sixty times allowable magnitude."

"Maybe you inverted the constant."

"Maybe moons made of dianthia blossoms. Constant is right. Action at a distance is wrong. Cannot be done."

"Can be done," she said, mimicking his accent. "Can be done, and we will do it. Drautzlab will do it. The ultimate weapon, Ayne, the weapon Sondak will use to put an end to all fighting, all war throughout the galaxy."

"Wonderful name," he said sarcastically, "ultimate weapon. Perfect for leading to ultimate death. Unfortunately, *ultimate* problem is that ultimate weapon will not work."

"Guntteray's theory says it will."

"Guntteray was a philosopher, not scientist."

"Guntteray was a brilliant man, Ayne, scientist or not. But if you're such a nonbeliever, why did you join this project? I know for a fact that Caugust offered you a choice of—"

"Joined for challenge. Challenge finished. Guntteray's theory is likely true as chances you will bed me."

No matter what the subject, Ayne managed to work in some reference to the fact that she refused to bed him. It did not matter to him that she morally opposed such bedding. He ignored her argument that bedding between co-workers made for bad work, and he did not appear to care that she was fifteen years his senior and only one year a widow. Ayne openly lusted after her without apology and without relief. Were he not such a fine scientist—and one whom Caugust had worked hard to recruit—she would have had him removed from the project.

Sjean frowned. Regardless of his impeccable credentials, and his famous dissertation on spacetime, she was rapidly losing her respect for Ayne. Yet she found him attractive in his own bizarre way. "The theory holds. Try the numbers again using Planck's constant in place of Hareshi's."

With a scowl of disgust Ayne said, "Planck's constant is bad number—sloppy, crude, mushy number."

"No one asked your opinion of it."

"Opinion holds. Is bad number."

"Use it anyway." Without waiting for a response, Sjean turned and left the room.

Ayne cursed softly in his native Tyawese as he placed his fingers on the keyboard and called up the initial formulas. Planck's constant was a number for children playing math games. Guntteray's theory was a fantasy. Instantaneous action at a distance was a joke. But Sjean Birkie transcended all his rational objections to continuing with this stupid project.

He would show her he was right. Then he would take advantage of her moment of disappointment to comfort her—and bed her. He would show her what the ultimate weapon really was.

*   *   *

Delightful Childe wrapped seven fingers of one hand around his proboscis and stroked its soft ridges thoughtfully. Those who knew him well recognized the mannerism as one which indicated deep concern. Indeed, Delightful Childe was in a quandary. He was a neutral space merchant temporarily representing Sondak. But by a gross stroke of ill luck, he had captured the U.C.S. scientific station on a miserable little planet called Alexvieux Five.

Captured wasn't exactly the right word. After he had landed the *Nazzarone* in response to an emergency beacon, he had informed the scientists that he was a temporary representative of Sondak. The station chief, a Dr. Hachihaguri, had then inexplicably surrendered the scientists and the station to Delightful Childe and his crew.

Only then did Delightful Childe learn that a war had started between Sondak and the U.C.S. Apparently some difficulty caused by their war had delayed or diverted the supplies which should have arrived on Alexvieux months before. Dr. Hachihaguri and the four hundred-odd Chadiverians manning the station were on the verge of starvation. The muddled human logic which had led them to surrender only deepened Delightful Childe's dilemma.

As a neutral Oinaise he was obligated only to render whatever immediate assistance he could under the circumstances, and then he would be free to depart. This he had done, grateful that *Nazzarone* had more than enough capability to feed four hundred extra mouths.

In order to represent Sondak, he had signed a contract that stated in its sub-subclauses that he would render no assistance to any enemy of Sondak during time of war. These sub-subclauses he had chosen to ignore, basing his decision to do so on the tenets of a higher moral law.

The difficulty arose, however, in what to do next. His ship could produce enough food day in and day out to feed Dr. Hachihaguri and his people indefinitely. But *Nazzarone* had on hand supplies which would last the poor scientists of Alexvieux no more than a month at best.

If Delightful Childe gave them those supplies and left to complete his contract with Sondak, what would happen to those people? Suppose their resupply ships never came? He might be condemning them to a slow death. But with this stupid war now going on, if he sent a message to the nearest U.C.S. post, what guarantees would he have that . . .

With a sigh Delightful Childe touched his throatone. "Please send Dr. Hachihaguri to me at once."

Several minutes later the short, plump human was escorted into the office by a crew member. "Greetings, Benevolent One," Hachihaguri said with a low bow.

"Greetings, Doctor. Please be seated."

"You are most kind, Benevolent One," Hachihaguri said as he tried to make himself comfortable on the edge of a basee that was obviously too high off the deck for him.

"I would rather that you stop calling me that," Delightful Childe said firmly.

"Most certainly, ah . . . Honored Sir. I have no wish to displease my captor."

"I am not your captor!" Delightful Childe screamed in Vardequerqueglot. Then he caught himself and switched back to U.C. Standard. "Forgive me, Doctor. It is against my honor to raise my voice to you. But I am caught between a barb and a hook, and your insistence on titles does nothing to alleviate my discomfort."

"My apologies, Merchant Captain," Hachihaguri said with an awkward bow that almost caused him to fall off the basee. "However, is it not true that you have been benevolent to us?"

"No. I have only done my moral duty."

"To do such duty is to be benevolent by definition."

"That does not mean that you have to call me that."

"As you wish. However, did you not accept our surrender?"

"I accepted your needs as an obligation to be fulfilled, nothing more than that. I am not your captor. In fact, I called you here to help me determine how we can best ensure that you will be able to get back to Chadiver."

"You could take us, Merchant Captain."

"I cannot. I am under contract to the government of Sondak."

"You could use your long band transmitter to send for assistance."

"What if that assistance does not come? Should I just leave you here to die?"

"That is what we were doing before you came. We can do it again if necessary."

Delightful Childe snorted in frustration.

The vibrato sound caused Hachihaguri to throw his hands over his ears. "Stop! Please!"

"Then help me, human! We have a mutual problem that begs to be solved."

Slowly Hachihaguri lowered his hands and stared at Delightful Childe's deeply wrinkled face with its long, pale snout. "I have been cooperating as best as I know how, Merchant Captain. It is not clear to me how I may do more."

"I believe you, Doctor. Again I must ask your forgiveness—and your further cooperation," he continued before Hachihaguri could answer. "Is there any way you and your people could sustain yourselves here?"

The human rubbed the back of one tiny hand against his prominent chin bone. "If we had the proper equipment," he said after a long pause, "and, of course, sufficient weapons with which to hunt our food, then, yes, we could make such an attempt."

"There is no way I can give you weapons. You know that. What other kinds of equipment would you need?"

"Colonial tools," Hachihaguri said simply, "things I am sure you do not have—tillers, seeds, fertilizers, enzymes, planthuts—things like that."

Delightful Childe bared two rows of blunt, yellow teeth on both sides of his proboscis. "Do not underestimate the *Nazzarone*, Doctor. We might, in fact, be able to supply you with many of those things."

"We will still need weapons," Hachihaguri said flatly.

"I told you that was impossible."

"Then we cannot sustain ourselves."

"Why?"

"Because the only sources we would have for the necessary trace elements in our diet would be what we can kill and grow. The soil of this planet is too poor to provide those for us in sufficient quantities through the plants. That is why there is no colony here. Only in animal flesh can we find suitable concentrations of those elements. Even then, only the largest of the carnivores are really useful—"

"Why?"

Hachihaguri looked at the Oinaise captain as though searching for an answer. "Because the largest carnivores eat smaller ones, which eat smaller ones, which eat herbivores. In each instance the concentration of trace elements in the muscles of the dominant beasts is greatly increased. The musterroon weigh better than one ton apiece. In order for each of my people to survive on Alexvieux, they will each have to consume approximately two kilograms of musterroon meat per day. That will take a lot of hunting."

"Then we are at an impasse," Delightful Childe said calmly. "We cannot rescue you. We cannot render you aid which will ensure your survival after we leave. Most certainly we cannot abandon you to a slow death. Nor can we stay indefinitely and feed you. Definitely an impasse."

"Ship requesting permission to land, Captain," a voice said through the tiny speaker under Delightful Childe's single ear.

"Then again, Doctor, perhaps a solution is at hand. I will talk to you later. Thank you."

Frye Charltos awoke with a start. Instinctively he reached out to touch Vinita. A dark hollow swallowed his heart when he touched the emptiness beside him. With a low, growling sigh, he dropped back to the hard mattress and clenched his hands across his chest. Anger burned in him, anger for which there was still no release.

Forty, he thought. It has been forty days since she died, forty days since I killed her . . . forty endless days with only Vinita's ghost and the sadness of his memories to keep him company. If only Lisa Cay were here to help . . .

Lisa Cay. Every night he thought about her, wondered where she was and if she could keep her promise. Frye did not doubt that she would keep the promise if there were any way for her to get to him. But could she? It had been more than five local years since they had heard from her, five years without having any idea of where she was or what she was doing. Even when that message had come five years ago, it had been typically Lisa Cay—brief, vague, and full of love.

With a second, quieter sigh, Frye rolled over and got out of bed. There were other things he had to think about now. This was the day of his major announcement to Bridgeforce. In less than five hours he would tell them about his plans to attack the Matthews system. But as he cleansed away the residue of another restless night, he kept seeing Vinita's face in the mirror, and behind her, the smiling image of Lisa Cay.

By the time Frye arrived at his office, the darkness in his heart had hardened like the black coating behind a mirror, allowing only reflections of the outside world while protecting him from their intrusive glare. As dawn slid under the clouds and washed the ice-capped Irkbie Mountains with brilliant flows of burnt-orange light, Frye darkened his window. Vinita had loved dawn over the mountains, and had led him to love it. Now those colors which had thrilled her so only made him more aware of her absence and the anger which built steadily within him.

"Reporting for duty, sir," AOCO Melliman's soft voice said through the desk speaker.

"Thank you," Frye replied quietly into his lapelcom. "I want the overnights as soon as they are compiled."

"I've already fed them into your microspooler, sir."

"Any changes?"

"Nothing major, sir. But you might want to check the update on the Matthews system. There's been some increased activity there which I think you will find significant."

"Very good, Melliman. Check and see if Admiral Tuuneo has arrived, and if he has, request permission for me to talk to him in one hour."

"Will do, sir. Anything else I can get for you?"

Something in the tone of her voice set off an annoying alarm in the back of Frye's mind, an alarm she had set off several times since Vinita's death. He knew Melliman was only trying to be kind to him, but there was a tone of, well—He shut that thought off. "Nothing else for now, AOCO, Thank you."

Even as she signed off, Frye felt a momentary conflict of emotions about Melliman. As his Aide-of-Commander and most trusted subordinate, she was invaluable. But the fact that she was attractive, unmarried, and apparently unattached, added a new dimension to their relationship which Frye had never before given any thought to. Maybe he was just being overly sensitive, reading things in her words and actions which had no significance except that which he gave them.

With a flick of his wrist he turned on his microspooler and waded into the overnight reports, starting, as Melliman had suggested, with the status reports on the Matthews system. If there was unusual activity there, he had damn well better know about it before his presentation of the plan to Bridgeforce.

What he read startled him. In addition to an increased number of freighters entering Matthews system, the U.C.S.

agents in place reported the arrival of several Sondak garrison ships.

"Melliman, get in here."

"Yes sir." Moments later she entered his office and stood before him.

"Sit down and tell me what you make of these reports from Matthews."

"Hard to say with any certainty, sir," Melliman said.

Frye would have been hard pressed to miss the eagerness in her voice. "But you suspect something?"

"Two things actually, sir. Either Sondak is reinforcing the Matthews system in preparation for an attack, or they are getting ready to evacuate their military forces and concede the system."

"Conceding the system to us seems a little extreme, doesn't it, AOCO? What would they have to gain from that?"

"Consolidation of their forces, sir, and a shortening of their supply lines."

"And a blow to their morale," Frye added.

"I suppose so, sir. But if I were their commander, I would rather take that blow now than later."

"Why?"

"Because I think it would be easier to overcome now."

Fry valued his Aide-of-Commander precisely because she told him what she thought in a way that few of his previous AOCOs had been willing or able to do. Yet neither of her choices made as much sense as they should have. Reinforcing the Matthews system would cost Sondak an investment in personnel and equipment they could hardly afford after the losses they had suffered. Conceding the system, especially its principal planet, Reckynop, with its established lightspeed service base, could be an irreparable blow to Sondak's morale, especially their military morale.

There had to be another answer, but the report offered no clues, and Frye could not pull a reasonable explanation off the top of his head. Better to let it sink in, he thought.

"Look for another reason, Melliman. And if you think of one, tell me immediately. I have a feeling we have missed something. That will be all."

"Aye, aye, sir."

The look on her face was one of controlled disappointment,

but Frye knew she would come up with a list of other possibilities. She understood strategy better than half the admirals and commanders he knew, and she was proud of that
understanding. Melliman would sift through the accumulated
data until she found other answers.

Frye turned to the rest of the overnights and scanned them
for any information which might affect his attack plan. Aside
from the continuing requests from his task-force leaders for
permission to hold their extended positions rather than regroup, there was little in the overnights of immediate con-
sequence.

The task-force leaders would have to be dealt with firmly. If
they hesitated too long in following his orders, they would
surely throw off the timing for the attack. On the other hand,
Frye thought with a quiet smile, if his own subordinates did
not see that the next logical objective was to regroup and strike
in an unexpected place, then perhaps Sondak would not see
that either. Suppose Sondak had some plan for a retaliatory
strike? That could certainly explain a buildup in the Matthews
system, and confirmation of that theory could give the U.C.S.
the advantage it needed to—

"Admiral Tuuneo on the vidphone for you, sir."

"Yes, sir," Frye said as he turned on his vidphone.

"Are we ready, Commander?"

"I believe so, sir. But there are a few things I would like to
talk to you about before I present my plan."

"Any time you're ready, Commander."

"Thank you, sir. I will be there shortly."

Frye gathered his plan and the supplementary information
he had accumulated, then gave Melliman an urgent message
for all the task-force leaders, telling them to execute his orders
without delay. As soon as he was finished, she cocked one of
her bright auburn eyebrows at him. "A question, Melliman?"

"No, sir. Just a sudden thought. Suppose Sondak's actions in
the Matthews system are a ruse of some sort? We have no
positive information that those garrison ships are full of troops,
and none about what those additional freighters are carrying. I
mean, sir—"

"Suppose you see what else you can find to support that
idea, AOCO. You just might be headed in the right direction."
Frye gave her an approving smile. "But now I have to find out
what direction Bridgeforce wants to take this war."

*　　*　　*

Leri Gish Geril paused and stared as Sondak's most recent ambassador squirmed in his protective suit. Humans, Leri thought, good-for-the-worst humans. "By what right does Sondak plan to expropriate our methane? Or doesn't it think it needs such a right, Ambassador?"

"Please, Proctor," the ambassador's voice droned through the translator. "Sondak would never do anything to—"

"Lies," Leri said calmly. Then just as calmly she generated a little oxygen, mixed it in the dual chambers behind her gills, sparked her teeth, and spat a small fireball at the ambassador.

It gave her little joy when the human jumped and uttered some untranslatable word. Humans rarely gave joy to anything. The skittery little aliens were too busy lying, cheating, fighting, killing, and propagating their irritatingly powerful race to find much joy in anything. No wonder they were rarely fun to play with.

"What you have told me, Ambassador Fushtig, is that your military has determined that it needs billions of cubic hexameters of methane which it can use for your short-range fighters. Consequently, your scientists determined that just such a quantity of methane was available in the surface of our atmosphere. How convenient."

Fushtig had rather bravely resumed his position directly in front of Leri, and when he spoke, the translator indicated no signs of fear in his voice. "I assure you, Proctor, that no such thing happened. Your planetary council has been exporting methane for centuries and—"

"At a controlled rate."

"Exactly. We only wish your assistance in increasing that rate of export within safe guidelines for all—"

"A two-thousandfold increase is hardly what we would consider safe."

"But, Proctor, we have presented the data to your own experts, and they have indicated—"

"They are still analyzing it."

"But they have indicated that their preliminary study confirms our findings."

Leri took a deep breath and pursed the membranes at the end of her tubular mouth. Fushtig tensed, but held his ground and stared back at her through the clear faceplate of his helmet. Leri blew a steady series of little fireballs over his head. To the ambassador's credit he did not flinch this time until the twentieth almost grazed him.

"Stop it!" his voice screeched through the translator.

"Why?" Leri asked. "Will you stop pirating our methane if we tell you to? Of course not. You control the process as you always have. You control the stations. Your technology makes it all work. Why do you bother to ask our permission or pay us at all? Why do you not just take all you want and be done with it?"

They both knew the answer to that question, but Leri wanted to hear this ambassador's response. His predecessors had recited Sondak's fair-trade policy by rote—complete with a self-serving revisionist history of their assistance to Cloise. Their crude tale of political and economic entanglement always amused her. That it was at least half true annoyed her.

"I don't know, Proctor," Fushtig said. "It would certainly be simpler than negotiating with you. And as you say, the advantage is ours."

Leri gulped and burped in quick succession, a sure sign to anyone who knew her that she was both amused and angered. "Not totally," she said. Her next fireball consumed Ambassador Fushtig who struggled only briefly before his suit exploded.

"You will have to break that habit," a mildly disapproving voice said from behind Leri.

"I know. I know. But you must admit that these humans are a most irritating race. Yet I suppose you are right, Ranas, if only because they are beginning to grow suspicious."

"And impatient with us," Ranas added.

"So they are, my love. So they are." Leri started her personal music, lowered the meditative curtain, and shut herself off from Ranas and the ambassador's charred remains. Then she curled her long, narrow body into a tight coil. It was time to pray for Fushtig's soul as duty required.

Leri was in no way convinced that individual members of the human race had souls. They might have a collective soul as the Verfen did, or they might be altogether without souls like those pitiful aliens who called themselves the Oinaise. But she refused to offend the Elett by not following the dictates of her religion. Better to pray for the soul of a creature with none, than to risk having to serve that soul in the eternal seas of the hereafter.

In the middle of her prayers Leri shuddered with pleasure and immediately changed to the litany of delight. Her time had come. She shifted her coils to form a shallow bowl shape and sang her joy to the gracious Elett, asking their blessings and their love.

Moments later she gave birth to a clutch of daughters. As the last of seven squirmed free from her body, Leri was filled with maternal happiness. Yet she knew in some deep, intuitive way that one of these guplings of hers had an ambassador's soul. That knowledge tempered her joy.

*   *   *

"Captain Mica Gilbert, reporting as ordered, sir." Mica executed a perfect salute and stood at rigid attention in front of Admiral Stonefield. Despite the fact that he had known her since she was a child when he had been her father's first commanding officer, she had never felt comfortable alone in his presence.

"At ease, Captain. Have a seat. There is no need for you to be so formal."

"Thank you, sir," Mica said carefully, making sure that her posture was straight and correct in the oversoft chair in front of his desk.

Admiral Stonefield laughed. "You always were a strange girl, Mica, but I suppose it's in your blood—your father's, I mean. It's the Gilbert independence mixed with military descipline, I guess. Makes for an interesting combination."

Mica resented the casual way he criticized her and her father, but she smiled and said, "The family traits have been commented on before, sir."

"Yes, I'm sure they have. You know your father's coming back here, don't you? Of course you do. But did you also know that he has requested that you join his staff?"

The surprise shifted her face before she could catch and suppress it. "No, sir, I didn't. I thought that—"

"It is against regulations, Mica. At least it usually is. But in this instance, as in all instances of war, regulations get set aside for the good of the service. How would you feel about serving under your father?"

"I'm not sure, sir." Mica hesitated. Admiral Stonefield knew she would like nothing better. Why was he asking such a stupid question? "Serving under my father would be an honor and privilege that I dared not even dream about. But if it would cause problems, I, uh—"

Stonefield snorted. "Let me worry about the problems. If you think you could serve under your father as well as under any other officer, that is all that matters." He looked at her sternly for a moment, then smiled. "However, there is another complication in this matter."

"Sir?"

"Commander Rochmon has also requested that you be transferred to his staff. His chief communications officer will be moving to CENFLEET as soon as we can replace him."

That information did not surprise Mica. Rochmon had told her he might put in a request for her, but knowing the ways of the military all too well, she had decided not to think about that until it happened. Now she had two opportunities, both of which greatly appealed to her.

"Well, Mica? Which would you rather do?"

Something in Stonefield's tone made her pause before answering. Her first choice by far would be to serve under her father. But perhaps—"Which would be better for the service, sir?" she asked quietly. "Isn't that really the question?"

Stonefield smiled again. "An excellent question, Mica, one which I am not sure I can answer. However, I don't expect you to answer it either. Unless you have some serious objection, I am going to have you assigned as communications officer for Cryptography Headquarters. That's where the service needs you the most at the moment. Later we might need you elsewhere."

Mica knew she had given the correct response, but that did not alleviate the sense of disappointment she felt. Under any other circumstances she would have jumped at the chance to serve under Rochmon. Now, well, now she almost wished he had not asked for her.

"Thank you, sir," she said, as she rose from her chair and pulled herself to attention.

"That's not all, Mica. Please, sit down."

What else could there be? she wondered as she sat back down and returned Admiral Stonefield's even gaze.

"There is something we need for you to do for us."

The look on the admiral's face put her immediately on the alert. "We, sir?" she asked hesitantly.

"Yes, Captain, we—the Joint Chiefs. We want you to serve in a dual function on Commander Rochmon's staff."

"In what way, sir?" Mica was not sure she wanted to hear his answer.

"As honor trustee," he said without inflection.

Mica was shocked. To be an honor trustee on Rochmon's staff meant that she would be spying on them for the Joint Chiefs. Surely they didn't suspect that—

"Perhaps I should have prepared you for that," Stonefield said as he looked steadily into her eyes, "but I see by your expression that—well, never mind. Rest assured, Captain, that we in no way doubt the loyalty of Commander Rochmon. However, the surprise attacks have caused the Joint Chiefs to question whether all the necessary information about the Ukes has been getting through to him, and thus to us. As communications officer, you will be in an ideal position to monitor what goes in and out of that headquarters. Should you detect anything suspicious, anything at all, you are to report it directly to me—if, of course, you accept this duty."

There was no way she could refuse it, not in time of war. Yet Mica wanted to with all her heart. Even if Stonefield said Rochmon was above suspicion, he would still expect reports on everyone in Cryptography. Everyone. Rochmon included. She would be spying on all of them.

"I understand the difficulty of your position, Captain, but I must remind you that we are engaged in a war, a war which we are by no means guaranteed of winning. Under such circumstances, we are all called upon to do things which are onerous to us."

"Yes, sir," Mica said as evenly as she could. There was no way out of the dilemma. An age-old military tradition which she had been introduced to on her first day in StarFleet Academy dictated that she accept. "What are the procedures?"

Even as Admiral Stonefield explained exactly how she was to report to him and what criteria she was to use, Mica's stomach churned with ugly anticipation of what she had agreed to do.

*   *   *

"Get closer before you fire." Commander Zupanch's voice was calm as she attempted to direct her fleet, but inside she felt the sharp anticipation of loss.

The Uke launchship was already spewing flight after flight of attack ships through her thin defense net. Commander Rankin and Graczyski's defenders might stop a few of the Ukes, but

Zupanch knew they would be hard pressed to do more than offer token resistance.

Half of her fleet consisted of hastily trained civilians flying station shuttles and personal craft with crudely mounted rocket launchers and industrial pulse lasers. Rankin's fleet was almost totally civilian. Yet Zupanch refused to give in to her feelings. She had argued as well and as hard as she knew how for an alliance with Sondak—knowing for decades that Cczwyck could never adequately defend itself. Now it was too late. If they lost, they lost, but at least they would defend their home with every resource they had.

"Watch out! Here they come!" a voice crackled over the transceiver. "Hundreds of them!"

"Maintain formation and speed, and prepare to fire on my command."

Zupanch recognized the voice of one of her spacecorps leaders and sought for an instant to remember his name.

Then in front of her, *Tiernan*'s viewscreens filled with the scenes of battle. Rockets exploded in ephemeral rosettes of color against the bright backdrop of stars. Flashes of orange light erupted from the sides of the Uke launchship.

A babble of voices filled with terror and triumph vibrated the speakers. One ship crippled. A scream of anger. Another ship gone. Then another. Then ten. Then thirty.

Through the chatter of commands and the cacophony of reports in *Tiernan*'s battle center, Zupanch heard someone sobbing.

Cries of panic preceded the desertion of several civilian ships. They were quickly joined by several more, despite orders and curses for them to stay.

The Spacecorps hung grimly in the center of the battle with the majority of the civilians fighting beside them. For every ship they lost they seemed to be taking three or four of the Ukes with them. But the odds were just too overwhelming.

"Withdraw to Graczyski," Zupanch ordered. "All ships withdraw to Graczyski."

With deadly slowness a long thin swarm of ships followed her command and headed back toward the center of the system, harassed from all sides by the relentless Ukes. The *Tiernan* was the last to turn as Zupanch used her multiple guns in a hopeless attempt to ward off the attackers.

5

There were more military personnel in the halls of Drautzlab than Ayne Wallen had seen since he had begun working there.

The war, he thought disdainfully. They should be out fighting the war instead of hanging around here looking for some magic solution to their problems. He knew for a fact that Sondak was conscripting throughout his domain, even on his sparsely populated Be-Tyaw. If they were that much in need of bodies to fight against the Ukes, surely some of these military people hanging around the lab were needed also.

When he entered his office, he was surprised to find Sjean Birkie waiting for him.

"Where are they?" she asked before he could offer his greeting. "You said they would be ready yesterday."

"Ah, Sjean, my impatient. Good numbers hard to find. Sometimes takes months to find one."

"Which means that you haven't done what I told you to," she said without anger. "Why not?"

"Please, to sit," Ayne said as he moved past her and sat down behind his immaculately arranged desk. "Did all that you asked. Did it twice to be sure. Still no—"

"Using Planck's constant?"

"Certainly, impatient one. Those were your instructions."

"I want to see your datafeed."

Ayne knew he was in trouble, but did not care. Let her demand anything she wanted to. "Scrubbed," he said quietly.

"Scrubbed? Scrubbed! What in Heisenberg's name is that supposed to mean?"

"Gone. Erased. Deleted," he said much more calmly than

he felt. "Numbers no good, so datafeed no good. Erased all junk and am starting with fresh."

Under the delay of a deep breath of frustration Sjean looked at him in wonder. What was the matter with this man? Was he such a poor scientist that he did not understand the value of a datafeed? Or was he up to something else entirely? At the moment it didn't matter. His actions were beyond her jurisdiction.

"You will have to explain that to Caugust," she said quietly. "And probably to Scientific Security, too. No one scrubs data on a project this important without having to pay for it."

Ayne gave her an innocent grin. Behind that front his pulse thumped against his jawbone. He hadn't thought about Scientific Security when he scrubbed the datafeed. All he had thought about was demonstrating to Sjean that he was not some hireman she could boss as she pleased. He hadn't thought of Caugust either.

"Smile if you want to," Sjean said as she stepped toward the door, "but hope you have enough credits to get back to Be-Tyaw. Otherwise you might find yourself conscripted."

"Perhaps," he said softly, "there is an alternative."

"Not for you, Ayne. We've put up with a lot from you, made adjustments for you we did not have to. But there is absolutely no adjustment we can make for this kind of negligence."

"Was not negligence."

"Then it was sheer stupidity. Have a nice trip." She walked quickly out of the office and slammed the door behind her.

As soon as she left, Ayne turned to his computer console and rapidly called up a display of his last equations. They were pristine and empty, waiting for him to enter the appropriate values. He knew they were empty. But they were also valuable.

With those equations he could push Guntteray's theory and Drautzlab's research a giant step forward. If he scrubbed them, too, it might take Sjean and the rest of them years to discover what he had accidentally stumbled upon the day before.

Ayne smiled to himself. The ultimate weapon might just be possible after all. Simultaneous action at a distance was still a joke, but the backside of Guntteray's theory might hold a better, more powerful secret—reciprocal action at a distance.

As he stared at the equations, he hesitated. One impulse

was to erase them and deny anyone else access to their beauty. The stronger impulse was to take them and flaunt them in Sjean's and Caugust's faces. For the moment he could do nothing but gaze on them with a fondness only a scientist could have for such abstract balance and harmony.

He pushed aside his personal feelings and considerations. Duty and honor demanded that he do what he had sworn to do. When the combuzzer called him to report to Caugust's office, he turned the display off and left his office with the air of a man going to sneer at his enemy's feeble threats.

* * *

Lucky and Marsha sat perplexed in front of Delightful Childe. "I'm afraid we don't understand what you are asking of us," Marsha said finally.

"Ah, yes, well, that," Delightful Childe said slowly as he stroked his long proboscis, "that is a point I have yet to make. However, we must first ensure that we totally understand each other's positions. You wish to contact someone on the central U.C.S. planets. We wish to be relieved of the burden laid on us by Dr. Hachihaguri and his people. Our respective—"

"Pardon me for interrupting," Lucky said, "but we've been over all of that. Why don't you just tell us what you think we can do to help?"

Delightful Childe suppressed a sigh. "Do you have tillers?"

Marsha laughed. "No. What would we—"

"We do. Do you have planet seed?"

"No," Lucky and Marsha said together.

"We do." Delightful Childe said holding up his seven-fingered hand. "We also have enzymes, planthuts, generators, and miscellaneous other equipment which might prove useful to Dr. Hachihaguri. We do not, however, have weapons. Do you have weapons? Lots of weapons?"

When they hesitated, Delightful Childe bared his yellow teeth in what passed for a smile. "Ah! So you do have weapons. Good. Weapons are exactly what Dr. Hachihaguri's people need to survive. You give him your weapons, and I will send his messages and yours on *Nazzarone*'s long band transmitter." Delightful Childe leaned back and hooked a finger of each hand in the folds of flesh hiding his neck. He was pleased.

"We can't do that," Lucky said quietly. "We paid a lot of good credits for those weapons, and besides—"

"You think our tillers, seeds, and supplies were free?" Delightful Childe asked in a voice somewhat louder than he intended. His pleasure had been short-lived.

"No, but you're probably insured for something like this. As independent lightspeed freighters, we—"

"You have an obligation. Are these not your own people?"

"They're mine, not his," Marsha said quickly.

"Did you not describe yourselves to me as partners?"

"Yes, but—"

"Then they are his people, too. And your weapons to give if you so choose. Must I lecture you on moral duty? Did your primitive societies teach you nothing about a higher law?"

"You don't have to lecture us."

"Someone should!" Delightful Childe caught himself before saying more. Arguing with them would do nothing to resolve his problem or Hachihaguri's.

"Perhaps he's right." Marsha looked straight into Lucky's pale blue eyes. "Perhaps we do need to be reminded of—"

"Oh, no!" Lucky said as he stood up. "I don't have to listen to this." He was suddenly aware of how uncomfortable he was in Delightful Childe's presence. Now Marsha was siding with that presumptuous alien. "You want to give up your share of the weapons? That's fine with me. And you can stay here on Alexvieux if you want to." As soon as he said that, he regretted it. The pained look on Marsha's face as she rose beside him stabbed his conscience, but it was too late to turn back now.

"Look," he said as he turned to face Delightful Childe, "you have supplies, and weapons, too, I'll bet. Why can't you just take care of these people? What's the matter with your higher laws? Don't they cover humans?"

"You try my patience, Captain Teeman. Should I choose to do so, in the name of all that is holy, of course, I could take your weapons—and your ship—and serve that which is right without the least thought to your inconvenience. But I was suffering under the misapprehension that I was dealing with a civilized human."

Lucky glanced quickly around, his body tense with anger. The immensity of the *Nazzarone* had impressed him when they landed *Graycloud* beside it. Now the size of this room seemed to reinforce Delightful Childe's threat. He probably could and would take whatever he wanted, whether Lucky liked it or not.

"Please, Lucky? You said you were willing to help whichever side paid the highest price." Marsha grabbed his arms and forced him to look at her. "Don't you understand? The price we're talking about here is measured in lives."

The implication that it was their own lives as much as those of the scientists was not lost on him. With a deep breath Lucky let the tension go. He looked at Marsha, looked into that face which had brought him so much unexpected joy, and knew she was right. "I'm sorry," he said quietly. "I guess I just—"

"There is no need for you to apologize," Delightful Childe interrupted. "If you will but agree to my suggestion, we can make the necessary arrangements immediately."

Lucky resented this alien, resented the twist he had forced on their plans, and resented his high-handed threat. But most of all, he resented having said what he did to Marsha. He blamed that on Delightful Childe.

"On condition," Lucky said as evenly as he could.

"Yes? You have some difficulty we have not discussed?"

"We'll send our own message through your transmitter— with none of your personnel around."

Delightful Childe bared his teeth again. "How quaint your suspicions are, Captain Teeman. No, no," he said with a wave of his hand that barred interruption, "do not get excited again. We accept your condition . . . and impose one of our own."

"Which is?"

"That your message include a report of what the *Nazzarone* has done to whomever you are contacting in the U.C.S. Does that meet with your approval?"

"But of course," Marsha said before Lucky could answer.

"Good. Then let us proceed with the details. I will send for Doctor Hachihaguri immediately. In the meantime, perhaps you would care for some edibles?"

When they assented, Delightful Childe felt like a great burden was about to be lifted from him. Yet his training and experience refused to allow him to celebrate until *Nazzarone* was clear of Alexvieux.

When he was sure he had done all he could and *Nazzarone* was well away in space, he would report first to his immediate superiors and then to his employers in Sondak. Those two acts would satisfy all the obligations incurred by this annoying side trip to Alexvieux. Then, and only then, would he be able to relax and savor the rewards of benevolence.

*   *   *

"No, sha," Frye said quietly, "there was no way we could plan beyond that point with any certainty. As I explained before, part of our actions will depend on the losses we incur in the Matthews operation." As he spoke, Frye reminded himself again that these military leaders had been chosen as heads of their respective services based on politics, not on military ability.

"That sounds like a very dangerous approach to strategy," Marshall Judoff said.

"All strategy is dangerous, sha."

"But as Commander Kuskuvyet noted earlier, this operation of yours will require the majority of our heavy forces. Is that not a terribly high risk?"

Frye stared at her for a moment before answering. Tuuneo had said he could control Judoff, so— "Everything we decide has its risk factors, Marshall Judoff. The greater the rewards to be gained, the greater the risks which must be taken." How foolish to have to quote cliches to her, he thought.

"Perhaps I should put it this way, Marshall Judoff. We know we cannot win a prolonged war with Sondak. Their resources and their production capabilities far exceed ours. We have crippled them momentarily, but now is the time to follow up on our success and gain control of central space. Once we've done that, Sondak will necessarily be on the defensive and we can—"

"Cornered," Kuskuvyet said, "and fighting like animals."

"No, Commander. If we control the Matthews system, Sondak will not be cornered—but they will be outflanked. Their polar systems will be vulnerable. Their refitting base on Roberg will be within easy range of our medium attack ships. And," Frye said with a chop of his hand, "their morale will be devastated."

"No need to get so emphatic, Commander," Judoff said in a silky tone of amusement.

Frye gave her a smile without humor. After two days of defending his plan to the Bridgeforce commanders and their nitpicking staffs, he was finding little humor in anything. "Perhaps not, sha, but there is no need for most of the questions which have been asked today, either."

A murmur of protest rose from around the table.

"I agree," Admiral Tuuneo said immediately, speaking for

the first time in the last several hours. All heads turned in his direction. "It appears that we are all agreed that the Matthews system should be attacked, captured, and held. I'm sure that Commander Charltos has gained some valuable suggestions that he can use in attaining that goal. But in the end, it is his responsibility to work out the exact details."

"But, Admiral—"

"Let me finish, Judoff. You've had your say." A quick glance at the other members of Bridgeforce left no question that he had their attention. "When we chose our Joint Force Commander, we agreed that the final strategical and tactical decisions had to be his. Too many of us remembered what happened in the last war."

"This is not the last war," Judoff said firmly.

"No, sha, it is not. And so long as I am chairman of Bridgeforce, we will do nothing to let it turn into that kind of war. What in Decie's name has happened to your memories? Have you forgotten how our services were almost destroyed by the Amarcouncil's constant attempts to second-guess us? Have you forgotten why Bridgeforce was formed?"

His question hung in the air without an answer.

"Then I say we approve Commander Charltos's plan and let him begin its execution."

"But, sir?"

"Yes, Marshall Judoff?"

"Shouldn't we be kept informed on a daily basis on how the plan is developing so that we can make adjustments to the—"

"If you demand that, I'll disband Bridgeforce."

"You cannot do that," several people said at once.

For the first time Frye felt a real smile rework his lips. Now he knew one of the ways Tuuneo was going to control them.

"I certainly can," Tuuneo said sternly. "Read the regulations. As senior commander of all the services and as chairman of Bridgeforce, I have the full right in times of armed conflict to disband this body and select a staff of *my personal choosing* to assist me in directing *all* war efforts in the U.C.S."

"That's dictatorship."

"No, just war, Marshall Judoff, and the rules of war tend to get very simple and very strict. But I'd forgotten. You missed the last war, didn't you?"

Judoff flushed with anger, but to Frye's surprise she said nothing. Although her allegiance in the last war had never been questioned, there was a fair amount of public evidence that she and the paramilitary force she led at the time had never actually engaged the enemy.

"I call for a vote," Admiral Tuuneo said quietly. "All in favor of supporting Commander Charltos's plan so signify."

The plan carried by a vote of eight to zero. Marshall Judoff abstained and left the room as soon as the meeting adjourned. Kuskuvyet followed in her wake like a dull asteroid caught in her gravity.

Frye watched them go with relief and concern, neither of which explained the sense of distraction he felt.

"An excellent presentation and defense, Commander."

"Thank you, Admiral," Frye said, allowing himself the faintest of smiles. "But I have a question, sir. Did you expect Bridgeforce to work this plan over for two days?"

Tuuneo did not return his smile. "Actually, Commander, I expected it to take longer. If Judoff and her puppet hadn't been so impatient, they might have gathered more support. Their crudeness surprised me."

Frye knew immediately what the admiral referred to. Judoff had ignored customs and traditions which formed the heart of Tuuneo's military background. Nothing she could have done or said would have disturbed him more than that. "To ignore tradition," he had once told Frye, "is to walk blindfolded into the night of ignorance."

"Nevertheless," Tuuneo continued, "we accomplished our goals, and you have your assignment waiting for you. Will you come pray with me before you go back to work?"

"Certainly," Frye said without hesitation. He had not done much praying since Vinita's death, but his current lack of spiritual fervor could not be reflected publicly, especially in Tuuneo's presence. All the traditionalists insisted that the gods and war were interwoven in essential ways. Tuuneo might be too rational to believe that the gods controlled wars, but his belief in them made the gods a part of everything he did.

"Good. We will use my basili."

As Frye followed Tuuneo from the room and toward the shuttle tubes which would take them up to Tuuneo's office and his private basili, he wondered why he was being accorded this honor. It was highly unusual for anyone other than family to be invited to use a private basili, and— Suddenly Frye knew. Tuuneo's invitation to pray was not only his personal stamp of approval on Frye's plan, but also an acknowledgement of how much was at stake for the U.C.S. in this operation.

For Admiral Tuuneo, his prayers for blessing and assistance were more than just a formality. They were a necessity.

6

The sun did a slow boil into the sea, casting its last orange light through the single window of the cliffside residence. Hew Rochmon lay sated in the warm glow with his arms around a naked wisp of a woman. Slowly and silently she faded away as her time expired, and his arms collapsed around nothing.

Rochmon wondered why he bothered with ephemera at all, and why he didn't buy ones that lasted longer. The answer had something to do with shame and confusion, anger and lust, all mixed with an alien image so erotic even after all these years that it always caused a physical stirring in his loins.

The light in the room faded to reflections of reds and purples before the insistent dinging of his milcom pulled Rochmon from his reverie. He hated that thing, hated his agreement to having it installed, and hated the war which made it necessary for him to be always within reach of headquarters—his headquarters. With a sigh he stood up and moved to the back wall of the room where the milcom rested beside his bed.

"Rochmon," he said firmly, after he keyed the transmitter.

"Captain Gilbert, Commander. Your pardon, sir, for bothering you at home, but Admiral Stonefield said—"

"No apology necessary, Mica. Stony told you to contact me immediately, which means that you've agreed to join my staff."

"Yes, sir. Right on both counts."

"So now what are you going to do?"

Mica thought she detected a sarcastic note in his voice, but dismissed it as caused by the communications equipment. "I don't know exactly what you mean, sir?"

"I mean, Captain Gilbert, are you going down to headquarters and hang around like some fleety on first duty, or are you coming here so that we can celebrate?"

"Uh, sir, I—well, I'm already *at* headquarters."

Rochmon laughed. "Doesn't surprise me. You get a driver to bring you over here topspeed, and I'll gather some of my off-duty staff at the Officer's Center."

"But sir, I thought—"

"This is your first official order, Captain. You wouldn't want to start off with the wrong wing forward, would you?"

"I'm on my way, sir."

"Good." Rochmon broke the connection and immediately questioned his motives. Never before had he welcomed an addition to his staff with any kind of reception, informal or otherwise. Why had he decided to make an exception in Mica's case? Because it's Mica, he thought as he stepped into his shower. Just because it is Mica.

As Mica waited for the driver to bring her skimmer around, she was full of her own questions. As much as she liked Rochmon and was pleased to be assigned to his staff, she did not like the underlying tone in Rochmon's voice when he ordered her to the O.C. There had been something unprofessional about it, something she had no way of evaluating, but something her instincts told her was dangerous.

Rochmon dangerous? That was stupid. Admiral Stonefield's demand that she become an honor trustee must have worked deeper into her thoughts than she realized.

The skimmer pulled up, and her concentration was broken for the moment. As she strapped herself in, she tried to dismiss all the questions. Rochmon was an old friend of her father, a friend who had a special interest in her for that reason, and that reason only. There was nothing wrong with his wanting to celebrate. It would be rude of her to spoil a gathering in her honor with groundless worrying about tone of voice or anything else so insignificant.

At least that is what she told herself over and over again as the skimmer hummed through the dark on the way out to the Officer's Center . . . what she tried to make herself believe.

When Rochmon greeted her at the door with a glass of wine and a wrong-handed salute, she almost did believe that nothing was wrong. After a dozen introductions and several more glasses of what turned out to be very strong wine, Mica realized she was slipping back into her old attitude toward

Rochmon, the one she had carried with her since girlhood. He was wonderful. He had always been wonderful. But if he was so damned wonderful, why couldn't she let the nagging, annoying feelings go by the board?

"And last, but by no means least," Rochmon said as he pulled a woman of indeterminate age in front of Mica, "this vision of stern beauty is Jectiverdifiaad Barrabockerman Montivillieo Questen Pasqualini."

"He's the only one at HQ who can remember that much of my name," the woman said with a tight smile and an extended hand. "You can call me Bock."

"Bock, the civilian rock of cryptography," Rochmon said.

"Pleased to meet you, Bock," Mica said.

"Of course you're pleased to meet her. Now you two talk. I have some subordinates to dress down." Rochmon's eyes twinkled as he turned and left them.

"He's had a little too much to drink," Bock said quietly. "In fact, I don't think I've ever seen him drink this much."

"My fault," Mica blurted without thinking.

"How so, Captain? Have you been using your charms on our handsome commander?"

Mica felt the cutting edge under Bock's words and caught herself before she responded. "Certainly not. Have you?"

Bock laughed oddly. "Fair shot. I've tried," she said with a quick glance across the room where Rochmon was talking earnestly with one of his officers. "Several times, as a matter of fact. But . . . I don't think I'm his type."

After waiting for Bock to add something, Mica finally said, "He's one of my father's old protégés."

"And now you're one of his."

"I beg your pardon," Mica said as the anger flushed her cheeks, "but if you have some reason to say these things, then I suggest you get them out in the open right now. I do not see what right you have—"

"Don't get defensive, Captain. Rule number one: Keep others on the defensive, but never become defensive yourself. May I find you some more wine?"

"You may not," Mica said firmly. This woman with her finely etched skin and odd sense of humor needed to be avoided. "But I thank you just the same. Now, I think it is time for me to leave. If you'll excuse me?"

"Absolutely. You are a very excusable woman."

Before Mica could respond, Bock turned, slipped past two people who had been standing behind her, and was gone. Mica did want another glass of wine, if only to wash the sour taste out of her mouth. But the way her nose tingled told her she had already had more than enough to drink.

As gracefully as she could, she made her way across the room to Rochmon's side. For a moment he did not seem to notice her. Then he stopped in the middle of a sentence and looked into her eyes for a brief, piercing moment.

"We'll finish this discussion tomorrow, Lajardy," he said to the young officer. Then he turned back to Mica. "You are getting ready to leave, aren't you?" he asked.

"Yes, Commander. I think I've had enough to drink."

"Bock didn't bite you, did she?"

"Of course not. She's a, hmm, very interesting woman."

"She's a cryptographical genius whose gonads have gone berserk. Did she tell you she'd seduced half the people in this room? Male and female? And a dozen or so aliens, just that we know about?" Rochmon laughed. "And you think I've had enough to drink."

Mica returned his gaze, but refused to answer. This all seemed like a terribly wrong way to begin her new assignment.

"Actually, Mica, I've only had one drink all day, and that one was before you called. The rest has been, shall we say, a slight act for the sake of these nice people who came on short notice during their off-hours to meet you."

Confusion encompassed her fully now. All this made very little sense, but she knew that if she did not leave immediately, she would be in trouble. "I really do have to go, sir."

"Of course you do. But first there's something I have to show you. Follow me, please."

The sudden change in his tone startled her again. She followed him quickly through a door, down a short hall, and over to a slide chute. Moments later, they dropped through a tunnel in the cliff and came to a gentle rest at the door to Rochmon's quarters. He opened the door to the dimly lit room and Mica stepped in without hesitation. A pleasantly musky male odor mixed with a scent she couldn't identify gave her a slight shiver of fear.

Rochmon stepped past her and sat in one of the chairs in front of the window which looked out over the ocean. "Sit down, Mica," he said with a wave toward the other chairs.

"Perhaps I shouldn't stay, sir. I mean, how would it look, sir, to your—"

"How would it look to have my new communications officer turn out to be an honor trustee?"

Mica sucked in her breath. "You know, sir?"

Rochmon laughed bitterly. "Found out right after I talked to you. Hard to keep secrets around my people."

Mica nodded in the direction of the O.C. "You mean they all . . .?"

"No. Just Bock and me. Now sit down, Mica. There are some things I need to know about this."

"I'll have to report this conversation, sir," Mica said as she sat in one of the chairs facing him.

"That is your duty. But you are my subordinate, and at the moment, I don't care what you report to the Joint Chiefs. The only thing I care about is what they instructed you to do." He paused and let his body relax slightly in the chair. Despite his reasons for having brought her here, Rochmon liked having Mica in his quarters.

Mica felt strangely calm. Whatever else happened, at least all this would be out in the open between them. " I was told that you were above suspicion, sir, if that's what has you concerned. I was also told that you were absolutely the only one I should consider above suspicion."

Rochmon snorted. "Until I do something you do not understand. If I am above suspicion, why didn't they tell me about you? Answer me that one, Captain."

"You've answered it yourself, sir. Someone obviously did tell you, maybe in the only way they could—" Mica stopped on a sudden suspicion of her own. Then she added, "Because they were so far away." She looked steadily at Rochmon in the dim light for signs of reaction. Rochmon returned her gaze, then sighed softly and seemed to struggle momentarily with something in himself.

"Your father," he said finally. "How'd you guess?"

"I didn't. You told me. I just suspected that he was the only one who would do it this way." But how? she wondered, There had been so little time.

"He's still a tough old bird. Told me to grill you if necessary." Rochmon smiled.

Mica returned his smile, but had to force it at the edges. A tense awareness pushed past the alcohol in her system and demanded her attention. She had missed some signal from Rochmon, and she did not want to miss it again. "That's all right, sir. He told me to kick back if you got too rough," she said.

"Which leaves us with you as an honor trustee spying on my staff whether I like it or not."

"Nobody asked me if *I* liked the idea, sir. They just told me to do it."

* * *

Twenty tiny ships drifted into the fringes of the Matthews system, braked almost imperceptibly, then settled into their designated observation points. Each ship carried one crew member who had volunteered for a mission which meant certain death. If they were discovered, they would almost certainly be blasted from space. If they were not discovered, they would die with their ships, ships incapable of getting them across the Matthews system, much less back to U.C.S. space.

There was no rescue planned for these observers. The mother ship which had launched them had only paused long enough to spit them out and disappear back into the void of subspace. They were expendable from the moment they volunteered, and they knew it.

None of the crew members cared about that. Each had personal reasons for being there, reasons that could all be summed up in one word: revenge. Their lives were of little importance in comparison to the greater goal of wreaking havoc on the Matthews system and establishing a base of operations from which the U.C.S. could bring its full fury against Sondak's heart.

Only Frye Charltos and a few select members of his command knew about their existence and their mission. He alone knew that they served a dual purpose. If they failed in their secondary mission, only he would know. If they succeeded, their names would be added to the long list of those who had made the ultimate sacrifice for the United Central Systems and for a greater cause of peace in the galaxy.

* * *

Post Admiral Pajandcan bounced neatly off the walls of her office in an impressive low gravity release of highly controlled frustration.

"How in the name of anything holy"—pause-bounce—"am I supposed to defend Reckynop"—pause-bounce—"much less the whole of the Matthews system"—pause-bounce—"with the mite-poor ships, troops"—pause-bounce-bounce—"and supplies you've allocated us?" she asked her visitor in a surprisingly even tone of voice.

Her visitor was too busy ducking to answer.

"Who do you think we are fooling"—pause-bounce—"by shuttling all those empty ships through the system?" She flipped over once, landed in her chair, and stared calmly at her nervous visitor. "Well, dirtsider? You have any answers to those questions? Of course you don't, *Mister* Dawson," she said before he could respond, "'cause there aren't any. Not a damn one. So why'd they send you out here?"

"With the admiral's permission," Dawson said as firmly as he could, "I am to be your new defense coordinator."

Pajandcan cursed softly. "A blinking civilian dirtsider is supposed to help me defend this whole poked-up system? Drone ships I could have used. Rim satellites I could have used. Old, spaceworn battle cruisers I could have used. But how am I supposed to make use of you, Mr. Dawson? And how are you going to help us? How?" She stared at him with unveiled disgust.

"I don't know that yet, Admiral. I've done a preliminary analysis, but until I get more detailed information locally, I won't be able to—"

"You won't be able to defend beggars from children. Admit it, Dawson, you're just one more ruse they're throwing out here to keep me from deserting my post and taking everyone with me."

Dawson opened his mouth, then shut it quickly.

"What experience do you have, Dawson?"

"I was war-games coordinator for the last two full-fleet exercises," he said quietly.

"Oh, well, drip on my deck, then," Pajandcan said. "You're a blinking expert then, aren't you? What was the last real war you were in? You do know what a *real* war is, don't you, Mr. Dawson?"

"The Salimar Rebellion, twenty-five through twenty-seven."

"And what were your rank and duties there?"

"Defense coordinator for the Gyle Coalition."

Pajandcan kept the surprise off her face. "How old were you then, Dawson, fifteen?"

"Forty-eight, Admiral," he said with a slight smile, "that is forty-eight of Salimar's years which would be about sixty-some-odd universal years."

Again Pajandcan held her surprise in check, but she looked at Dawson with the beginnings of new respect. It was hard to believe that he was as old as he claimed, but it had been just as hard to believe that the Gyle Coalition had agreed to a truce. Their defenses had been more than adequate in the three systems they had controlled, but the truce had been an economic necessity for their continued survival.

"I suppose all of that is here in your records," she said quietly, "and if I hadn't been so angry, I might have read that before letting go at you?"

The question was rhetorical, and Dawson had the good sense not to respond to it.

"Very well then, Mr. Dawson, perhaps we should discuss the possibility of your becoming defense coordinator. Then we might talk about exactly what you need to know. But, before we do that, I want you to go eat a solid meal and let the medlab give you the standard checkup. I don't want you getting sick on me in the middle of my defenses."

"As you wish, Admiral. When shall I report back to you?"

"I'll call for you, Dawson. I'll call for you."

As soon as he left her office, she picked up his file and broke the seal. After skimming the usual transmittal forms, she plugged Dawson's datacard into the slot at the base of her screen and watched the first bank of information roll into place.

Pajandcan whistled through her pointed teeth. Dawson was *homo communis*, ninety-three universal years old, born on Salimar III (Croate), educated there, etcetera, etcetera. The next bank told the part of the story she was interested in.

Not only had Dawson organized and directed the overall defense plan for the Gyle Coalition, he had also commanded the task force which had defeated Admiral Y'Ott's final attack on Granser's planet.

I'm losing my edge out here, she thought. Too many years stuck in the middle of nowhere. She read on.

Dawson was under special contract to Sondak's Joint Military Command, a paid consultant for spitting in space! But he'd done everything he'd told her he'd done, and more—much more.

Pajandcan turned off the viewer and yanked Dawson's card out of the slot. What did Sondak need her for if they had this genius dirtsider to coordinate her defenses? Maybe she should apply for a fleet job commanding a bucket somewhere. Might even have enough of her reflexes left to be a pipe jockey. At least then she might see some action and take her chances on going out with style instead of . . . instead of what?

With a grim smile she twisted her limber body, pulled her feet behind her head, and leaned back in her chair in a position only she would have thought of as comfortable. What would Josiah Gilbert say if he could hear me thinking like this? she wondered. The old toad is just as isolated as I am, commanding a haphazard assembly of scrounged-up ships that they dare to call Polar Fleet. But he would still probably give her his usual lecture on duty, service, and honor if he knew what she was thinking.

But he didn't know. And if she ever saw him again, she wouldn't tell him. If she ever saw him again, there were too many things she wanted to tell him, like what a bastard he was, and how much she hated his guts, and how much she respected him as a man of integrity.

And how much she had loved him once?

No. He didn't need to know that. Neither did she. That was a long past chapter in both their lives when she had been too proud and he had been too honorable, and they both had been too stubborn to quit the military and too weak to grab each other and run for the stars.

Pajandcan laughed. What wonderful romantics they had been, he the *homo sapien,* bound and braced by traditions he didn't even understand; she the *homo electus,* convinced that she was one of the chosen people, unwilling to break that myth for the love of a lesser man. But Josiah had been anything but lesser.

Too late she understood how much alike they truly were and how closely their feelings and philosophies paralleled one another. Too late she had come to her senses only to find herself separated from him by endless parsecs. When she had finally sent him that message of apology and invitation, he replied point-blank that it was too late—much too late.

Slowly Pajandcan unwound her feet from behind her neck and lowered them to the deck. She only hoped it wasn't too late to set up some real defenses for the Matthews system. If this Dawson could do the job with the equipment she had available, more power to him.

But she suspected that whenever the Ukes were ready, they were going to come bounding out of space with lasers blazing and neutronics burning the skies. All they had to do was capture seven key space stations and Reckynop Command, and they would have effective control of Matthews system. With that accomplished, they could mop up the resistance on Reckynop and the minor bases at their leisure. The only thing Pajandcan didn't understand was what the Ukes were waiting for.

7————————

Frye read the message with a sharp mixture of elation and anger. Lisa Cay was safe, but she was being held at some place called Alexvieux pending confirmation of relief for a party of stranded scientists. It was bad enough that some Oinaise merchant was involved, but her message also asked for safe passage for a lightspeed freighter with Sondak registry. What in Decie's name had she gotten herself involved in?

There was no time to worry about that. "Melliman!"

Moments later Melliman stood perfectly at attention before him. "Sir?"

"Relax, Melliman. Take a seat, and tell me what you make of this message."

"It appears authentic, sir," Melliman said as she sat in her usual place beside his desk, "in spite of the fact that we haven't used that code base for almost—"

"Ten years," Frye said quietly. "Ten years."

"The reference to Alexvieux Five is real enough, sir," she continued. "Chadiver has had a series of scientific missions there over the past several decades."

"I thought all those scientific missions had been ordered recalled?"

"Alexvieux Five was one of the exceptions, sir."

"By whose order?"

"The record doesn't indicate. However, I believe Marshall Judoff has an interest in Alexvieux."

"And why do you believe that, AOCO?" Frye was suddenly curious about Melliman's information.

"Because she believes Alexvieux has military potential, sir.

She said as much in front of me one day when I was in her office picking up those Deo-D records for you."

"She told you that?"

"No, sir. She was showing off that new holospan galactic map of hers to a subordinate and explaining how Alexvieux could one day prove of great strategic value to the U.C.S."

"Do you think that's true, AOCO?" He watched her as she thought carefully before answering.

"Any place can have strategic value, if for no other reason than because it appears not to have strategic value."

"Very well. We'll let that rest for the moment. What other information can you add to the contents of this message?"

"Exceedingly little, sir. The Oinaise ship satisfied all security checks before leaving Quadulbank, and would have been within range of an emergency beacon from Alexvieux on its scheduled course. There is almost no information on the Sondak ship except that it also has U.C.S. trading registry."

Frye cocked an eyebrow. "That means . . .?"

"That it is an officially recognized trading vessel."

"Except in time of war," Frye added with a smile. "Anything else, Melliman?" For an instant he was aware of how close he was to her and leaned back in his chair.

"Nothing that you don't already know, sir. The message was sent by your daughter."

"And how did *you* know that, Melliman?"

"Because she slipped and used the patfam form of address. Who else would address you as father?"

Frye smiled. Melliman would be shocked if he gave her the true answer to that. "Who else, indeed? Well done, Melliman. Now, what is being done by Chadiver to relieve or rescue those scientists?"

"I'm afraid nothing at the moment, sir. MILCOM Chadiver is responsible for defending a double expanse in that sector, and they just do not have ships to spare."

Frye's smile quickly turned into a frown. "You mean MILCOM Chadiver was going to sacrifice a scientific expedition without so much as an attempt to rescue them?"

"I don't think they had a choice, sir. They didn't have ships of their own to effect a rescue, and there were none close enough to loan for such an effort."

Melliman spoke matter-of-factly, but Frye could tell that her instincts were with his. They both hated the waste of human lives. "All right. Let's send some messages. The first to my daughter telling her to remain there and render whatever assistance she can until relief arrives from Chadiver. The second to the Oinaise—the usual thanks, good wishes, and be gone. The third to MILCOM Chadiver. Tell them to pull a ship from the line and get those people off Alexvieux."

"What about the safe passage request, sir?"

"Approved. No, make that tentatively approved pending final confirmation from this command. I want to think about that. But go ahead and add their registration info to the next update."

Melliman stood up. "Anything else, sir?"

"Yes. We're going to be working late again this evening. Durham's bringing his staff in for briefing and evaluation, so if you're going to eat, you'd better do it now."

"What about you, sir? Can I bring you something, something special perhaps?"

Frye immediately cut off his cold reaction to the warm tone of her voice. "Just the usual," he said quietly without meeting her gaze.

As soon as she left, he cursed softly. Melliman might prove to be expendable after all. He rejected that thought as soon as it arose. She had done nothing, absolutely nothing wrong, and she was the best AOCO he was going to find any time soon. The fault, whatever it was, was in himself. For reasons that he didn't yet understand, Melliman had been setting off cold bursts of fury in him like bombs exploding in a vacuum.

Yet it was his reaction that was at fault. He knew that. Not once had she acted in anything but the most professional military manner toward him. Not once had she given him cause to reprimand her. As an Aide-of-Commander, she was damned near perfect. It would be stupid to transfer her somewhere else because he failed to control his personal reactions.

But it would be more stupid to keep her around if her presence kept annoying him, for he certainly didn't have time to waste trying to analyze his feelings. There were other AOCOs who would suffice if necessary.

*   *   *

General Mari stared into the viewscreen and waited impatiently for the com-window to resolve itself. The independent systems of Cczwyck and Fernandez had both fallen to the Ukes, and now it looked like Matthews system might be their next target, but Mari refused to believe that they would really be so foolish.

Finally a voice broke through the static, but the picture on the viewscreen remained jumbled with harsh, jagged lines.

"Post Admiral Pajandcan for you, sir," the distorted voice said in his earpiece.

"We've got no picture," he said to the technician working beside him.

"No picture here, either," a new voice said in his ear.

"That you, Pajandcan?"

"It was . . . went to sleep, General."

"Yes, of course," Mari said quickly. "Forgot to figure the time difference."

"Say again, sir?"

"The time difference, Pajandcan. Oh, never mind. We need a report from our consultant."

"Can't scramble . . . channel . . . to through Dawson . . . by the measure of it . . ."

"Your transmission is breaking up. Repeat what—" Mari cut himself off in midsentence. The static in his ear went flat, and the screen went blank.

"Lost them, sir," the technician beside him said. "We knew it would be a dirty com-window when we tried it."

"So get them back."

"We can't sir. The window was closing when we started. It's gone now."

Mari flushed with anger. "When can we get her back?"

"On synchronous com?" the tech asked incredulously.

"Yes, on synchronous com," Mari said in disgust.

"The next good window we'll have, sir, will be in about one hundred eighty hours. Until then we'll have to use relays. Shall I call them back on the relay, sir?"

"No," Mari snapped. "I don't want to talk to them on relay. I want to talk to them directly." He stood up, stared at the technician, and swore to himself that the inferior races like these pikeans would be weeded out of the service as soon as this war was over. "Where's Captain Gilbert?" he demanded.

"Uh, she transferred out, sir. To Cryptography, I think."

"Then who's running this section now?" In his anger Mari had forgotten all about Gilbert's transfer. That was something else he didn't approve of. Why should Rochmon have gotten her instead of him?

"Captain Londron, sir, but he's not here at the moment."

"Dammit! Who's here now?" Mari was fast losing control and didn't like it.

"Group Leader Baret, sir," the technician said hesitantly. "Shall I get him?"

"You'd better if you don't want to be busted back down to fleety."

The tech gave him a quick salute and immediately left the room. Mari stared at the communications equipment and tried to calm himself. It had all been happening too damned fast, and for the first time in Mari's career he felt unprepared to deal with the events which swirled around him.

First there had been the surprise attacks which negated all his arguments for the past three years. Then he had been forced to take totally unnecessary abuse from those incompetents from the TriCameral and the Combined Committees. All the while it had become more and more obvious that he was in the minority with the Joint Chiefs. His frustration and anger had mounted accordingly without finding a good outlet.

"Captain Londron, sir," a voice said from behind him.

Mari spun around and found himself face to face with another pikean inferior.

"I was told you wanted to see Group Leader Baret."

"You'll do just fine, Captain. If, that is, you can tell me why we can't get through to the Matthews system."

"It's a matter of com-windows, sir," Londron said with a shrug. "I don't pretend to understand all the physics of it. I just know how to manipulate our communications to—"

"To do everything to frustrate the war effort!" Mari exploded. "I want to be notified the moment you have one of your precious windows to the Matthews system. Is that understood?"

"Yessir!"

"And I want you to notify me, Captain, not some tech or some group leader. You."

"Will do, sir."

"Excellent." Mari left the room without returning Londron's salute and made his way quickly out of the communications center. In the back of his mind he knew he shouldn't have directed his anger at the communications officer, but he didn't care.

He was going to his quarters where Giselda would be waiting to service him. The thought of the gentle, witless pikean brought a thin smile to his lips. Giselda would take his anger and frustration and find her own pleasure in it while he got roaring drunk.

* * *

Quarter Admiral Ingrivia had been addicted to gorlet for more than ten years—addicted to its subtle tranquilizing effects. But it was an addiction she understood and controlled with a self-discipline as rigid as a code of honor. Admitting her addiction to her superiors yet refusing to give up the gorlet had halted the progress of her military career—that, and the anti-pikean sentiments at the higher levels of command. Unable to force her out of the service because of her previous record, her superiors had given her the isolated command of Ca-Ryn.

Once the Ukes ran over Fernandez and took Cczwyck, Admiral Ingrivia made the supreme sacrifice for Sondak. Through three days of vomiting, diarrhea, and hot and cold sweats she had purged her system of the residue of gorlet.

Now the Ukes were approaching Ca-Ryn, and despite her discipline, she longed for one rich, sweet bite of the Oinaise candy and the tranquility that came with it. Instead, she chewed cafpicks, drank liters of herbal tea, and worked for days without sleep to prepare the defenses for Ca-Ryn and Umboolu.

Her efforts paid off. The defense fleet off Umboolu caught the Ukes from behind and severely crippled them. Umboolu eventually fell, but the time gained there had helped her shore up Ca-Ryn's defenses. However, nothing she could have done prepared her for the first sighting of the Uke fleet coming around Ca-Ryn's sun.

"Two launchships and twenty cruisers, Admiral."

"Reinforcements," she said softly. "But from where?"

She had no time to wait for an answer. The first Uke missile tore off the bow of her command ship. Shaken and angry, she immediately started giving rapid-fire orders that sent her own missiles and ships in reply.

With the Flight Corps in the lead of two hundred well-trained, armed civilian pilots, Ca-Ryn's defenders gave the Ukes a fierce and terrible battle.

At the end of the first day, one Uke launchship and seven of its cruisers were out of action.

At the end of the third day, Admiral Ingrivia had withdrawn

her forces into a tight defense of Ca-Ryn itself and was sending them planetside one by one for the final defense.

At the end of ten days, she was commanding the ground troops and had managed to contain every Uke force that landed.

She smiled grimly at the small group of her officers outside her hillside headquarters. "The Ukes may control our space," she said with a half-wave at the sky, "and they may cut us off from the rest of the galaxy, but they'll never control Ca-Ryn itself. Not as long as I am in command. Whatever else we do—"

A thunderous explosion rocked the hillside, and only one officer lived to remember her words.

* * *

Leri buried the second gupling with the same resignation as she had buried the first. Her only serious disappointment had been that the one she suspected of carrying the ambassador's soul still lived. But it was not for her to question the ways of the Elett.

Ranas curled by her side, unspeaking as the rituals demanded, but with an strong attitude of censure that he transferred to her through the scent of his skin. Leri knew that Ranas was disturbed by her actions, and she knew that sooner or later she would have to face the problems she had created by killing the four ambassadors.

Yet Leri was consumed by a vision which had pushed everything else aside for her. After the birth of her guplings, she had dreamed of a path through the mists, a way to lead her race free from the humans and Sondak. Since then the dream kept recurring, each time a little clearer and more compelling.

"It is done," she said quietly as she sealed the narrow grave with the mucus from her body. "So be it."

"So be it," Ranas echoed.

"You are angry," Leri said.

"I have no right to be angry."

"You are still angry. I can smell it on you."

"You smell your own discontent, my mate."

"I smell your anger and disapproval," Leri snapped as she slid away from him and flashed her lean body back toward their nest and her remaining guplings.

"I will listen when you are ready to talk," he called after her, "and soon you must talk."

"Go away," she hissed quietly, knowing he could not hear her and hoping that he would follow. She did need to talk. She needed to tell someone about the vision, if not Ranas, then perhaps one of the Confidantes. If the vision became much stronger, there was danger that she would succumb to it and be led away from her duties as proctor. Some way had to be found to combine the vision with the duty and make them both—

The roar of an approaching human craft broke her thoughts and made her hurry the last few meters to the nest. They were returning much sooner than she expected, much sooner than she was ready for them.

She had barely settled around her daughters when Ranas slid in and announced the arrival of the new ambassador.

"Send him away. I am not prepared."

"You cannot dismiss this one so easily," Ranas said with a heavy tone of amusement.

"What do you mean? I can dismiss them all."

"This one is not human. It is Castorian."

Leri shuddered. "Are you sure? How can you be sure?"

"It told me," Ranas said. "And it warned me not to try to kill it."

"They are soulless," Leri protested.

"We are not," a crablike creature from behind Ranas said in a piercing voice. "We are no more soulless than you are."

Leri shuddered again. This was not part of her vision. "Why have you come here?"

"To breathe your sweet methane, Proctor," the crab said with a rapid clack, "and to intercede for Sondak."

"Do all your people sell themselves in such a way, Ambassador?" Leri coiled tighter around her guplings, suddenly frightened for them and for herself.

"When necessary," the crab answered. "However, I am not an ambassador. I am a scientist and a scholar."

"One of those who evaluated our atmosphere," Leri said.

"Yes, I have done that. I have also been studying your race. From a distance, of course. Most interesting."

"Do you have a name, Castorian?"

"None which translates well. The humans call me Exeter. That will do as well as anything else."

"And what have your human masters sent you to tell us, Castorian Exeter?"

"They are not my masters, and they gave me no instructions.

Such would not be proper, nor would they believe me willing to follow them. I merely offered to speak with you and to determine, if possible, why so many of their ambassadors have suffered, uh, accidents."

"They were clumsy."

"They were human," Exeter said, "but they cannot help that."

"Clumsy. Human. The words are interchangeable."

"Add dangerous to your synonyms, Proctor."

Leri tensed. "Is that a threat?"

"It is a fact, Honored One. The humans will do whatever they feel they must to get what they want. If you obstruct them, you will find them as dangerous as they are clumsy."

"You are threatening us! Leave! Leave our planet immediately!" Leri spat a fireball at him.

Exeter spat a fireball back at her. "A simple trick, Proctor. Is that how the ambassadors had their accidents?"

Leri whistled humorously, suddenly glad to have this Castorian to deal with rather than the stupid humans. "Perhaps their suits were inadequate," she said.

"And perhaps you treated them rather harshly—by their standards, not yours," Exeter added quickly.

"Shall we discuss it, Castorian Exeter?"

"That seems reasonable."

"Good. Tell us first what makes you believe that Castorians have souls."

* * *

Lucky stood on the hill in the fading light and shook his head sadly. He was by no means a talented hunter, but these scientists were even worse. They showed almost no signs of becoming effective with the laser rifles. In eleven local hours the two teams he was assisting had only managed to kill four musterroon. They had taken countless shots and scattered several other herds but brought down no more meat. With the rate of success they had been having for the past ten days, they would all starve to death very quickly.

How did I let myself get talked into this, he wondered? As if in answer to his question, Marsha joined him on the hill.

"Did you live up to your name today?" she asked him as she took his arm.

"I'd have to live up to Benjamin," he said with a slight shake of his head, "because there's no luck to be made here."

"You give up too easily."

"It's been ten days, Marsha! For walking in space! How long do we have to give these chipheads?"

"As long as it takes," she said quietly. "And don't call them that. They're good people, and they're trying hard. You just have to remember that this is very new to them."

"Well, it's new to me, too, but I can see right now that if we armed them all and sat them down in the middle of a herd, most of them would still starve to death."

She squeezed his arm and gave him a mysterious smile, knowing that she shouldn't tease him, but unable to resist the temptation. "Then we'll have to help them as best we can until some relief arrives."

He pulled slightly away and looked at her carefully. "Did we get an answer, Mars?"

"We did. My father's sending help. He asked us to stay until they get here. Then we're to proceed on to Hiifi-11."

"Two points for your father. But where in the galaxy is Hiifi-11? Or is that a secret?"

"No secret, my love, but not an easy place to find."

"Like not in our standard galactic directory," Lucky said with a shiver. "Like a military base, right?"

"Right. Are you cold?"

"I am now." He looked down the hill with a grim smile. At least the chipheads knew how to butcher what they had killed. "Let's go back to the ship."

"Maybe we should see Delightful Childe first," Marsha said as they started walking down the hill. "He said he would be leaving as quickly as possible."

"What? These people can't survive on their own yet, Mars. He should know that."

"He does, my love, and he's leaving what supplies he can to supplement the hunting. However, Father's message was explicit. Delightful Childe has to leave now."

"But that's stupid!"

"No it's not. It's war."

"So all these people, all these innocents from the planet where you were born, their survival doesn't count for anything."

Marsha laughed. "Listen to you! You were the one who was willing to fly out of here and let Delightful Childe cope with the problem. Now you're saying someone has to take responsibility? Why the change? You beginning to like these people or something?" She knew the answer, but she wanted to make him say it.

"Got me. I was wrong before, that's all. There's not one of these people I really like, with the possible exception of Doctor Hachihaguri, but there are none of them I'd abandon when they're in such obvious trouble. You laughing at me for that?"

"I'm laughing because I love you and I—" Marsha paused and cocked her head. "Do you hear that?"

The echoes of hundreds of angry, shouting voices drifted faintly through the still twilight from over the next rise where *Graycloud* and *Nazzarone* rested side by side.

"Sounds like trouble of some kind, but still doesn't make sense, Mars."

"Then we'd better hurry. I suspect they found out the *Nazzarone* is leaving." Marsha dropped his hand, and they started running along the wide trail the musterroon had worn through the thin soil.

8

For seemingly endless weeks the Ukes' major code, the Q-2, splintered and chipped under Cryptography's relentless efforts, but it refused to break.

Mica began a project of refining Cryptography's intercept methods and kept the information pouring into the databanks. Despite the continuing sense of uneasiness she felt around Rochmon, she was glad she had accepted the transfer. She liked the creative tension in Cryptography. She also liked the people and had even grown to admire Bock, who seemed to be everywhere at once and always on duty.

But Mica was totally unprepared when Bock, dark and angry, came roaring up to her one morning, shaking a reel of captape in her face as though Mica should understand why.

"What in the bed of fornicating Castorians is this supposed to be?" Bock demanded, holding the tape within inches of Mica's nose.

Mica bristled for an instant, then remembered who she was dealing with. She stepped back slightly and reached for the tape, turning it so she could read the label. "Just what it says, I suppose. That's the most recent tape of Uke transmissions picked up by ComScan on Reckynop. Is there something wrong, Bock?"

"Is Rochmon horny? Of course there's something wrong, you idiot. This tape has been edited!"

"Not by my staff," Mica said firmly. "We only receive, copy, and dump. Where did you get that tape?"

"An urchin sold it to me this morning! Where I always get my tapes—straight from Depository, of course."

"Then you'd better talk to them."

"I think we'd both better talk to Rochmon," Bock said in a suddenly quiet voice.

Mica knew immediately what Bock was thinking and didn't like it. Bock knew that she was an honor trustee, and now Bock was thinking there was cause.

"Is he here?" Mica asked. "I haven't seen him yet this morning."

"If he's not, we'll get him here." Bock turned and headed toward the corridor that led to Rochmon's office.

Mica signalled a subordinate to assume command and followed Bock as quickly as she could. There was no way her staff could have edited the tapes. They didn't have the time, or the equipment, or the opportunity. Besides, for someone to have edited the tapes, the coded contents of the messages would have to be clear to them.

For the first time since Admiral Stonefield had laid the extra duty on her, she understood why. If someone had edited the tapes, that someone already knew the Ukes' codes, knew them well enough to make quick deletions or changes. Suddenly Mica realized that they could be dealing with the worst kind of Uke agent, one who had been planted years before and was only now being used. She shivered and almost ran into Bock.

"He's here," Bock said, giving her a strange look.

Within minutes they were sitting at the console in Rochmon's office as he started the tape.

"There's the first edit," Bock said when a series of clicks and chirps paused abruptly and then resumed again.

Rochmon stopped the tape. "How do you know it's not just a flaw in the tape? Or in receiving?"

"Listen some more."

After listening for three or four minutes it was obvious even to Mica that the gaps on the tapes were going to be difficult to explain as anything other than editing. In all of her experience, she had never known a piece of communications equipment to cause problems like that, nor had she ever heard transmission gaps so clean. As her mind raced through every possibility, she glanced over to Rochmon and realized he was watching her.

"Editing," she said simply. "But by whom? And when?"

"Good questions," Rochmon said as he turned off the tape. "Add *where* to your list, and we're on the right track."

"Reckynop," Bock said suddenly.

Rochmon and Mica both turned to her.

"It has to be, don't you see? I'm sorry for jumping on you like that, Mica, but it didn't hit me until just this moment. We tape the messages as received, then load them in the databank—"

"Sometimes simultaneously," Mica offered.

"Exactly."

"You mean you don't think it happened at this end?" Rochmon asked.

"We don't know that for sure, sir," Mica said before Bock could respond, "but it would be much easier to tamper with the data before it reaches us than to alter it once it has been received and logged."

"You'd have a hard time convincing me that it's happening at ComScan on Reckynop." Rochmon knew he had to consider that possibility, but he would need more than a little evidence to take it seriously. "Brill Whitdworf runs that station, and she's one of the toughest by-the-book people we have."

"That doesn't mean a damn thing," Bock said.

"It had better. Half of what makes this department work is trust in one another's judgments."

"Bock's right, sir," Mica said with more conviction than she felt. "But so are you. It doesn't make any difference how tight an operation Whitdworf runs. And it does make a difference that you have to trust the head of every ComScan unit."

"Are you suggesting something happened between here and there? That is the most ridiculous thing I ever—"

"No it's not, Bock. Listen to me for a minute. The windows we get to Matthews are too few and too short to use them for routine code traffic, so it all comes to us by relay. Every bit of it. If the Ukes control just one relay station, or even just a key person in one station, they could control all the data we receive. It's that simple."

"How many relays do we normally use?" Rochmon asked quietly.

"Three. But for the past two weeks we've had to use five to get around the interference from the Margaritte Cloud."

"Which means one of the two new relays—"

"Three new relays, sir. We've been using the south polar route because there's less interference that way."

"Then one of the three new relays is suspect," Rochmon said.

"They all are," Bock added. "We have no way of eliminating any of them."

There was a long pause as each of them considered the implications of what they had deduced. Finally Rochmon looked at each of them and asked, "Suggestions?"

"It'll take a test . . . with a built-in trap," Mica offered, "but it will be difficult to set one up without warning whoever is responsible."

"Not if we had the Q-2 code," Bock said quietly.

"Lots of things would be easier if we had that damn code, Bock. The question is, what can we do without it?"

"I think we almost have it."

Rochmon and Mica both looked at her with surprise.

"That's why I checked this tape out of Depository. Spaulding and I stumbled across what looks like a new cycling key yesterday, but we wanted to verify it with this tape. I got so angry when I realized the tape had been edited, that for the moment I forgot all about the key."

Rochmon's eyes reflected his excitement. "How close do you think you are?"

"Close enough so that I think we can break it even with an edited tape."

"How long?"

Bock snorted. "You know better than to ask that. As long as it takes. Two days? A week? I don't know. But it won't take more than a couple of days to know if we're really on the right track."

"And when you break it, we get two rewards instead of just one," Rochmon said with a grim smile. "We get to tap the main channels of Uke information, and we get to catch ourselves a traitor."

Or a spy, Mica thought, unwilling to say the word aloud.

*   *   *

Sjean watched with an uneasy sense of satisfaction as the equations again filled the screen. She had copied Ayne Wallen's files as a routine precaution, fearing that he might very well dump all of them after Caugust fired him. She had been right about that. With typical Tyawese efficiency he had purged the computer of everything under his operating code except an arrogantly annotated copy of his resume. But she had been wrong to delay checking Ayne's files to see what they contained.

They had lost two months of valuable time working in directions that his equations emphatically indicated would lead them nowhere. Yet now that she had found the equations and begun to grasp their significance, Sjean wished she had been able to copy Ayne's thoughts as well as his files. There was too much missing there, too many assumptions behind the equations and implications within them that were totally unclear to her.

But Ayne's basic theory was as plain and simple as the empty equations before her were beautiful. If his equations proved to be appropriate and accurate, reciprocal action at a distance offered a path of research with far more possibilities of success than everything Drautzlab had done in the past five years on simultaneous action at a distance.

What had fooled her at first was the asymmetrical nature of the middle equations. That apparent imbalance had fooled her so well that she had quickly dismissed them as scratchscreen work and gone on to scan the rest of his files. Minutes later as she had paused to examine some curious datafields, she had that odd feeling which hits every research scientist once in a great while—the feeling that she had skipped over something important—something very important.

Now she knew what that something was, and it was time to inform Caugust. It startled her when he answered his own vidphone. "I hate to bother you, sir, but I believe I've found some extremely important equations in Wallen's files."

"Explain," Caugust said in his usual terse way.

"If your terminal is clear, I'll copy them to you first."

"Ready."

Sjean punched in Caugust's code, hit the transfer button, and seconds later heard him say, "I have them, Birkie. What do they mean?"

"Well, sir, if I'm correct in my preliminary analysis, they mean that Wallen found another way to approach the action at a distance problem—a radical way, to be sure, but one which certainly has a nice curve on its theoretical surface."

There was a pause as Caugust scanned his screen. "What is that reverse symbol down in the, uh, sixth set I guess it is?"

"I wondered about that, too, until I read through the middle section. It appears to be Wallen's symbol for the negative exponent that Guntteray theorized would have to exist to account for the dilatation of mass at the moment of ignition."

"Thought we ruled that out last year."

"We did, sir, but only in the standard equations. We never had to evaluate it in this kind of relationship."

"But if the exponent is negative . . ."

"The effect will eventually be reversed," Sjean said with a sudden sense of certainty. "Which means that if these equations test out, they could very well lead to an ultimate weapon which shoots backward and causes a reciprocal action rather than a simultaneous one."

Caugust combed his heavy white beard with his fingers as he again scanned his screen. Then his face broke into one of his rare, wrinkled smiles.

"Looks like you have a new project, Birkie. I'll get Noel to supervise your other projects. Keep me posted on your results."

He signed off before Sjean had a chance to respond. As much as she liked the old man, he frustrated the physics out of her sometimes. She didn't want to abandon her other projects, but she didn't want to give this one to anyone else either.

For the second time since Ayne had left, Sjean was sorry that he had been stupid enough to get himself dismissed. Then she looked at the equations and knew that he had unwillingly given Drautzlab more of his genius than he had ever intended to share. However obnoxious the rest of his legacy was, she knew in a deep, irrational way that he had made one extremely significant contributon to Drautzlab's efforts.

Now it was up to her to move that contribution toward the Ultimate Weapon and Sondak's final goal of permanent peace within the galaxy.

*   *   *

Delightful Childe screamed first in Vardequerqueglot, then in gentongue, then in U. C. Standard, but the face on his viewscreen remained impassive. "What in your mother's ooze do you want us to do?"

"Return and render aid," the checkdroid said.

"But we haven't left yet! Aren't you listening to me? We are still here on Alexvieux Five. However, we are planning to leave as soon as possible because we were ordered to leave. Our conscience is clear that we have done all we can and that further assistance for these people is forthcoming."

"Return and render aid," the checkdroid repeated.

"Agreed," Delightful Childe said with a sudden idea. "Then what shall we do once our aid is no longer needed?"

"Proceed at once to Tomottac, and release your cargo per the specifications of your contract."

"Very well. Anything else?"

"Report as appropriate."

"Thank you. *Nazzarone* out."

Delightful Childe's proboscis fluttered in a deep, rumbling sigh. He had no idea why Buttonface had sought out the *Nazzarone*, but the fact that they were looking for his ship meant nothing but bureaucratic trouble even under the most ordinary circumstances. Now with the bolker shortage and the increasing number of checkdroids taking their places, previous bureaucratic nightmares were beginning to look like the fair days of pleasant dreams.

With a second sigh he flipped on his external viewscreen and looked with dismay and despair at the humans still camped tightly around his ship. Why was it so difficult for them to understand that *Nazzarone* had to leave and that they would be all right? Why were these humans so fearful and dependent? Was it because they were scientists, unused to coping with the realities of the external world? Or was it because they were humans, so caught up in their me-my-us culture that they dared not think, much less work, beyond their own self-interest?

He decided it was because they were human.

Thus he would have to find a human solution. "Send for Doctor Hachihaguri," he said into his throatone.

While he waited for Hachihaguri to come, Delightful Childe comtemplated his two navels, wishing at once that his paternal navel were larger and more aesthetically pleasing, and also that his maternal navel had grown just a shade more red over the years. Actually, he admitted to himself, they were fairly acceptable as navels went, but he felt that with a little cosmetic surgery, they could be aesthetically much more pleasing.

He had always secretly believed that one of the reasons he had only had seventeen mates was because his navels were less than totally attractive. Yet Duvvenay had navels that could truly be considered ugly, and Duvvenay had mated fifty or sixty times and was a full decade younger than Delightful Childe.

No, perhaps ugly navels are not the answer, he thought with grim self-honesty. Perhaps I will have to reconsider the idea of commitment to offspring. And of commitment to mates.

Juices bubbled noisily in his gonad string. A gentle shiver shook his body at the dismal thought of commitment. But he had more than enough time to recover his composure before Hachihaguri was announced into the cabin—more than enough time to wonder what life would be like for a year linked to mate and offspring, and more than enough time to become thoroughly depressed by the whole idea as his juices continued to bubble uncontrollably.

"Greetings, Benevolent One," Hachihaguri said in his normal, cheerful tone.

"Bite dirt," Delightful Childe barked.

"Pardon, Benevolent One?"

"I said, bite dirt, you stupid human. Then tell your people that this ship is lifting planet at sunrise tomorrow. If they refuse to move by then, they won't have to worry any more."

"But, Benevolent One, I—"

"Stop calling me that!" Delightful Childe screamed.

Hachihaguri fell to his knees and covered his ears, his face distorted with intense pain.

"And stop being such a limberneck! Tell your people to move, now! And rumble their turshes if they are too slow about it! Do you understand that, Doctor?" he finished in a slightly lower voice.

A quiet whimper escaped Hachihaguri as he looked up at Delightful Childe with tear-filled eyes. Delightful Childe felt only the slightest pang of sympathy, and no remorse for causing Hachihaguri's painful discomfort. His emotions were still darkly shadowed by thoughts of mates and offspring.

"I understand, Merchant Captain," Hachihaguri said finally, "but I cannot force them to move."

"Then they will die, good doctor, and you will be responsible."

"But, sir—"

"That is all," Delightful Childe said with an annoyed flick of his seven-fingered hand along the fold of skin just above his bubbling gonads. "Sunrise tomorrow. Tell them. Tell them I will not even check to see if they have moved. Tell them I am leaving whether they have moved or not. Is that clear?"

"Yes, sir. But what about Captain Teeman and—"

"Tell them, too. No. I will tell them. You will have quite enough to do between now and sunrise." Delightful Childe felt a twinge of pity for Dr. Hachihaguri, but quickly stifled it. This was no time for pity.

"Now go, Doctor, and take my best wishes with you."

Hachihaguri rose slowly to his feet and gave Delightful Childe an exaggerated bow. "Our thanks for all your kindness, Merchant Captain. In the annals of charity you will—"

"Your thanks are noted. Good-bye."

Hachihaguri looked offended, but he bowed again and left the room, much to Delightful Childe's relief. Humans, he thought with a shuddering sigh. What a dreadful fate to be born human.

Now all he had to do was alert the other two and prepare *Nazzarone* for departure. He would make sure that the humans had moved, that Hachihaguri had done as instructed before he lifted off, but he wanted nothing more to do with them. For the moment his first priority was to quiet the bubbling of his gonad string before his crew heard its embarrassing noise.

The deftly erotic movements of his fourteen fingers came as naturally to Delightful Childe as years of practice in the solitude of space could make them. Yet as his body tensed on the edge of relief, he knew deep inside that sooner or later he would have to mate again—to mate and have offspring.

The vision of himself planetbound came just at the moment of release, and Delightful Childe's body quivered out of harmony with his mind.

9

Admiral Pajandcan read the message with more than a little dismay. It was bad enough that Stonefield and the Joint Chiefs expected her to defend the system with insufficient ships, personnel, and supplies. It was worse that they had stuck her with Dirtsider Dawson, the defensive whiz who seemed to have far more questions than answers. But this—the idiotic directive—this topped everything!

How in the name of suffering humanity was she supposed to "give full and complete attention to resisting the invasion of Reckynop" if she was supposed to defend all of Matthews system? Did they think Dawson was going to perform some miracle and free up the ships she would need to even begin to thwart an invasion? Was that it?

But no. The directive didn't say anything about Dawson.

Suddenly Pajandcan understood. They were telling her that she was relieved of system defense and responsible only for the planet. Anger and frustration burned in her gut.

She hadn't made post admiral by being stupid. If they didn't need her for system defense, then they didn't need her at all! That was what they were telling her. She wasn't needed.

With a swift kick and a curse she bounced out of her chair and hit the overhead with feet together, knees flexed. As she pushed off, she tapped a switch on her belt, and the door to her office popped open. Without hesitation she dove through it, past her startled aide, and landed neatly beside her communications chief forty meters away.

"When's the next window to Nordeen?" she demanded.

He glanced at a digital display and said, "Four hours, Admiral, but—"

"But what?"

"Well, uh, unless you have something really hot to send, we've got priority traffic for every second of that window."

"Oh, it's hot, Torgy, it's really hot. But I'll make it as brief as I can. How about twenty seconds?"

"No problem," Torgy said sharply.

"Good."

Since her office was closer to the hub, it took her two jumps to return to her chair. As soon as the door closed behind her, she began drafting her message. Twenty seconds gave her about a thousand words, enough so she could burn tails and collect ashes all in the same burst message.

An hour later she almost had the wording down exactly as she wanted it, when the defense perimeter alarms went off over her console. She started and thought, so this is it.

Pajandcan immediately switched on the emergency net and scanned the status board. All systems and stations appeared to be responding properly. Pipe jockeys were already launching from the command station. Reckynop's alert net was on-line. The cruisers *Rankin* and *Gephardt* reported battle station preparation commencing. But there was something wrong. It took her a moment to understand what it was, then she switched her viewscreen to Battlecommand.

The face that appeared on the screen was Dawson's—his face looking perfectly calm and self-satisfied. "What is the meaning of this, Mr. Dawson?" she asked as she overrode the channel.

"A test, Admiral. It appears that all systems are functioning properly."

"A test? A test? Get your ass into my office immediately! No one authorized you to test anything, mister!"

When his face disappeared, she said, "All clear and secure. Repeat. All clear and secure." Then she slammed off the screen and spun in her chair. A test? What was that damned dirtsider thinking? Didn't he know what would happen if the perimeter alarms sounded?

That was just it. He probably didn't know. Maybe that was why he ran the test—to find out. But the arrogant idiot should have gotten her approval first. Or was her reaction part of the test? Now that he was in charge of defense, was that it? Was he trying to put her on the defensive?

"An angry defense is no defense." Josiah Gilbert's words echoed in her thoughts as though he had just spoken them. No matter how many parsecs and years separated them, she could still hear his calm voice and steady tone whenever . . . almost whenever she needed him.

Sometimes she resented that. Sometimes she wished he had never been her friend and mentor, because somewhere in their relationship she had built up a resentment of his calmness, of his patient ability to lead her through a crisis in a carefully measured way. Somewhere in the midst of all that she had broken part of herself away from him and denied his right to contribute to her life.

But whether Pajandcan liked it or not, Josiah had been right too often for her to ignore it. And she knew his words that echoed in her head were right again.

She cursed him for that, then began the slow ritual of calming herself down. When Dawson entered her office thirty minutes later, she was in total control.

"Sit down, Mr. Dawson," she said quietly, "and explain to me, if you can, why and under whose authority you tested our defense systems? Then tell me why I shouldn't ship you dirtside until some space tramp can haul you out of here."

Dawson looked slightly amused. "Same reason for both, Admiral. I was ordered here to be your defense coordinator. How can I coordinate a defense system that I've never seen operate?"

"I'll ask the questions, mister. You stick to answering them. What made you think you had the authority to run that test?"

"The admiral told me I was free to observe all functioning systems. Put it on disk," he said smugly, holding out the security disk she had authorized for him.

"But that was never meant to include—"

"I thought it was, Admiral."

Pajandcan looked at him carefully. No matter how impressive his record was, and no matter how hard she tried to like him, there was something about Dawson which irritated the base of her soul. But she was not going to let him get the upper hand in this—not yet, anyway.

"Perhaps you should think again, Mister. Until I receive orders to the contrary, everything within the Matthews system falls under my jurisdiction. Everything—including arrogant civilians who take license where it was never intended."

"But, Admiral—"

"Hear me out, Dawson. Or pack your kit. Those are the only choices you have at the moment."

He stared at her with the strange little smile still flickering at the corners of his mouth, then said, "Very well, Admiral. Everything falls under your jurisdiction."

The repetition of her words, as though he were prompting a child with a lesson, only irritated her further. "Good," she said slowly, "I'm glad you are beginning to understand. But not only does every *thing* fall under my jurisdiction, so does every *person*. That means you, Mister Dawson. In fact, at the moment that especially means you. Is that clear?"

"But of course, Admiral."

"Then there's only one more thing you have to understand for now. If you do anything, anything at all which even faintly resembles this test stunt you just pulled, I will ship you out of here so fast that you'll barely have time to suit up before the vacuum sucks you dry." She stared at him for a moment, waiting for him to respond. Finally she said, "I'll take that security disk now."

"Ah," he said with his disquieting smile growing again, "I wondered if it wouldn't come down to that. You can have this one, Admiral," he said as he handed it to her, "but you may not have this one." Dawson pulled another security disk from his pocket and put its light chain around his neck.

"Mister," Pajandcan said quietly, "I can have anything I want. Apparently you weren't listening very well."

"Oh, I was, Admiral. I was." He took the disk off and handed it to her. "You may certainly look at that disk, and you may verify its authenticity as much as you deem necessary, but you may not have it."

It only took one second for her to recognize the Joint Chiefs seal on the disk, and another second for her tired brain to tell her that there was probably little doubt that it would prove to be valid. On a sudden impulse, she opened the disposal chute at the corner of her desk and dropped both disks in.

Dawson jumped from the chair, then caught himself and slowly sat back down. The smile was gone from his face.

"There, Mr. Dawson. If I may not have that disk, neither may you. That seems fair enough, doesn't it?"

He stared at her in disbelief.

"Now, Mr. Dawson. Explain to me very carefully on what authority you plan to operate in the future."

For a long moment he just looked at her with his expression frozen in place. Then slowly, ever so slowly, his smile crept back to the corners of his mouth. "Your authority, Admiral," he said with a hint of amusement in his voice, "yours and yours alone. Did I get it right?"

"Indeed you did." Pajandcan leaned back with her own quiet sense of amusement. "Do you have any more surprises for us, Mr. Dawson? Like more security disks, perhaps?"

"I wish I did."

"Then you won't mind if we search you, and your quarters, and your personal gear for something that, uh, might not belong to you?"

Dawson's smile grew wider. "Not at all, Admiral."

"Excellent. Now perhaps you would like to explain why you were so eager to test the security systems that you failed to check with me first."

"It's fairly straightforward, Admiral. When I was asked to come here, Admiral Stonefield told me that I was to use every opportunity to evaluate—"

Two defense perimeter alarms squawked in concert with a panel of flashing lights.

Pajandcan hesitated for a split second. Dawson again? The look on his face told her no.

"The real thing," she said as she spun in her chair and flicked on the security net. Again the status board indicated all systems operating according to plans. But again she sensed something wrong. "You again?" she asked, half-turning in Dawson's direction.

"Not this time, Admiral. Looks like the real thing to me."

"Looks like it, but it isn't. Battlecommand," she said as she turned back to the console, "what is your status?"

"Two unconfirmed neutronic missiles."

"How can you have unconfirmed neutronics, Zennte?"

"Don't know, Admiral, but that was the initial report from sector ER-24."

"I'll monitor, Captain Zennte."

"Aye-aye."

"You stay where you are, Mr. Dawson," she said quickly

when she saw him rise from his chair. "I'm still not convinced that this isn't part of your exercise. But if it isn't, if this is the beginning of the Uke attack, you might as well watch the action from the top. Right?"

Dawson sat back down and nodded, the smile gone from his lips, his brow deeply furrowed with concern, his eyes watching the screens intently.

* * *

Lucky flopped into bed, bone-weary and angry.

He had returned from the daily hunting trip to discover a Uke rescue ship resting a thousand meters up the hill from *Graycloud*. A few questions to Dr. Hachihaguri's people revealed that Marsha and Hachihaguri were both aboard the Uke ship. But after Lucky had dragged his fatigued body up the hill, two armed guards had very rudely turned him away and ordered him to return to the encampment. Their response to his demand to talk to their superior was to order him to drop his pistol.

In the face of two blasters he had done exactly what they told him to, but all the way back down the hill he thought of the things he would liked to have done to them. He even thought about taking one of the rifles and making them do a long-distance dance, but he was just too damned tired to make the effort—and too sensible to run the risk, he admitted to himself as he closed his eyes and waited for sleep.

Sleep wouldn't come. All he could think about was Marsha, and those stupid Uke guards. He had hardly had time to talk to her since Delightful Childe had blasted unceremoniously into space the week before. Hunting had taken every moment of their days from dawn to dusk. When they met each evening aboard *Graycloud*, neither of them had had energy for much more than a cursory meal, a quick cleanse, and sleep.

Every muscle in Lucky's body ached with the dull pain of overuse. Dirtside was no place for a spacer, especially a dirtside planet like Alexvieux where the gravity was one-point-three times what he maintained aboard *Graycloud*. He was out of shape, totally out of shape for this kind of physical exertion, and longed . . . to get back into space, he thought, get free of this gravity . . . free of hunting . . . free of every day trying to feed Hachihaguri's people.

Why hadn't Marsha left word . . . for him to join them? Or

was it because . . . of course! The war . . . the damned war. He was from Sondak. They were Ukes. Didn't matter a dust speck in space that he had helped them . . . their people.

The last of his anger died for want of energy. Marsha's face drifted through his dreams, smiling, changing, unhappy, crying. He awoke to the sound of her sobs.

"Mars? Mars? What's the matter?" he asked as he pulled her into his arms.

"It's—oh, Lucky, I'm sorry."

He held her as the sobs wracked her body, willing to let her cry it out, his brain still heavy with fatigue, his thoughts dark and afraid for her—and for them. Finally she calmed down.

"Can you tell me about it?"

"I have to," she said with a quiet sniff, "but I don't know how to. And I don't know what to do."

The whine of uncertainty he heard in her voice was totally unlike her. But Lucky hesitated to ask her anything. The questions rippling through his mind were full of anger and implications he did not want to face.

Finally she whispered, "They say you can't come."

"What do you mean?"

"They say you can't come any farther into the U.C.S."

"What about your father's promise?"

"My father—my father told them to turn you back."

Her whisper was edged with bitterness that ate into his heart. There was nothing he could say, nothing that made any sense, nothing that would help either of them, but he had to try.

"We knew there was a chance this would happen," he said as calmly as he could.

"I didn't. I trusted him. Lucky, I'm going with you."

His hopes jumped, but he dared not believe that she meant it. "Is that what you want, Mars? What you really want?"

"Dammit, Lucky, I don't *know* what I want."

"We came here so you could be reunited with your father, to keep your promise, remember?"

"But I thought—"

"You thought we could do it together. Well, we can't." Even as he said that, Lucky remembered their trip to Alexvieux and the doubts which had nagged at him then.

Marsha pulled herself away from him and propped herself

up on one elbow. "You mean you'd leave me?" There was anger and accusation in her voice.

"I mean we don't have a choice. Look, Mars, we busted away from Roberg to get you home. Now there's a Uke ship waiting to take you there. I'll be all right. And so will you. Besides, this war can't last very long, and—"

"You don't want me to go."

It was not a question—it was a statement, an emotional challenge she had hurled at him. "Of course—no, that's not true. You're right. I don't want you to go, because if you go with me you will be miserable, always doubting yourself, always wondering if you'd done the right thing. Don't you see that?"

She pulled her arms around herself and lay back, staring at the overhead. Sometimes Lucky seemed like a reverse image of her father—acting the same way toward her for totally different reasons. "I don't see that. All I see is that neither of you gives a damn about me. Neither of you cares what I think and feel about all this."

"Then what was I just talking about?" he asked angrily. "I was just talking about how you would think and feel if you didn't go home. Or was I just talking to the bulkheads?"

After waiting a moment for her to respond, he moved closer to her and put his arm around her waist. "Look, Mars," he said quietly, "I'll go along with whatever you decide. But I want you to be sure, damned sure, that you can accept the consequences of either decision. I can't make this any easier for you. I don't know how." Lucky heard his own voice breaking and paused.

"I love you, lady, love you like I've never loved anyone else in my life. And no matter what happens, I'll treasure these years we've had together." As he rested his head on the cushion beside her, he knew he had to stop. There was nothing else he could say, nothing that would be fair to her. Yet inside he wanted to say, *Yes, yes, come with me. Forget about your father and come with me.*

Marsha sensed his need for her—sensed the kind of love that she had always wanted and never had before. Yet there had to be more to it than that. Deep in her heart she was torn in two directions. "Make love to me, Lucky," she whispered fiercely. "Make love to me now."

Despite his efforts to slow the pace, their emotions drove

them to a physical frenzy as they sought not pleasure, but a
greater escape from the universe which surrounded them.
When they finally lay spent and exhausted in each other's
arms, Lucky knew something had changed between them,
something that would never be the same again. She was leaving not just him and their partnership, but part of herself that
she could not take home with her. And he was letting her do it.

*   *   *

The first of the observer ships exploded behind the sixth
planet, close enough to the surface that it escaped detection.

The second exploded in open space after its scanners revealed that escape and evasion was impossible. The Sondak
ships had it triangulated and were closing too fast. Its crewman
grimaced slightly, sent the prepared message for relay back to
its base, and with grim determination flicked the detonator.

For a few brief moments the night sky above Reckynop had a
new star. Then it faded and was gone. The cruiser *Gephardt*
slowed, unwilling to get too close to the radioactive debris, and
immediately started tracking the largest pieces. There weren't
many. What few they managed to locate and retrieve told them
nothing useful beyond what they already knew.

The Ukes had sent a neutronic missile into the Matthews
system, a missile so small that it had been detected totally by
accident. Why it had exploded prematurely no one could even
guess, but if there were more, if the system had been seeded
with such missiles, defense was going to be even more impossible than it already was.

Long after the perimeter alert was eased back to ready status, Admiral Pajandcan and Mr. Dawson sat hunched at her
consoles, reexamining every detail of the defense plan, hoping
to discover some clue which might give them the slightest advantage. When they finally gave up in exhaustion and turned
the project over to others, they had no more hope than when
they started.

If anything, Pajandcan and Dawson now believed that Reckynop and the Matthews system were even more vulnerable
than all their previous assessments had indicated. When the
Ukes came, they would have a field day.

10

The explosion shook the observers platform, and Frye gripped the safety rail with a grim smile. Had he not seen the charge himself, he never would have believed that something so small could have caused so much destruction.

Melliman stood beside him, her pale complexion flushed with a brightness that Frye thought could be either excitement or fear. "Well, AOCO, what do you think of that?"

She took a deep breath before she answered, the front of her uniform pressing against her in a very pleasing way.

"Impressive, sir, but unless the delivery system is equally as small, I do not see how we will benefit from it except for use by the invasion forces."

"Exactly, Melliman. Exactly. You saw the size of the charge which caused that. If every landing squad had two or three projectile weapons of that kind of destruction, who would be able to stop them?"

Melliman looked at him curiously. "Mobile artillery, sir?"

"Something like that. It could decimate the enemy in seconds." He winced with perverse pleasure at the thought, knowing the prototypes were already proving their worth in the battle for Ca-Ryn system.

"And cost a lot of lives, sir."

"Or save them. Depends on who has it, doesn't it, Melliman? And how you use them, he added to himself, suddenly aware of how prepared he was to use them in the most reckless way. "Weapons always depend on who controls them. Watch this."

Regardless of whatever else Vinita's death had done to him,

it had made him more than willing to sacrifice whatever lives were necessary to accomplish his goals and get their revenge. He understood now how truly ephemeral and insignificant any one life was.

The second demonstration was a typical landing squad of twenty-three troops, all armed with the standard lasers and blasters except for three who carried odd, long-barreled rifles. They approached to within a kilometer of the target buildings, then the three new riflemen moved to the front of the squad, took up firing positions, and loosed one three-shot barrage. The nearest building disintegrated in a ferocious explosion of plasteel and rock. Again the viewers' platform shook.

When Frye looked at her, Melliman spoke first. "How many rounds can each man carry, sir?"

"Maximum one hundred. But the squad can carry an additional two hundred for each gunner. That's a lot of firepower." Frye was glad he had brought Melliman along for the demonstration. For reasons he refused to explore, he enjoyed having her close to him.

"What next?" she asked.

"The shielded wall."

The squad had moved another hundred meters closer and again arranged itself so that the gunners were in front. The shielded wall was easily forty meters high and eighty long, but after three earth-shaking volleys, it gaped, sagged, and twisted into smoking chunks of hot metal.

Frye had a brief vision of what would happen to anyone behind such a wall when it was attacked, then immediately brushed it from his mind. The only people behind such a wall would be the enemy.

"Show's over," he said quickly as he brushed the dust from his uniform. "Time for us to get back to work."

"How many of these new weapons will we have in time for the invasion of Reckynop?" Melliman asked as they descended from the platform.

"Not as many as I'd like, but enough to give us one more advantage, AOCO."

They rode in silence back to headquarters, and Frye was tempted to ask Melliman if she would like to have dinner with him. But as soon as that thought crossed his mind, he remembered Vinita, and a coldness crept through him that froze out the idea of doing anything with Melliman.

When they entered his office, Frye asked, "What is the update on the rescue of those scientists?"

Melliman went immediately to her console and coded in a request. After a moment the information came up on her screen, and she said, "They should be arriving any time now, sir."

"And they have instructions to notify us as soon as they arrive?"

"Of course, sir."

"What about reports from Umboolu?"

"Umboolu and Ca-Ryn systems are both now under our control, sir, as of this report," she said tearing a pink update sheet from his imager.

Frye allowed himself a smile of pleasure and looked forward to reading the detailed reports later. "Any further messages from my daughter?" He knew there would be a delay in receiving any messages from Alexvieux, but he was impatient to hear from Lisa Cay.

"No, sir."

"Very well, Melliman. That will be all for now." Frye watched her leave with a hint of anger. At first he thought it was because he had not heard from Lisa Cay again, but a few moments reflection told him it was something far more nebulous than that. He really did not expect to hear anything from her until the rescue ship arrived on Alexvieux. So what was it?

Melliman again.

The answer popped into his thoughts followed by a confused wash of emotions. It took all his concentration to push his personal feelings down and look for a rational reason for this constant reaction to Melliman.

Then he saw it and felt like a fool for not understanding it sooner. In his mind's eye two images crossed and merged, one of a very young Vinita in the uniform of the home guard, and one of Melliman the day she had first reported to him for duty. It wasn't a physical resemblance between them which linked the images as much as a similar military bearing.

Oh, Vinita had been so correct and proper in her uniform, so exact in the way she wore it and in her reaction to him.

Frye remembered telling Vinita years later that Melliman had reminded him of her that first day. Vinita had laughed, saying that it was Melliman's youth and uniform which attracted him. But it had been more than that, and Frye had buried his reaction under his love for Vinita and laughed with her.

Now it all made sense. Now he understood what it was which angered him so unexpectedly about Melliman's presence. And maybe now he could come to terms with those reactions. If not, then Melliman would have to go.

Lisa Cay could take her place. They'd make a tremendous team, father and daughter. He knew that without having any evidence to support it. Yes, a tremendous team.

"Sir?" Melliman's voice interrupted his thoughts.

"What is it?"

"Marshall Judoff is here to see you, sir."

Judoff? What did she want? "Send her in, Melliman, and don't disturb us unless it is absolutely necessary."

"Aye, sir."

Judoff was through the door almost before Melliman's voice died in the speaker. Frye rose to meet her.

"To what do I owe this honor, Marshal Judoff?"

"It is no honor, and you owe me nothing more than explanations, Commander Charltos," she said, taking a chair before he could offer it to her. "Two of your observers in the Matthews system have disappeared."

He wondered how she had found out, but the tone of her voice and her general attitude warned him he would have to be even more cautious than usual with her. "I know that, sha."

"Then why wasn't Bridgeforce informed?"

"Because Admiral Tuuneo made it plain to me that I did not have to report every daily incident in this war to—"

"Well, he didn't make it plain to me, Commander. I want to know what happened to them and what your plans are."

Frye knew better than to try to give her a fast answer. This woman would jump on anything he told her. "I plan to give a complete report to Bridgeforce tomorrow," he said quietly. "However, since you are here, I will be glad to tell you what little we know. Apparently two of the observer ships were discovered during some routine drill Reckynop's defense forces were going through. Per our plan they self-destructed."

"But that's terrible," Judoff said.

Her voice rang false in his ear, and Frye wondered what the real purpose of her visit was. "A necessary precaution, sha. If

Reckynop's forces had managed to capture one of those ships, it would have been far more terrible. As it is, we still have eighteen in place, and another twenty which we will insert shortly before the attack begins."

"At what expense, Commander?"

Frye wasn't sure what she meant and hesitated.

"I asked you a question, Commander. What will it cost us to protect those observers in place and insert twenty new ones?"

"We're not protecting them," Frye said simply. "The insertion of the others will involve one—"

"Not protecting them? Isn't that rather foolish, Commander?"

"Begging your pardon, sha, but I do not understand what this is all about. Perhaps you should save your questions for the Bridgeforce meeting tomorrow."

Judoff stood with a sneer on her face. "And perhaps you should have some better answers by then, Charltos. Good day."

Frye watched her go with a serious sense of confusion. Whatever her intent had been, he had missed it completely. But she had given him a valuable suggestion. He would be better prepared for her questions tomorrow.

"Melliman," he said into his lapelcom, "I'm taking you to dinner."

"Sir?"

"Then we're coming back here and working, until dawn if necessary, to get ready for Bridgeforce."

"Yes, sir."

If there was pleasure in her voice, Frye couldn't hear it. His mind had already jumped ahead to what they would have to do. He wasn't even surprised that he had invited her to dinner. Wouldn't hurt to be nice to her for the little while she had remaining on his staff. Might even find out who else she would like to work for.

* * *

As Admiral Josiah Gilbert rose to speak before the Joint Chiefs, he was pleased to see Mica smiling at him from behind Commander Rochmon.

Duty and circumstances had kept them from sharing any more than a few brief vidcom conversations during the three days he had been down on Nordeen. But if everything worked as planned, they would have at least part of this evening together. He quickly put the thought of that pleasure aside and began his presentation.

"At Admiral Stonefield's request, I have prepared what I believe will be the best possible defense of the Matthews system, one which my staff and I hope will catch the Ukes by surprise and give us the valuable time we need to bring our fleets back up to fighting strength."

"Pardon me, Admiral," General Mari said from the far end of the table, "but would you tell us first why you think the Matthews system should be defended at all? There are some of us who are not sure that it should be defended, much less that it can be."

Mica was surprised by Mari's question, but from the look on her father's face, apparently he was prepared for it.

"Certainly, General—with the group's permission, of course." Affirmative nods around the table gave him the impression that they were all interested in his views, and Gilbert allowed himself a small smile before continuing.

"Firstly, if we successfully defend the Matthews system while at the same time rendering a serious blow to the Uke forces, then we will not only gain much needed time to rejuvenate our fleet as I mentioned before, but we will also gain a victory for the morale of our forces.

"Secondly, if we were to abandon the Matthews system, as I know some of my colleagues have recommended, then we would be signalling the Ukes that we are unwilling or incapable of engaging them in a serious battle."

"What about the south polar systems?" Admiral Lindshaw asked. "Aren't we on the verge of engaging them there?"

"Yes, it appears that way. But unless Commander Rochmon has information to the contrary, the Ukes do not have sufficient forces in the south polar sector to engage in anything more than attacks on those independent systems they have claimed as their own since the last war."

General Mari coughed quietly. "But didn't you once say, Admiral, that those systems were extremely important to the security of Sondak?"

"I certainly did, General Mari, but perhaps I should continue with the whole plan we have devised so that you see how it all fits together."

"By all means." Stonefield's tone indicated an impatience with the interruptions.

As Mica watched her father's carefully controlled reaction, she was suddenly aware of how old he looked. Not old, just tired, she thought, as though it was somehow wrong to think of him as getting old.

"Thank you, sir." Gilbert had hoped his old friend Stonefield would be working with him in this meeting, but with Stony one could never be sure until the shields were down.

"The third, and final goal of this plan is to make the Ukes believe that we suffered fewer losses than they think they caused with their surprise attacks.

"Consequently, the essence of our proposal is fairly simple. We suggest that the main battle groups from CENFLEET, POLFLEET, and HOMFLEET set up skirmish sectors—"

Several gasps broke his concentration for a moment, but he continued. "Set up skirmish sectors along the most likely routes of Uke attack. This will include subspace detection screening as well as widespread standard operations to include—"

"That's insane," Avitor Hilldill whispered, but everyone in the room heard him.

"Perhaps, Avitor," Gilbert said before anyone else could speak, "but it is our opinion that the Ukes will believe exactly the same thing."

"But sir, if it doesn't work . . . if we should fail in this, then the path would be open to the heart of Sondak."

"No doubt, Avitor, no doubt. But if we leave our forces scattered as they are, the Ukes are quite capable of punching holes through them at will. Better that we make a stand around the Matthews system than to stretch ourselves so thinly as to have no real defense at all."

"Suppose they don't attack the Matthews system?" General Mari asked. He had a nightmare vision of Uke forces circling around Matthews. "Suppose they bypass Matthews and strike the First Fringe systems? Do you realize the resources we'd lose, not to mention the blow that would be to morale?"

"Every plan has its risks, General," Gilbert said calmly, "and so far this isn't even a plan. It's just a proposal. But if the Ukes were foolish enough to do what you suggested while we had our combined battlegroups at Matthews, then the heart of the

U.C.S. would be open to us. I suspect we would give better than we got from them."

"What makes you so sure they'll strike Matthews anyway?" Admiral Eresser asked. It was the first time she had spoken and all heads turned in her direction. "Oh, I know we have Commander Rochmon's intercepts, and I've read the decoded Q-2 reports from their group leaders, but how do we know all of this isn't just a ruse?"

"Perhaps I should answer that, Admiral," Rochmon said. "It's more than just reports, ma'am. When we broke the Q-2 code, we tapped into their routine traffic as well, all the forcekeeping information which gives them daily status on all their ships and personnel. The Ukes are very systematic about all that, Admiral. Very systematic. There hasn't been time to translate all of their messages, but constant throughout what we have translated is their massing of two main battle fleets, the smaller one under the command of Kuskuvyet, and the other under an unnamed commander that we believe will be Charltos."

"Would they dare risk him in battle?" Hilldill asked.

Hilldill had been following Charltos's career almost as long as Rochmon had, and Rochmon knew the question was very valid. "I don't think it's a question of dare," Rochmon said. "I think it's a question of Uke tradition. The planner of the battle is required by tradition to participate. I'm betting my credits on Charltos, because Kuskuvyet is a political commander, not a military one."

"And you believe this battle fleet with the mystery commander will attack Matthews system?"

"If they don't, General, they will have wasted a lot of time and effort getting ready to do it. But I'll tell you what the biggest clue is, sir. The A-fleet—that's what we call the big one— the A-fleet is drawing more than its share of medium-range attack ships. We did some quick figuring and decided that the only reason those ships would be needed was if the Ukes had a base from which to use them. And the only suitable base which would give them the ability to attack systems over half the length of the First Fringe is Reckynop."

Mica had heard this line of reasoning earlier in the day, but she enjoyed hearing Rochmon present it again in front of the Joint Chiefs.

"If they control Reckynop, they can harass twenty major systems and another fifteen smaller ones from there. No other location gives them that kind of ability." Rochmon looked around the table and saw the looks of concern. "Sorry, Admiral Gilbert. Perhaps I've said too much." Abruptly he sat down, knowing he had left Admiral Gilbert back in the position of authority.

"Not at all, Commander." Gilbert wanted to slap his former protégé on the back with joy. If the Joint Chiefs weren't convinced now that Matthews system needed defending, nothing he could add was going to impress them.

"How detailed are your plans, Admiral Gilbert?" Stonefield asked after a long pause.

"Not nearly as much as they should be, sir. There was no way, of course, that I could keep up with our current situation while on my way here, so by necessity I had to make certain assumptions which proved invalid once I arrived. However," he added quickly, "it would not take long to formulate the specifics once we had the proper authorization."

"Thank you, Josiah," Stonefield said as he shifted the focus of the meeting to himself. "I'm sure there are a great number of questions we could ask—and no doubt will ask if we approve this course of action. But for the moment, I think you and Commander Rochmon have laid the situation out for us fairly well.

"Now, unless someone has further comment or objection, I think it is time we decided exactly what we are going to do about the Matthews system."

"I do have one further question," General Mari said, "but I am not sure this is where it fits in."

"Go ahead, General."

"What about Admiral Pajandcan's report this morning, sir? If the Ukes have seeded the Matthews system with neutronic missiles, what effect should that have on our decision?"

"None," Gilbert said quickly. "Sorry, sir," he added with a nod to Stonefield. "It wasn't my place to answer that question, but regardless of what lengths the Ukes are willing to go to in the Matthews system, our decision should be made on what is best for Sondak."

"And if they have seeded the system," Stonefield said quietly, "that would probably be further confirmation of Commander Rochmon's assessment of the situation. They would have to be pretty serious about wanting Reckynop in any condition in order to use neutronics. Does that satisfy you, Mari?"

"Yes, I suppose it does, and I have to admit that despite some severe reservations about stripping our active forces to defend Matthews, I think the defense itself is our best course of action."

Mica and Rochmon shared a look that said they both knew how hard it had been for Mari to make that statement.

After a few minutes of further discussion, the Joint Chiefs voted six to one in favor of making the defense of Matthews system their first priority. Josiah Gilbert heaved an internal sigh of relief.

"So, Josiah," Stonefield said almost informally, "you have our full resources at your disposal. How soon can you have a preliminary plan for us?"

"Two days, sir. Three at most."

"Make it two, Josiah. We have no idea how much time we have before the Ukes strike."

"Yes, sir."

"And," he said, leaning on his hands and facing the entire table, "I want recommendations from each of you as to who should command this combined battle fleet."

For the first time since the meeting had begun, Josiah Gilbert was caught by surprise. He had assumed that if they accepted his plan, he would be the battle fleet commander. But Stony certainly understood the politics of this decision much better than he did. Better to wait and see what happened than to say anything now, he thought.

"Then I think that concludes the major business of the day. Commander Rochmon, if you would escort Admiral Gilbert to your headquarters and help him in any way you can, we would all appreciate it."

Mica followed Rochmon and her father out of the meeting room with a sense of pride in what she had witnessed. Her feeling was tempered by the understanding that Sondak was about to take a huge risk—and if their gamble did not pay off, her father's career would go down in ruins. But when the door closed behind them and her father turned and held out his arms to her, nothing else in the universe mattered for the moment.

11————————————

During her weeks of negotiating with Exeter the Castorian, Leri reviewed Cloise's long history of petty mistreatment at the hands of Sondak's economic pirates. She reminded him that only Cloise's dependence on Sondak for the agricultural assistance now necessary to support Cloise's growing population gave them reason to continue such a relationship.

Yet as Leri renewed her hate for Sondak and all humans, she also gained a great deal of respect for Exeter. She had to admit that the implacable crab definitely had traits worth admiring, and a better sense of humor than ten or twenty humans combined.

With a great concern that she not offend him, she had chosen the music for this season's meeting very carefully—a subdued but uplifting piece by Shetotum with classical overtones that would give appropriate background to half a season's conversation. If their meeting lasted longer than those ten hours, she had programmed the music to repeat.

Now as he faced her, she chose her words just as carefully as she had chosen the music, and wished, not for the first time in the last few seasons, that her term as proctor was over.

"Despite your best efforts to intercede for Sondak, my gracious and intelligent friend, I am afraid we must decline this offer your human, uh, allies have described as their last. Better that they rob us of our atmosphere than of our honor."

"But I still do not understand how your honor is at stake here, Proctor. I apologize for that, knowing it is a deficiency on my part, but since I have agreed to relay this message, it would behoove me to try one more time to comprehend exactly what your objections are."

The music swelled just as Exeter finished speaking, and for a brief moment Leri suspected she had chosen poorly. However, before she could answer him, Ranas slithered into the chamber.

Ignoring Exeter, he slid up beside Leri and hissed, "They have begun."

"Begun what? And why do you interrupt us like this?"

"The tankers have arrived. They have begun collecting."

Leri stared at Exeter and saw that he had politely pulled his head back into his shell. "Exeter!" she screamed, sending a small fireball over his head for its dramatic effect, "I demand an explanation!"

His head popped out of his shell as though his tail had been stung. "Pardon, Proctor? An explanation for what?"

"Ranas informs me that the Sondak tankers have arrived, and their collectors have already begun working." She let the natural gruffness of her voice rise slightly as she spoke, hoping Exeter would sense her anger and dismay.

"But Proctor, that is within the limits of the previous agreement."

"It certainly is not!" she screamed again. Her voice rose another octave, and a froth of fire sputtered from her mouth. "You will return to your treacherous human *friends*, now, and you will demand that they immediately cease their collection efforts. Otherwise all these negotiations end. Now. Forever. We have certain steps we can take to safeguard—"

"No, Leri."

"Hush!" she hissed at Ranas. "As Proctor, it must be my decision." She swiveled her long head back to Exeter. "Do you understand me, Castorian?"

"I understand only that you are upset, Proctor, and that there has been some misunderstanding—"

"There is no misunderstanding, Exeter. Tell them to stop, or we will ignite the surface." There, she thought, I have said the magic words. Now let us see—

"Leri!" Ranas said in his most deeply anguished tones. "You cannot!"

"But I can. And I will." I should have warned him, she thought, but now—

"It would kill us!"

"Hush, Ranas, and leave us. Your emotionalism disturbs me. We have ignited the surface before, and we can do it again. Let Sondak gather its methane elsewhere." She had hoped he would understand what she was doing, but the fierce scent of disapproval from his skin told her otherwise.

Exeter made quiet chattering sounds to himself as Ranas slid sullenly out the back entrance of the chamber. "Forgive me, Proctor," Exeter said finally, "but by your own records—the Isthian records—the last ignition of your atmosphere's surface almost decimated your race."

"So it did, Exeter the Castorian, and so it might again. But it also stopped another group of pirates, those who would have stolen an equally precious resource from us."

The music swelled again, and Leri was not sure her tone had been quite right, so she waited a moment for him to respond. When he didn't, she spoke with all the sternness she could muster in her voice. "Go now, Exeter, before I lose patience."

"As you will, Proctor. But may I return once they have ceased collecting your methane?"

His tone had altered also, but Leri had no idea what that signified. "Only if you return with guarantees," she said quietly and with just the proper touch of sadness.

Exeter clacked something unintelligible with his claws over his head, as was his wont in taking leave of her, then scuttled from the chamber to the fading strains of Shetotum's overture.

Leri was annoyed and distressed. She had fully expected Sondak to try something of this nature, and she was thoroughly prepared to lay her bluff on Exeter's shell as soon as they did it. If Sondak's tankers refused to stop collecting, she would order the surface ignited to prove her sincerity to them. What they could not know, of course, was that her own Isthian scientists had discovered a way to extinguish such fires.

Those were not the things which distressed her. Ranas upset her most—Ranas her beloved mate, father of her guplings, troubled emotionalist—Ranas who no longer held the center of her affections, who would be deeply hurt if he knew that the young Weecs had slithered into her chambers and into her heart. But Ranas presented the most complicated of her problems, so she pushed thoughts of him aside until she could meditate on him later with less distraction.

Another annoyance came with her vision of the future which had grown alternately cloudy and clear during her dealings with Exeter. She knew the vision was important. Yet she knew there was no way to force it into the open where she could better examine it and use it to guide her path.

The guplings were next, especially Voneri, the one she was now positive was possessed by Ambassador Fushtig's soul. Custom demanded that she kill Voneri within the next ten seasons or acknowledge her right to live with whatever soul she possessed. Leri was still undecided about what to do, and Ranas had been little or no help with that serious concern either.

Last was her growing impatience with her duties as proctor. The vision showed her continuing with those duties, but Leri was no longer comfortable or content with what was demanded of her in this position. It was almost as though some external force demanded that she split herself in two, serving the vision with one part of herself and the rest of her life with the other.

Yet sometimes it was all she could do to serve one side.

Weecs represented part of her problems as well—and part of one possible solution. Their first meeting had been a wild intellectual affair at Lucase, where she had offered a pun in rebuttal to some laughing remark of his one morning, and a full season later they had found themselves curled quietly together in the first green shades of dawn, laughing, talking, and sharing a joy of discovery that Leri had never dared dream would happen to her again. Only as an afterthought had they drawn their tired bodies together and coupled, as though physically sealing the intellectual bond that had formed between them.

Leri had coupled with others outside the nest, others who had caught her fancy and been willing and available partners when she most needed their companionship to counterbalance Ranas's sexual indifference. But never before Weecs had she felt such a tremendous sense of oneness, a sense she had dared not believe until the two of them had repeatedly reaffirmed not only their physical bond, but their intellectual one as well.

Yet Weecs lived halfway round the world, and he had no reason or resources to bring him closer where they might share in the delight of each other's presence more frequently. And for all her power as proctor, Leri had yet to find a way to help him come which would not be transparent to anyone who examined it—but most of all, transparent to Ranas.

As her closest advisor, Ranas would be the first to understand that Weecs was something other than a young, ambitious historian come to watch The Proctor in action.

Leri uncoiled herself and stretched her long, narrow body, seeking physical relief from the tension. With a slight smile she pulled her body into an oval and scratched her shrinking teats, glad that her daughters would soon be totally weaned.

Yes, Weecs did provide a possible answer. She could decline the automatic offer of continuation when it came, slide down from her office as proctor, make her apologies to Ranas, their families and friends, and flee to some remote place where she could reevaluate her life. If in time Weecs could join her there, so much the better. And if he could not . . . she refused to consider that possibility.

Weecs meant something to her that she had been afraid to admit even to herself, something which was more wonderful—

The announcement chime rang, and Leri sighed as she resumed her station. Duty always seemed to interrupt the best thoughts at the worst times.

She pushed the button announcing her readiness and was surprised when Exeter scuttled back in. Surely he had not been gone long enough to—

"My apologies for the delay, Proctor," Exeter said with a sincere clack, "but communications being what they are, it took more time than I had hoped to make the arrangements."

"The guarantees?" Leri asked, unwilling to believe that he had accomplished his mission so quickly.

"Ah, here," Exeter said as he reached under his carapace and pulled forth a small black folder. "A facsimile, of course, but I will deliver the original at our next meeting."

Leri took the folder and opened it. The folder exploded. Dark fumes filled the chamber. Leri lunged for the floor, desperate for methane.

The lights dimmed. Her thoughts faded as someone . . . who someone? Someone dragged her into blackness.

* * *

As the *Nazzarone* settled into orbit around Tomottac, Delightful Childe praised his crew and thanked the gods that they had arrived before the penalty date. When their landing clearance arrived, he would prepare his report for Complete Center, confirm the disposition of his cargo, and begin to think about the future.

The message terminal beside him flashed with a priority notice and Delightful Childe flinched. The last thing he needed was some checkdroid sending him a priority message. With great reluctance he opened the terminal for reception and watched the message splat onto the viewer like the droppings of an ill gummer.

The message was in basecode, so it was with even greater reluctance that he placed the sixth finger of his left hand on the recognition plate and touched the decoder key.

What he read stunned him. The message was written in the spare prose only a communicator could love.

> *Dispose of all cargo immediately.*
> *Return to Oina.*
> *Conflict is imminent.*
> *Acknowledge without reference.*

He whispered a curse in Vardequerqueglot, then asked himself the most important question the message failed to answer. Conflict with whom?

The Oinaise, like the Castorians, the Verfen, and the dispicable Cloise with their Isthian symbiotes were determinedly neutral. So who could they possibly be in conflict with? Or could this be some delayed message referring to the war between Sondak and the Ukes?

Delightful Childe checked the universal date. No, this message was less than five extracts old. The checkdroid he had spoken to seventeen extracts before had not only known about the Uke-Sondak war, he had even passed on the new name for this latest insanity between the humans. Called it the Double Spiral War, as though the whole galaxy were involved.

Conflict is imminent.

The phrase hung in Delightful Childe's mind like a dark stain on the white vestments of Oina's future. The command to acknowledge without reference only made the stain darker and more loathsome. It meant that Oinaise neutrality might be jeopardized by any reply which mentioned the supposed conflict, and that meant someone, somewhere—someone with the worst intentions had access to the basecode.

Delightful Childe shivered once, then again.

What was happening to everyone? Why this sudden belligerence from all sides of the galaxy? Had no one learned anything from the last war? It was not totally surprising that the humans could not learn from their past mistakes, but Delightful Childe expected much better things from his own people. There was something wrong here—something dreadfully wrong.

After reading the message one more time, almost daring to hope that there was a hidden meaning he had missed, Delightful Childe erased it from the screen. There was no hidden meaning, no disguised release from this dreadful news that might relieve the anxiety he felt. *Conflict is imminent*.

But wait, he thought suddenly, if someone had access to the basecode, might not they have sent the message?

It only took a moment for him to reject that thought. Who would have anything to gain from such an action? Surely neither Sondak nor the U.C.S. would profit by sending the Oinaise home. Both had controlled all the neutrals very effectively in the last war, although Sondak had been perhaps more efficient than the U.C.S. But both governments had sworn not to use the neutrals in any future conflict. Then again, they had also agreed there would be no future conflicts.

Just as he decided to suspend his questions, the message terminal flashed with a second priority notice. Delightful Childe winced, then opened the terminal again. This message was also in basecode, and he was surprised at the anger he felt when he fingered the decoder.

Conflict has been initiated.
Oina attacked.
Return with caution.
Acknowledge without reference.

Delightful Childe stared at the message in anger and amazement. Who would dare attack Oina?

Without hesitation he called communications. "Notify Tomottac that we must land immediately to make emergency repairs," he said curtly.

"Yes, sir," came the automatic reply.

Next he called his loadmaster. "Prepare to jettison all non-military cargo as soon as possible after landing," he said quickly, "and do not worry about receipts."

"But Senior Merchant, we must—"

"Do as ordered!" Delightful Childe cut the contact before

his well-meaning loadmaster could respond. This was no time to worry about rules or to abide insubordination. If Oina had indeed been attacked, *Nazzarone*'s place was at home, not here serving the humans who had precipitated this outrage.

Someone had dared attack Oina! It was incredible! So was the growing heat of hatred and revenge that simmered under Delightful Childe's heart.

*   *   *

General Mari read the latest Joint Chiefs situation reports without expression, but his gut churned in anger and fear. In addition to Cczywyck, Fernandez, Umboolu, and Ca-Ryn systems, the Ukes had taken Pierce system, the Ivy chain, and both water planets around Thayne-G.

BORFLEET was stretched beyond its limits fighting skirmishes along two hundred million tachymeters of space, each of its elements totally vulnerable to even half a normal Uke battle group.

What Mari couldn't understand was why the Ukes had spread their attacks over such a wide area. Oh, he knew that all the systems they had taken were ones to which the U.C.S. had traditionally claimed sovereignty, but they could have taken any of them whenever it pleased them. Why were they taking them all at once? What did they believe they were gaining from that?

None of the BORFLEET patrols had encountered overwhelming Uke forces, but rather the commanders seemed to be consistently reporting facing enemy groups just sufficiently larger than Sondak's to ensure either victory or a Sondak retreat. Per instructions from the Joint Chiefs, Sondak's patrols had retreated, but none of the commanders were too pleased with that. Along with the situation reports came their requests for permission to engage the Ukes in decisive battles.

Mari shook his head sadly and felt the knot tighten in his stomach. Sondak could not afford such decisive battles. And part of that was his fault. It was he who had led efforts to trim the services, decommissioning many able ships in order to save credits for other uses, because he had been convinced that Sondak would have sufficient warning to strengthen the fleets should the Ukes again indicate signs of hostility.

Suddenly he understood what Frye Charltos was doing with his Uke forces and an involuntary smile crept to Mari's lips. "Get me Admiral Gilbert," he said into his vidcom.

As soon as Gilbert came on the line, Mari said, "Have you seen the latest situation reports, Josiah?"

"Yes, sir, I have."

"What are your thoughts on the Uke actions?"

"They confirm what I've suspected, General. Charltos is reinforcing his perimeters."

"Exactly. Every one of those outer systems they take and garrison now will provide a strong point in their defenses that we will either have to bypass or attempt to capture later."

"Agreed, sir. And if we bypass any of those systems, we could never be sure that our rear and flanks were secure."

"But if we attack them, the Ukes would be able to slow any counterattack, system by system—and maybe stop us cold. All at a miminal cost to themselves."

"It fits the Charltos pattern," Gilbert said. "That's one of the reasons our defense of Matthews system is so important."

"I still question that, Admiral," Mari said quietly. "Looks more and more to me like the Ukes are preparing for defense rather than offense. By your own admission—"

"Begging your pardon, sir, but just because they've taken the perimeter systems does not mean they are ready to fall back into a defensive mode. Revenge is still a big part of their code, and we would be foolish to forget that."

Mari reddened. "Are you suggesting, Admiral, that I might need some basic instruction in—"

"I'm not suggesting anything personal, sir—just pointing out the situation as I see it. It seems imperative to me—"

"We'll talk about this later, Admiral." Mari cut the connection before Gilbert could add anything else and cursed silently. Gilbert was one of those people who fostered the inferiors in the service and should have been drummed out after his insane proposal of alliance with the Castorians. It was bad enough that this war was all wrong without allowing sloppy thinkers like Stonefield and Gilbert to make it worse.

The Ukes were building for defense, not offense. That was obvious. Consequently, it was foolish to send the heart of Sondak's forces to defend Matthews system from an attack which would never come. The thing to do was to pick the weakest point in the Uke defense and strike there—hard.

Mari pulled out his scribblepad and started making a list. It was time to call in some favors and make sure that Gilbert and Stonefield and their friends did not continue to get everything they wanted. With the forces allocated for the defense of Matthews, Mari could put together a strike force that might just throw the Ukes off stride. But if he was going to do it, there was no time to be wasted.

12

Frye caught her when she slipped on the thick carpet and pulled her close. Then suddenly he wanted her, wanted to feel her skin under his fingers, to kiss every inch of her and smother her in his lust.

Instinctively he kissed her. Without hesitation she pressed her body fiercely against his and kissed him back, and just as suddenly he knew she wanted the same thing.

There was no tenderness in their passion, only a desperate race toward fulfillment as they struggled out of their clothes and fought for a closeness that was too soon blown away in the explosions of their locked bodies.

When his thoughts returned, Frye looked at her tranquil face, her delighted eyes, and he felt only waves of confusion and sorrow. "Melliman . . . I . . ."

"Shhh," she whispered, putting a finger to his lips. "Don't. Don't say anything. I understand."

Frye freed himself from her gentle embrace and rolled to his back. He shut his eyes, knowing that *he* did not understand, and for the moment, did not want to understand what had happened.

Melliman pulled herself close beside him. "Just relax and listen to me," she whispered. "You are one of the most wonderful men I've ever known. I don't mean as an officer. I mean as a man. I respect you as both, but I love you as a man."

"Uh . . ." He was unsure of what to say.

"Please, let me finish. I don't want anything from you, sir, except your affection. I know I have no right to expect even that, but it would be unfair of me not to tell you how I feel, how I've felt for a long time. When I was first assigned to your staff . . ."

Frye heard her words, but they didn't mean anything in the presence of the dark, swirling images which crowded his thoughts. He saw Vinita, young and vivacious, calling to him from the top of a hill, heard her voice whispering in his ear, felt her hands circling lightly over his body. He responded as he always had to her with tenderness and patience, using every part of his body to bring her to the highest peak of ecstasy.

Even as he fell a second time into the mindless joy of orgasm, he knew he had not fooled himself, knew it was not Vinita he had made love to. But in that moment of release and oblivion when everything else in the galaxy dissolved into blindness, Frye Charltos the man did not care.

*　　*　　*

"So where will you go?" Marsha asked sadly.

"Oina, I think." Lucky put the last, tightly wrapped package in the bundle and answered without looking at her. "I need someplace quiet—someplace away from this damned war—and who knows, maybe Delightful Childe and I can set up some kind of freighting partnership."

"I thought you didn't like him?"

"Oh, he's all right." Lucky finished tying the small bundle and looked straight into her eyes. He felt like someone had put a restraining strap around his heart. "Besides, at least I don't have to worry about getting emotionally involved with an Oinaise." Looking down, he picked up the bundle and handed it to Marsha without meeting her eyes. "Here."

"Stop it, Lucky," she said as she automatically took the bundle. "That's not fair."

He paused before responding to her, feeling very vulnerable and full of caution. When he finally spoke, his voice was filled with a quiet, angry resignation. "Nothing's fair in this universe, Mars. Not a damned thing. So what?"

"You know what." She tried to tell him with her eyes as much as her voice, but the tears clouded her vision. "What is this?" she asked, hefting the bundle with one hand as she whipped the tears from her eyes with the other.

Lucky allowed himself a small smile. "That's all your personal stuff—things that would have been yours, anyway—things I was going to give you."

"But Lucky—"

"Take them. I don't have any use for them. You might."
Lucky heard the strain in his voice and fought to relax it. "Now
we'd better get you up to the *Tongasuk*."

"This is a hell of a way to say good-bye," she said in a tone
that was half joking and half sullen. Her weak attempt at
humor hid the raging sorrow she felt inside.

"Sure is, Mars. But it's a hell of a war, isn't it?" His gaze
rested on her eyes, and the strap around his heart tightened.
"Take care of yourself, Mars, good care. I'm going to miss you."

"Sure . . . for a while." She managed a brief smile through a
new wash of tears. "Then you'll find some cute young spacer
looking for adventure, and before you know what's happened
to you, you'll have a new partner."

"Yeah, maybe Delightful Childe knows some women
who . . ."

Suddenly they were in each other's arms with the bundle
between them as they hugged each other with hungry desperation.

"I love you, Mars," he whispered as he stroked her hair—
afraid to abandon the touch of her—afraid to hold on. His eyes
burned with dry pain.

"I love you, too. Oh, God, how I love you!"

Lucky took a deep breath and let it out very slowly. "We'll
look for each other?" He meant it as a statement, but it came
out as a question.

"When it's over," she said with a gentle sob.

"Good. Tell your father I hate him."

"I will."

After giving her several quick kisses on her forehead, he
pulled her tighter against him. He didn't know what else to
say. Finally he gently pushed her away and looked softly into
her eyes. "You really need to go."

She knew he was right, but she did not want to leave him.
"Walk me up to the ship?"

"No, I don't think so. I told *Tongasuk* I'd leave first. Seems
your people don't trust me. So as soon as you're clear, I'll be
taking off."

Without another word they walked arm-in-arm to the port,
each caught in a personal web of sad thoughts, each snagged
by possibilities of what might have been.

"I swear, Lucky, I'll—"

"Shhh," he said putting a finger over her lips. "No more

promises. After the war we'll look for each other. That's it.
Okay?" He kissed her softly on the chin.

"Okay," she said, moving her mouth to catch his lips.

Then she broke the kiss, turned, and ran down the ramp.
Moments later she disappeared around *Graycloud*'s side.

Lucky stared for a long minute at an empty landscape that
danced with images of everything he and Marsha had shared.
Then something violent snapped inside him, and the images
disappeared. With a harsh slap he hit the lever to close the
ramp and headed for the controls.

He wanted to be long gone before she reached the
Tongasuk. He wanted her to watch him leave and feel as de-
serted as the center of his heart felt.

Let her stand there staring up at the thin air over Alexvieux
watching *Graycloud* disappear into forever. Let her feel rotten,
guilty, and miserable standing all alone on that wretched little
planet. And let her cry in his dust as he would cry in the dust
of the void.

*   *   *

"Mr. Dawson, take a look at these," Admiral Pajandcan said
as she handed him a sheaf of messages. Despite his independent ways, she had learned to respect this dirtsider's way of
thinking. He had certainly made some basic improvements in
their defense posture, and several of his suggestions had made
her reevaluate her own concepts of defense. Anyone who made
her think, even a civilian, couldn't be all bad.

"Doesn't look like they're going to help much," Dawson said
quietly as he flipped through the last of the messages.

"You're right about that, mister. The Joint Chiefs, and especially Admiral Gilbert, are convinced that the Ukes have spy
ships in Matthews. If we start a buildup of supplies and personnel, the Ukes'll know it, and they'll know we suspect
they're going to hit us hard here. So the J.C.'s have decided to
make us look like an easy target."

"Wonderful," Dawson said without irony as he handed the
messages back to her. "I only get involved in the worst of situations."

"But Mister Dawson, had we all the resources we needed
here, we would not have needed you." She hoped he would
catch the levity in her tone, but from the expression on his
face, she knew he hadn't.

"That is true, Admiral," he said seriously, "but it would be nice, just once, to have the materials I need to conduct a truly superb defense."

"You and half the officers in the service."

Dawson sighed. "Very well. If we take what we now know, we are going to have to make a few more of those adjustments you and I talked about, especially in terms of pulling all our fighting ships back within a tighter perimeter."

Pajandcan wondered what his response was going to be to the surprise she had for him and laughed.

"I don't see what's so funny, Admiral."

"Nothing, Mister Dawson. Absolutely nothing. However, there is one more piece of information you need to evaluate and react to before you make any further plans."

"And that is?" He cocked one eyebrow at her as though he were skeptical of anything she might tell him.

"The Joint Chiefs have given me the discretion of putting you totally in charge of defense—if you're interested and willing, of course." For only the second time since she had met him, Dawson looked truly surprised.

"But, Admiral, wouldn't that usurp your . . . I mean, how would that look to the rest of the military if a civilian—"

"You wouldn't be a civy," she said with crinkling eyes. "They want to give you a reserve commission of Quarter Admiral with the concomitant pay and privileges."

"That's crazy! They're asking me to commit suicide!"

Pajandcan lost her smile. "Oh? Are you now saying that Matthews cannot be successfully defended?"

"I've been saying that all along. But you haven't been hearing me. Now with this 'easy target' plan of theirs, it ought to be pretty obvious to anyone with a brain that—"

"And are you suggesting that I don't have a brain?"

Dawson pulled his mouth shut and stared at her.

"Come now, Mister Dawson. Be honest with yourself and with me. You like all this defense planning. It brings your talents into action. I told you the J.C.'s were going to provide external support for the defense. Now I'll tell you the rest of it. I'm going to command that external force. I want you here, commanding the defense of Matthews."

"But why me?" he asked finally. "There are half a dozen of your officers quite capable of—"

"I know my officers, Mr. Dawson, and they're all capable and dedicated people. But not one of them has your imagination for defense. Certainly none of them have your experience." She paused and looked at him for a long moment.

"It's odd, Mister Dawson, but in spite of the fact that this has not been my favorite post in all my service years, I've become rather attached to the Matthews system. I like being able to go down to Reckynop and spend a week or two in the mountains. I like the people who live here, even if I don't totally approve of their anarchic form of government. I don't want anything to happen to those people."

"But, Admiral, if I—"

"Let me finish," she said more sternly than she meant to. "Now I have a chance to protect Matthews system by commanding the battle group which will lay in wait for the Ukes to attack. I also have the rare opportunity to choose who will lead the defense of the system itself. And I choose you, Mister Dawson—Croatean, Gyle Coalition, *homo communis* dirtsider that you are—I choose you because I think you are the best possible person for the job. Maybe the only person who can give us a chance of success."

She paused again, but he just stared back at her with an unreadable look in his eyes. "There, sir, I've revealed all my prejudices," she said quietly, "and I still want you to do this in spite of them. What do you have to say to that?"

"Nothing."

"Nothing?"

"There's nothing I can say, Admiral Pajandcan. You have me at a total disadvantage. I'm sure that if I should refuse Sondak's offer, that I would quickly find myself restricted to some corner of the galaxy or another where I would endure the local situation until the war's end."

He was wrong, but she let him continue.

"And if I agree, I'm probably condemning myself and thousands of others to death."

"Wrong on both counts," she said quietly. "Refuse, and you will remain here as defense coordinator under whoever takes command. Agree, and you could make a significant contribution to the conclusion of this war."

"I'm surprised by the first, and seriously doubt the second," he said bitterly.

"Then let me ask you something, Mister Dawson. Why did you agree to come here in the first place?"

He returned her steady gaze for a few moments before answering. "I thought I had a debt to settle, a debt I owed to Sondak for sparing my life. Now I'm not so sure."

Pajandcan waited for him to be more specific, then decided to prompt him. "So you've decided your debt is paid by spending a month or so here, sharing your *expertise* with us, then running off when the going got rough, is that it?"

Dawson gave her a grave smile. "Not at all, Admiral. I think I've just realized the true value of the debt. Your Admiral Y'Ott's forces could have killed me, but he chose to instruct them not to. So in a way, I owe Sondak my life. The only way I can repay the debt is by giving my life back to Sondak. The problem is . . . I wasn't quite ready to do that, not yet, but . . ."

She wanted to help him, but didn't have much to work with. "It's your decision, Mister Dawson, yours alone. I can't make it for you, or tell you what to do. I can only give you a few days to make it in. But when I tell you it's time to give me an answer, I'll want it then, one way or the other. Understood?"

Dawson gave her a small nod, his eyes closed, his head bowed, his thoughts a million parsecs away.

* * *

Frye hated himself as he left Melliman's quarters in the early morning light. He hated her, too—hated her for letting him . . . for giving him the opportunity . . . for inviting him to share his grief and loneliness. It was not fair to hate her because of the way *he* felt, but he did.

Yet he didn't. She had been compassionate, offering herself to him, not as a surrogate, but as a woman who cared deeply about him for herself. He had taken advantage of her emotions, of her devotion to him in a way that was totally inexcusable—personally or militarily.

She'll have to go, he thought as he returned home. There was no way he could face her every day, knowing how she felt, feeling his own shame, and still be able to function with her as his AOCO. It would be a great loss, but he would cope until Lisa Cay returned and could take over the job.

He quietly cursed his vulnerability, and stupidity, and lust, and lack of self-control as he bathed and changed clothes. Later, as he sat reading the latest field reports in his office, he tried to block Melliman from his mind, glad that he had told her not to report for duty until midday, and regretful that he had not told her to take the whole day off.

He didn't want to see her, didn't want to remember the loving body she hid under the crispness of her uniform. But most of all, he did not want to face the cold wave of anger that her presence would arouse in him.

Frye concentrated on the reports again and forcefully banished thoughts of Melliman from his mind.

The Pierce system had fallen almost without a serious fight, its inhabitants incapable of resisting even the small U.C.S. force Frye had sent against it. The five systems in the Ivy chain had put up extensive resistance, and according to the reports in Frye's hands, the planets themselves were probably unconquerable without using a considerably greater number of ships and more personnel and equipment than they were worth. So long as the U.C.S. ruled their space, he did not care what the groundlings in the Ivy chain did.

Ata One and Two, the water planets around Thayne-G, had capitulated as soon as the U.C.S. ships announced their presence in the system, but Frye was skeptical about the genuineness of their surrender. However slow and dim-witted the denizens of those two planets were, he knew from an early mission there as a cadet that they were fiercely antagonistic toward outsiders who had any notion of controlling them or their system. Best to send a message immediately, warning the garrison commander to be especially careful, or she might find herself with unwanted and unpleasant surprises on her hands.

With a faint smile Frye caught himself before calling Melliman to take the message, and a new emotion linked itself to her—chagrin. She had inadvertently taught him to be wary of his own weaknesses. One more credit for her. One more reason she had to go.

As he turned back to the reports, he quickly recognized what had been a growing concern about the limited engagements with Sondak's BORFLEET patrols. Despite all the reassurances from the sectors, he did not at any time believe that the surprise attacks had so weakened Sondak's forces that they could not put up more than token resistance.

What were Sondak's Joint Chiefs really up to? Why were their forces spread so thinly? Where were they planning their counteroffensive? And when?

Those questions had plagued him and his staff and would continue to plague them until the U.C.S. had successfully taken the Matthews system and established their forward base there. Then and only then would he feel comfortable enough to believe that Sondak could truly be defeated.

Frye set the reports aside, stood, straightened his uniform, and quickly ran through his mental checklist. He was prepared to answer any questions Admiral Tuuneo might have for him, so without hesitation he put the reports in their folder, tucked it under his arm, and left his office.

Melliman still had not arrived. But Frye knew that when he got back, he was going to have to perform the unpleasant task of telling her she would be reassigned. As he walked to Admiral Tuuneo's office he wondered if he should ask his senior . . . no. There was no reason to involve Tuuneo. This was something he had to do himself.

But he could ask Tuuneo if someone else needed a good AOCO. He could do that much for Melliman. He owed her at least that much of a courtesy.

13

Low, whispering sounds seeped persistently into her brain. Pale mists of pain shrouded her thoughts. The total blackness of insides surrounded her. The cool softness of fabric touched her sides. Slowly, ever so slowly, Leri pulled herself up into consciousness, aware at once of tight abrasive bindings around her body, and the close confines of her prison.

What had happened?

Exeter! The folder. Smoke and nothingness.

She remembered it all dimly, as though it had happened to someone else long before.

But why, why had it happened? Why? What burrowed reason could Exeter have for . . . The humans. Sondak. The methane collectors. All of that and more.

In her weak, queasy state it still did not make sense. Did they think that by capturing her and dragging her—she gulped, suddenly aware that the bindings served two purposes. Those queasy feelings had troubled her stomachs once before, the one time she had traveled into space.

Now she knew where they had taken her. Yet she had no better idea of why, or what they thought they would accomplish. Apparently they had a misconception of a proctor's importance.

"So, you are awake," said an all too familiar clacking voice close by her ear.

Leri tried hard to turn toward it, but the bindings locked against her skin. "I am awake," she said finally as she relaxed her straining muscles. "What new human treachery are you a part of now, Exeter the Castorian?"

"No treachery at all, Proctor. Sondak's humans know nothing of your, shall we say, visit?"

Confusion swirled in front of her lingering pain. "I do not believe you, Exeter. The humans must know what—"

"The humans are stupid—and naive, as usual. They believe whatever suits them at the moment, and what suits them is what I tell them—that you and I will be continuing our discussions next season."

"Then what is the purpose of this insanity? I demand that you take me home immediately."

"Now I could hardly do that," Exeter's voice said more softly, "could I? If I returned you to the surface, why you would cause immense trouble for me. No, Proctor, I'm afraid you will be staying with me for a little while yet." He laughed, as though he had made some joke.

"But why? Why?" she demanded.

"Because I have need of you—or at least parts of you, the most delicate, delicious parts of you."

Leri gasped. "You can't mean . . ." The strong, acrid scent of her fear flooded the confines of the chamber and almost choked her.

"Oh, but I do Proctor, I do. Each time I visited you I saw before me a living feast, food such as before I only dreamed of eating. I suspect you will be good, Proctor Leri, very good indeed, chilled slightly, of course, and served with a special sauce of my own making."

She gasped again, already chilled by the repulsiveness of his intentions. But deep within her, the heat of anger fought the chill and forced her mind to resist as his voice rolled on.

"Did I not tell you I had studied your people? Did not the acid bubble under my tongue at what I saw going to waste on your planet? Did I not hunger after you with a love deeper than any you could possibly imagine?" He paused, then whispered, "No mate could ever want you as much as I do, Leri Gish Geril."

The tone of his voice frightened her as much as his words. Exeter had totally lost control of himself. "I'll spoil myself," she said desperately. "In fact, I've already started doing it." Her fear-stench grew stronger even as she spoke. "Can you smell me, Exeter? Can you?"

There was a faint click, and the whispering hiss got louder. "That's right, Exeter. Take a good sniff. That's the smell of your feast spoiling. Spoiling, Exeter!" She laughed crazily, darkly, wildly, until the cacophony of her own voice pressed her mind back through the nightmare toward sanity.

"Then I shall have to gas you again, my dear Proctor," he said in a sad, quiet tone.

"It's too late, Exeter. My glands have done their job. How do you think my kind survived all these millennia? Because none of our predators wanted our bad tasting meat!"

She waited for him to respond, then, fearing the unknown, called to him. "Exeter? Exeter? Do you hear me? Do you understand? You might as well take me home. If you do that and leave our system, nothing will happen to you. I promise."

After a long pause he said, "Yes, I could arrange for that."

His voice was even fainter than before, and the sadness slowed and weighted his tones.

"If I push you out the lock, eventually gravity will take you home."

Leri could barely understand his last word, but she heard the click and caught the first hint of the gas in time to close her nostrils to it. Immediately she relaxed her body and began her meditation of peace, seeking suspension as the Confidantes had taught her when she reached maturity, seeking the stilling of her body that was her only defense.

She dared not think of what could happen next, dared not believe that he would actually cast her into space. But if he did, the thick mucus seeping from her pores and hardening on her body would protect her for . . . for how long? For how long in space before she dropped through the atmosphere?

Forcing herself to shut the questions out she sank deeper and deeper into tranquility, trusting in the only tunnel of survival open to her, until all but the most careful observers, or very knowledgeable biologists, or her own people would have thought her dead.

Less than four hundred kilometers away, Sondak's two massive collectors sucked thousands of cubic hexameters of methane per second from Cloise's atmosphere. They removed the free carbon dioxide, then remethane, purified, dehydrated it, cooled it, then magnetically ram-pumped it into fuel cylinders at a million grains of pressure per square centimeter for use by Sondak's short-range spacecraft.

The people who operated the collectors and loaded the tankers neither knew nor cared about anything else in this system.

They were rough men and women who enjoyed the pay and benefits of dangerous labor. They were also proud experts, specialists who gave all of their energy every shift to make their contribution to the war.

Sondak needed the gas, needed it in a hurry. These crews would collect it. Other crews of specialists would deliver it. It was as simple as that, an important job being done as quickly and efficiently as possible.

Even if they had known about Leri's plight, they would not have paused in their work, would not have given her a second's thought, much less considered assisting her. Such a suggestion would have made them laugh. Leri and her people were nothing more to them than alien salamanders whose lives had no meaning compared to humans. And never would.

* * *

"The politicians have to be convinced that we're actually doing something positive," Mari said quietly. "Otherwise"— he paused and looked around the room for any signs of allies— "otherwise we're liable to find ourselves up to our pockets with civilian observers wanting to know what's going on, and generally getting in the way."

"And you suggest we tell them everything?" Admiral Stonefield asked.

Mari did not like Stonefield's emphasis on the last word of his question, but he refused to step in the trap. "No, sir, I am only suggesting that as the Joint Chiefs, it is our responsibility to get them off the Service's backs. One way we can do that is to give them some idea of our overall strategy."

"And the Tellers, too," Lindshaw added. "My people are strained to the limit trying to keep them and their stories in line with reality. Have you seen some of those stories? 'Ukes Sweep Through Free Systems,' 'Sondak Services Demoralized,' and the best one came today because we wouldn't tell them anything yesterday, 'Joint Chiefs Paralyzed.'"

"Then get new people," Avitor Hilldill said.

"Smack an asteroid," Lindshaw snapped back at him.

"As you were, Avitor!" Stonefield barked in a voice that startled them all. "We have too much we need to accomplish," he continued, "without—"

"Up yours . . . sir," Hilldill said flatly, his stare steady and cold on Stonefield.

No one except Stonefield moved. He leaned back in his

chair, returned Hilldill's stare, then spoke in a voice that was almost a whisper. "Avitor Hilldill, while I am chairman of the Joint Chiefs you will show respect . . . or . . . you and your precious pipe jockeys will find yourselves on the short end of every compromise this body has to make. Do I make myself clear?"

Hilldill neither flinched nor hesitated. "Perfectly, Admiral. But since Flight Service is always on the short end anyway, I doubt that we'll suffer much."

After only the briefest pause, Stonefield gave him a tight-lipped smile. "How would you like to have to collect your own methane?" he asked. "Or how would you like to find your precious, archaic Flight Service dismantled wing by wing and put under direct fleet orders? Would you like that, sir? Because if you would, I believe that under the War Control Act I have quite enough power to do just that."

Hilldill turned red and sputtered.

"Oh, I know," Stonefield continued with his eyes growing narrower, "I know it would cause turmoil for a while—might even cost us the Matthews system if we weren't careful, but you know what, Hilldill, I might do it anyway, just to eliminate your continual complaints once and for all."

No one present believed Stonefield would do what he said, but none of them, especially Avitor Hilldill, was willing to risk testing him, or even, it seemed, to violate the uncomfortable silence that held them all in their place.

"Perhaps, sir," Mari finally said to break the tension, "perhaps we should return to the question of the politicians and the Tellers, and if I may, I'd like to make a suggestion." Despite the put-down of Hilldill, whom Mari considered a trustworthy friend, he admired the way Stonefield's whole expression changed when he turned to respond.

"Thank you, General. That is an excellent idea. Please, give us your suggestion."

The tension was still thick in the room, but Mari decided to talk through it. "Well, sir, it seems to me that we might solve both problems at once if we used the Efcorps as the official source of all information."

"But they're controlled by the politicians," Lindshaw objected.

"Exactly. Which means that the politicians control the news as we give it to them. And they'll only give the Tellers what makes them look good. But so long as the Efcorps was the one and only official source, the Services would be out from under direct pressure."

"That will raise a lot of constitutional and confederational questions," Lindshaw said.

"But maybe by the time they're settled, we will have won the war," Stonefield added, "and those questions won't matter."

"The Tellers will scream about freedom of information," Admiral Eresser said.

"Let them scream. We'll tell them to read the War Control Act." Mari didn't mean to salt Hilldill's fresh wound, but Stonefield had inadvertently given them a possible answer. He glanced quickly at Hilldill, but his friend was bent over the contents of a folder and didn't seem to react.

"It seems to me that only solves half of our problem, General," Lindshaw said. "If we control the news to the politicians and the politicians control it to the Tellers, we'll still have the politicians on our backs."

"Not if we tell them everything."

Heads snapped when he said that.

"Well, not exactly *everything*," he continued, "but enough so that both the Tri-Cameral and the Combined Committees were thoroughly briefed and had more information than they could safely release."

"What would keep them from releasing the information too early?" Stonefield asked.

"If we dump a lot on them now, sir, almost without warning, and keep dumping it on them, we control its timeliness."

"You're saying give them considerable old information now, and new information only after it becomes old. Is that right?"

"Yes, sir."

"I still say the Tellers won't stand for it."

"Oh, I think General Mari had the right answer for the Tellers, Admiral, and that gets you and your people off the block. I'm not saying that they won't be happy, but once it becomes obvious that the system has changed and the Efcorps—which will no doubt love its new power—is the place to go for their stories, I think it just might work."

The room buzzed with private comments.

"May I add to this discussion, sir?"

All eyes turned to Hilldill.

"Certainly, Avitor."

"Sir, colleagues, I do not doubt the immensity of the powers we were granted under the War Control Act, both to us as a body, and to our chairman in particular . . ."

Everyone waited. Don't push, Mari thought. For the sake of Sondak, don't push this.

"However," Hilldill continued, "I think it would serve us well to use those powers as judiciously as possible, lest we set dangerous precedents. I fully respect General Mari's intentions, and furthermore, I appreciate the practicality of his idea. But as Admiral Lindshaw indicated, we would arouse serious constitutional and confederational questions by such actions— not to mention the freedom of information problem—and if we can avoid those difficulties, I believe we should attempt by all means to do so."

"Is that all, Avitor?" Stonefield asked after a long pause.

"Yes, sir. That is all. For me, it is quite a lot."

Mari winced and held his breath as he waited tensely for Stonefield to react.

"Very well, then. I think you've made your position quite clear—as has Admiral Lindshaw. We will consider both before making our final decision."

With a low sigh Mari relaxed in his chair. He had hoped his complaint would bring some action, and now it looked like it would. There would be some interesting controversies stirred if the elitist Efcorps with its high-handed news reporters was given this job and brought under the intense scrutiny of its far more successful plebian competitor, the Official Tellers.

Once the Joint Chiefs settled this question, he planned to reintroduce the idea of abandoning Matthews system.

*   *   *

"But I thought you said—"

"I did, Caugust. I did. Don't let these equations fool you. What Ayne Wallen formulated for us is the basis for a reciprocal weapon." Sjean sighed. "I have to keep reminding myself of that. Too many years of looking at things from the wrong direction, I think. Anyway, if you can ignore the negative exponents for a moment and concentrate on the balance . . ."

She let her voice trail off as she recognized the look on Caugust's face. He was formulating something himself, and until he finished it, there would be no getting through to him. It was one of his most frustrating traits, one which made him look slow, even dim-witted at times, but Sjean had learned to adjust to it and patiently waited him out.

Finally he drew a large circle around one set of the equations, then looked up at her with an odd sparkle in his eyes.

"Wallen did more than that."

"Pardon?"

"Look, Sjean," he said, rapidly tapping the equations with a kind of nervous excitement, "if I understand what you've told me, and what these equations mean, not only did Wallen formulate the basis for the weapon itself, he also indicated a way to aim it."

"Now I don't understand, sir."

"All right, look. In Guntteray's prolegomenon to the basics of his theory, he stated . . ."

Six hours later Sjean returned to her rooms, tired to the bones, but understanding all too well what Caugust had seen in Ayne's equations. He was right, of course. There was a suggestion in the equations of how such a weapon might be aimed. But the path from the equations to an actual weapon looked longer and more arduous than ever.

In a week she would not only have to be able to explain all this in far less than six hours, she would also have to welcome the new additions to Drautzlab's staff. The seven expatriate physicists, four nonhuman and three human, and their families had fled from the U.C.S. along with thousands of other intellectuals to what they considered to be the morally right side of the war.

At least they all spoke gentongue, so she wouldn't have translators cluttering up the lab as well as seven lost scientists wandering around outside their normal space.

Sjean didn't know whether their coming would be a blessing or a curse, but she did know that her main project would suffer, and that made her slightly angry. Sondak needed the ultimate weapon as quickly as it could be developed. According to the Teller reports, the Ukes were doing just about whatever they damned well pleased in the galaxy, and there were all kinds of dire predictions about the possible outcomes of the war.

She did not want to hear any of that, but she couldn't ignore it. With two sisters in Flight Service and a dozen other relatives having just joined one or another of the services, family duty demanded that she do her part. Yet however much she accomplished each day, she never felt a sense of meeting the urgency of the war. Others at Drautzlab were producing real weapons systems for use in the very near future. She was struggling with a project that might never bring results.

But in spite of everything, she lay back on the bed and went to sleep with a slight smile on her face, a smile born of years of scientific patience. Not everyone can be in the battlespace, she reminded herself. Some of us have to build the ammunition. With that thought she fell asleep.

14

Lucky stared in disbelief at the picture that appeared on his viewscreen when *Graycloud* popped out of subspace. He immediately braked as hard as the shuddering dampers would allow, all the while keeping one grim eye on the space battle which raged between him and Oina.

"The Oinaise are neutral," he reminded himself aloud, as though by saying that the picture would change. It didn't.

Pinpoints of light grew to dazzling flashes against the background of stars, then traced bright lines that left afterimages on his retinas.

Brief spectroscopic explosions flowered brilliantly with startling hues of color. Then they dissolved into transparent pastel lenses through which shadows and light shifted at odd angles of optical illusion that made depth perception almost impossible.

In the midst of it all, Oina hung like a fragile, blue-green gem, caught in a conflict that all logic said should not have been taking place. But it was taking place. Neutral Oina was being attacked by someone, for some reason, and Lucky wanted to know who, and why.

With a reflex reaction, he started scanning the standard lightspeed communications channels as *Graycloud* vibrated violently against the full braking action of its engines.

The few channels that were active spurted equally violent messages into the cockpit. Lucky did not have to be able to understand the languages he heard to know what was going on. Battle communications in any language have harsh, staccato patterns of their own, all too easy for the experienced ear to recognize. It was Roberg all over again, but this time he had arrived in the middle of it.

Lucky eased the engines as *Graycloud* slowed, and the dampers responded by settling down to a deep hum that reached through the deck to the marrow of his bones. Who in the galaxy would be attacking Oina? And why? he wondered again. Then a voice spoke in clear gentongue from the communicator as though in answer to his questions.

"Withdraw! All timinos withdraw!"

Lucky thought he recognized the word. Timinos was a Uke military term for small fighting groups. But the timinos didn't look like they were withdrawing.

Graycloud was still much too far away from Oina even with the screen on full magnification for Lucky to see individual ships, but the flashes between them and random explosions of light told him that no one was paying much attention to the instructions. Now the question was, *why* were the Ukes attacking Oina?

"This is Commander Fugisho. All timinos withdraw!"

It would take *Graycloud* another thousand kilometers to stop at this rate, so Lucky again applied full braking power and watched with growing fascination as fewer and fewer flashes appeared on the screen. Then he gradually realized the battle flashes had stopped altogether and the lights he saw were the firing of warp engines.

Suddenly a ship loomed on the viewscreen, then just as suddenly it disappeared into subspace less than fifty kilometers from him. Lucky shuddered and resumed scanning the light-speed communications channels until he found a voice speaking in steady Vardequerqueglot. At least that's what he thought it was, because it sounded like Delightful Childe's language.

When the voice paused for a few seconds, he spoke quickly in gentongue. "This is Captain Teeman, lightspeed freighter *Graycloud*. May I be of assistance?"

The voice resumed speaking in Vardequerqueglot as though its owner hadn't heard an interruption. But when the voice paused again, Lucky repeated his message.

"Be still, human," a different, heavily accented voice answered in gentongue. "We will attend to you shortly."

Given the circumstances, Lucky decided the Oinaise were not being at all rude, so he diverted his attention to bringing *Graycloud* to a full stop while waiting for a response.

After an hour Lucky grabbed some flight rations and ate them cold. After two hours he started doing little shipkeeping chores to keep himself occupied. After three hours he had fidgeted himself closer and closer toward anger, but the response finally came.

"We have located your ship, Captain Teeman. By what authority have you entered our system?"

"I am a freespace lightspeed freighter. I've come looking for Captain Delightful Childe of the *Nazzarone*."

"We did not ask your purpose," a new, less accented voice said. "We asked by what authority you have entered."

Lucky was puzzled. He had never needed authority before to enter a neutral system, and he didn't remember anything in the Guidelines indicating a need for authority. But he had never been to Oina before, either, so perhaps their request was common practice. Or brought on by the war, stupid, he added to himself when the obvious smacked his brain.

"I have no authority," he said simply. "As I told you, this is a freespace freighter and I—"

"Permission to move, denied. Permission to leave, denied. Permission to proceed, denied," the voice said in a steady monotone. "Per Strictures Two-seventy-one and Three-three-four, your craft will be confiscated and impounded until a hearing can be held before the—"

"Repeat, please," he requested in disbelief.

"Your craft will be confiscated and impounded until—"

"Over my ship's rubble!" Lucky said when he realized that they were serious. "It'll be a clear day in subspace before you confiscate *Graycloud*." Even as he spoke, he hit the turning jets and began preparing to fire the engines. "Tell Captain Childe I stopped in to say good-bye."

I should have known better than to come here, he thought as he verified the preliminary heading which would take *Graycloud* out of the system. Who in the universe did the Oinaise think they were, anyway?

"A thousand pardons, Captain," a third voice said in an accent so thick that Lucky could hardly understand it, "but are you the same *Graycloud* that assisted Delightful Childe's benevolent mission on Alexvieux?"

"No. I'm Delightful Childe's grandmother," Lucky said as *Graycloud* steadied on the proper heading.

"Captain," the thick voice said, "there is no need for you to leave. The despicable Ukas have disrupted our protocol, for which we heartily apologize. Please be assured that you are certainly welcomed to be here."

"No thanks," Lucky said without hesitation. But he did not fire *Graycloud*'s warp engine. So it was the Ukes, or the Ukas as the accented voice called them. Seems like a stupid thing for them to do, he thought, about as stupid as me staying here. "I know where I'm welcome, and where I'm not. You want this ship, you're going to have catch us or blast us out of space."

"Do not be rude, Captain. It is not fair in the evidence of our apology. The forces of Oina have no intention of 'blasting you from space' as you so bluntly put it. You are welcomed here as a friend. Please accept that welcome."

Lucky hesitated. Was this some trick? Or did the Oinaise speaker really mean it?

With a sudden shrug of his shoulders he began turning *Graycloud* back toward Oina with an odd sense of resignation. "Very well," he said quietly. "I accept your welcome. Please send orbit and landing instructions."

"Yes, Captain Teeman. Yes we will. Channel nine-zero-point-five-five-three."

"Check," he replied as he tapped in the numbers. What difference did it make to him where he set *Graycloud* down? He had wanted someplace quiet. He had found a new corner of the war where there shouldn't have been war.

Maybe there is no quiet place, he thought as the instructions clicked into his computer. Maybe this war is going to consume the whole known galaxy. Then what difference does any of it make to us?

He looked up and beyond Oina toward the Spider Nebula with an odd sense of reassurance. Maybe he had come to the right place after all. If it wasn't safe here on the edge of explored space, at least they had a direction they could run in where groups of humans were not killing each other.

There was the Spider Nebula, the Double Spiral's closest neighbor, unexplored space with nothing stopping them except the black hole curtain and the knowledge that they would not have enough fuel to return.

"Just you and me, *Graycloud*," he said with a sudden, bitter laugh, "you and me popping through the black hole curtain and into the unknown. Bam! Just like that. We'll get away from them all!" When a tear ran down his cheek, he angrily wiped it away. "Just you and me against the whole damned universe."

* * *

"But Father," Mica said quickly, "wouldn't it be foolish—I mean, wouldn't you be taking an unnecessary risk joining the battle group?"

"Perhaps, Mica, but I think Hew would agree with me that there are times when a commander has to be with the fleet in order to ensure the greatest chance of victory."

"Oh, I do agree, sir," Rochmon said as he set a tray of drinks carefully on the table between them. "However, if you are with the battle group, won't that make Admiral Pajandcan's position rather awkward? It seems to me, sir—"

"I've thought about that, Hew. And I appreciate what you and Mica are saying. But I won't exactly be with the battle group. I'll be aboard the cruiser *Janet* with a small escort somewhere between the battle group and Matthews."

"With the subspace monitors?" Mica asked suddenly.

"Yes." Josiah Gilbert was pleased that they had joined him for dinner and this discussion, but he had reservations about how much he could tell either of them.

"Here you are," Rochmon said as he handed each of them a glass, "the finest postdinner drink my famous grandmother ever concocted from distilled spirits."

Mica was grateful for the distraction of accepting the drink and tasting it. "Umm, delicious," she said after the sip of the semisweet concoction slid smoothly down her throat. Yet she could not really appreciate the drink as much as its exquisite flavor deserved. She knew her father was holding something back, but she was unsure if she should probe further now or wait until after Rochmon left.

"Quite good," Gilbert said, holding his glass up to the light to admire the swirling liquor. "What is it?"

"An old family recipe," Rochmon said brightly as he sat down. "Its flavor is rather like what you just told us, Admiral— half simple ingredients, and half deception. Fools the palate into thinking it's something that it's not."

Mica smiled and watched her father carefully. Looks like Rochmon is going to probe on his own, she thought.

Gilbert smiled at them both. "Not much good at fooling you two, am I? Well, I should have known that, but it really isn't a question of trying to fool you, you know. It's a matter of not compromising your integrity. What you don't know, you can't be forced to tell."

"I don't understand, Father. Who would try to force us to tell anything?"

"The J.C.," Rochmon said simply.

"General Mari and Avitor Hilldill, especially," Gilbert added. "Neither of them believes in this plan, and once they learn that I've left to join the action, they're going to dig for all the information they can get. What you don't know, you can't tell them. It's as simple as that."

"On the other hand," Mica said slowly, "if we don't know exactly what you are doing or planning to do, there's no way we can give you assistance if you need it."

Gilbert and Rochmon both laughed. "She remind you of anyone?" Gilbert asked.

"Uh, not that I can think of."

"You, Hew. She reminds me of you. Always looking past the obvious to find what's going on behind things. Makes the same kinds of observations you used to make."

"You don't have to talk about me like I'm not here." Mica was not sure she liked the comparison.

"No, we don't, daughter-of-mine. But you do remind me of Hew when he was younger and brasher."

"Hardly, sir," Rochmon said. He finished his drink and reached for the pitcher. "She has a lot more control and common sense than I had back then."

Gilbert laughed again, then saw the look on his daughter's face and abruptly stopped. "What do you want to know, Mica? Shall I tell you my plans in detail? Or shall I—"

"Stop it, Father. I don't want you to patronize me or compare me to Commander Rochmon. I only want to know what you expect to accomplish by going to Matthews and how we can help you with your plan. If you don't want to trust us with—"

"It's not a matter of trust, Mica. You of all people should understand that." Her comment made him angry, but he knew she meant for it to. Trust was one of those things which had kept them close after her mother died.

"I don't understand any of this," she said simply. That wasn't true. She understood that her father had stood alone with his convictions for so many years that he hesitated to involve others in anything he did which might be controversial. His fierce belief that Sondak should ally itself with the Castorians had almost cost him his career. It had cost him some of the gentleness and sensitivity she had loved in him as a child.

"How long before the battle group is assembled?" Rochmon asked in an attempt to break the tension he sensed between father and daughter.

"Ten days at the most. If the repairs to the *McQuay* go as scheduled, less than that."

"But the *McQuay* suffered forty percent damage when Roberg was hit," Mica said in surprise.

"Yes, but they've been working round the clock on her. She should be spaceworthy any day now."

"But will she be battleworthy?" Rochmon asked.

"She has to be. Our plan requires seven launchships, and she's the closest to completing the force."

"What about methane?"

"That's being taken care of. Admiral Eresser and I made arrangements with the diplomats for increased imports from Cloise. There were some minor difficulties"—he thought of the four ambassadors who had died trying to negotiate the increase—"but it's being collected and loaded now, and the methane tankers will meet the battle group in the rendezvous sector shortly after the group assembles."

"That's a long way to ship methane," Mica observed, wondering if her father was going to tell them his secret plan or let them find out when everyone else did.

"Everything's coming a long way, including three hundred short-range attack ships. I just hope the Ukes figure the logistics are too difficult for us to handle."

"New attack ships?" Mica was startled. "From where?"

"From all over—but not new, just extras we could scrounge up throughout the fleets."

"Sounds like a lot of things are going to be pretty tricky timing-wise," Rochmon said quietly. "The Ukes could be right."

"Sir!"

"It's all right, Mica," Gilbert said with a smile, "Hew has a good point. There are a great number of operations that have to come together exactly as we want them to for this to work."

Suddenly Mica knew. "That's what you're going to do! You're going to . . ." She couldn't say it.

"Run assembly and dispersion," Rochmon finished for her.

No, Mica thought, it's—

Gilbert chuckled. "If my plan is that transparent, maybe I'd better rethink it."

"There's more to it than that," Mica said angrily. "You're going to keep some of those attack ships in reserve, aren't you? You're setting up a nonrevertor group!"

"A suicide group?" Rochmon asked. "Surely, sir—"

Gilbert held up his hand. "You don't know any of this—either of you. No one knows anything about any nonrevertor group. There will be a launchship and a select group of short-range attack ships held in reserve to defend the assembly and dispersion force. That is all. Nothing else. Do both of you understand that?"

Mica didn't answer, and neither did Rochmon. Their individual affections for Josiah Gilbert made the idea of him leading a nonrevertor group the most chilling thing he could have told them.

"Look," Gilbert continued when he realized what they were thinking. "We have to have every option open to us. If Pajandcan's battle group gets in trouble within a parsec of Matthews, there has to be an emergency reserve to help them out."

"But the *McQuay* won't be in good enough shape to follow and retrieve the attack ships it launches," Rochmon said simply. "So attack ships will either have to get to one of Pajandcan's launchships or die out there in space."

"We don't know that for sure," Gilbert said. He refused to verify the truth for them. This hidden part of his plan was born of desperation, but as he saw it, Sondak was in desperate straits. If they didn't stop the Ukes at Matthews, the Ukes probably wouldn't be stoppable. The nonrevertor group would be a last resort attack force, one which might deal an unexpected blow to the Ukes and turn the momentum of a questionable battle.

"Father," Mica said slowly, "I've seen that look on your face before. You're determined to do something, and I know that nothing we say is going to change your mind." She hesitated, unsure for the first time since her commission of the protocol between daughter-captain and father-admiral. "With that as a given, and with Commander Rochmon's permission," she added with a glance at Rochmon, hoping he understood, "I am going to request a transfer to your command. If you're going to do this thing, I want to be with you."

"Absolutely not," Gilbert said. "Nothing would be served by your presence."

"I beg to differ, sir," Rochmon said before Mica could recover from the instant rebuff. "If Mica were temporarily attached to your command as liaison for Cryptography, there might be a great deal to be gained. You're going to have seventeen of my screening ships in the Matthews operation. I'd like to recommend Mica as coordinating commander of that detachment."

Now it was Gilbert who wasn't sure of the protocol. Rochmon could request the commander of his choosing. The Joint Chiefs might look with some skepticism on his choice, but with Stonefield's backing, they would probably approve. If Gilbert said no outright, he was sure that Rochmon would go around him. But if—

"I accept," Mica said with a grim smile. "If that's what it takes to be a part of this operation, I accept."

Gilbert sighed. "I'm not so sure . . ."

"I think you're outnumbered, sir," Rochmon said carefully. "Not outranked, just outnumbered."

"Maybe I am." He smiled slightly at Mica. "Maybe I am."

Mica wanted to jump up and hug them both, not out of joy, but out of relief. But all her training kept her firmly in her chair. "Father, I think we both have to recognize that this whole operation is far more important than either of us. But there is no one in this universe more important to me than you." Letting her father know how she felt in front of Rochmon somehow made it easier. "If you are right about how important the Matthews defense is, and I believe you are, then I'm proud to be a part of it, and I will be equally proud to serve Commander Rochmon while standing by your side."

Gilbert nodded, unable to answer, seeing in his daughter an officer he could respect as well as a daughter he loved.

Rochmon looked from one to the other, grinning from ear to ear. "Well then," he said, refilling their glasses from the pitcher, "I propose a toast to Sondak's newest secret weapon—the Gilberts."

15

As they finished the traditional ice-water ceremony, Frye was annoyed by the way Commander Kuskuvyet sat smugly comfortable across the table from him. The ceremony demanded a certain humble demeanor from each of the participants, yet Kuskuvyet acted as though he had deserved the honor, or worse as though he were honoring Frye by participating.

In the presence of Kuskuvyet's inappropriate attitude, Frye chose his words very carefully. "Your task force will be known as the Shakav in honor of that planet's outstanding history of contributions to our military. My task force will be—"

"Marshall Judoff will not be pleased by that," Kuskuvyet said matter-of-factly.

Frye stared at his fat colleague in disbelief. It was not Kuskuvyet's place to make such a comment, nor was it any of Marshall Judoff's business what Charltos called the task forces.

"She asked me to *request* that you call my task force the Qubee-Tah in honor of her father."

Frye was doubly incredulous. Qubee-Tah Judoff had been little more than a space pirate until by a freak chance he became the temporary dictator of a minor planet. The only thing which had saved him from a worse reputation is that one of his dissatisfied citizens had killed him. To name a task force after Qubee-Tah Judoff would be an insult to everyone involved.

With a silent curse he knew he now had to be twice as careful about anything he said. Kuskuvyet's ear might as well be Judoff's.

"Surely you see no harm in that," Kuskuvyet said when Frye

failed to reply. "After all, Marshall Judoff is a very powerful and respected member of Bridgeforce, and—"

"Your pardon, please, Commander Kuskuvyet, but while I understand Marshall Judoff's interest in this matter, I regret that I cannot accede to her request. Both the representatives from Shakav and Admiral Ushogi's family have been notified of the honor."

"Ushogi?" Kuskuvyet asked in a condescending tone. "You have named your task force after that foolish old—"

"Admiral Ushogi was one of the finest admirals ever to serve the U.C.S.," Frye said sternly. Kuskuvyet had trod on the edge of disrespect already, and Frye would stand for no more of it. "The matter is settled. You will convey my regrets to Marshall Judoff."

Kuskuvyet laughed. "You're a high-handed bastard, Charltos, and so damned old-fashioned that it makes me sick. It was people like you who lost the last war for us, and I sure as hell hope you don't lose this one."

Frye stood very slowly, one hand on the security button at the edge of the table, his eyes burning steadily at Kuskuvyet, his heart furiously pumping blood through the veins in his neck.

"Sir," he said with all the self-control he could muster, "you will apologize instantly . . . or I will see to it that you sit out this war commanding nothing more than the most remote supply depot in the Systems."

"Why you miserable—"

"Silence!" Frye roared as he pressed the security button.

Seconds later, two of his personal security guards rushed into the room with stunners in their hands.

"You will escort Commander Kuskuvyet to Marshall Judoff's offices," he said through clenched teeth. "He has a message to deliver. If he resists, shoot him. Is that understood?"

"Yessir!" they barked simultaneously.

"You'll never—"

"Shut up!" Every muscle in Frye's body trembled with anger. "Take him. Now!"

"Yessir!" they barked again as they grabbed Kuskuvyet by the arms and dragged him across the room.

Frye allowed himself a tight smile as Kuskuvyet sputtered indignantly.

"They will shoot you," Frye said as the trio reached the door. "They are loyal to me."

Kuskuvyet never had a chance to reply as they swiftly maneuvered his bulk through the door and shut it behind them.

With a growl of frustration Frye collapsed in his chair. What had just happened was so irrationally wrong that he had no experience to help him deal with it.

The audacity of the man! And of Judoff!

How dare they attempt such a thing? How dare Kuskuvyet allow himself to be used like that?

Something clicked in Frye's brain, and he paused in the midst of his anger. Who had been used? Kuskuvyet? Or him? Or both of them? Had Judoff set this up for some reason? It made no sense—none whatsoever. What could she hope to gain from such an irrational act?

His microspooler dinged insistently, and he reached out without thinking and flipped it on. After the formal command designation, an excited voice started babbling something about an attack on the neutral Oinaise. For the longest moment Frye did not understand what the voice was saying. Then the words hit him like a blow to the gut.

". . . attack forces under Commander Fugisho attempted to take control of Oina system but were repelled. Fugisho refuses to report to this command or to explain his actions. As of this time his whereabouts are unknown. Request immediate instructions as to how to deal with this situation. Admiral Kimmel, out."

Frye tried to clear his head with a quick shake. Commander Fugisho? Wasn't he one of Judoff's ex-mercenaries?

Quickly he rewound the message and replayed it, listening carefully to each word, wondering all the while if Judoff had lost her mind. After playing the message a second time, he called Admiral Tuuneo.

"Sir," he said as soon as the admiral's face came on the viewscreen, "something is terribly wrong around here and—"

"I just received Kimmel's message, and verified it," Tuuneo said grimly. "Do you have any explanation for this outrage?"

"None at all, sir." Frye cursed Kuskuvyet for upsetting him so much that he hadn't even thought of verifying the message. "I just received Kimmel's transmission two minutes ago—right after Commander Kuskuvyet disgraced himself in the ice-water ceremony and then insulted me, and Admiral Ushogi. I had to have him forcibly removed from my offices."

Admiral Tuuneo's eyes narrowed darkly. "Judoff," he said quietly. "She is finally making her move. 'And the fools shall dance with death in time to their own music,'" he added, quoting from the Concordance.

"Sir? I, uh . . ." The quotation only added to Frye's confusion. What in Decie's name was going on?

"I will explain it to you later, Commander. Remain available to me on immediate notice."

"Yes, sir," Frye said as the screen went blank.

Had a sudden fit of madness overtaken Judoff? What did Tuuneo mean that she was finally making her move?

Like oil soaking into leather, a great fatigue saturated Frye's body and seeped glistening from his pores. Blank lethargy filled his mind. For the briefest instant he had a vision of Melliman standing before him with tears in her eyes. Then it was gone, and he could think of nothing, nothing which fit any coherent pattern. All he wanted to do was escape to some place where things made sense again.

With a sigh of resignation he rubbed one hand over his face, trying to massage life back into his mind. Then he stood up, pulled back his shoulders, and forced himself to take three long, steady breaths.

He had no idea what was going on, but for the moment that concern had been transferred to Admiral Tuuneo. Frye would proceed with his preparations for joining Ushogi Force and hope, now almost against hope, that Lisa Cay would arrive before he had to leave.

One way or another she would join him. The orders had been prepared and cut, awaiting her arrival. But he desperately wanted her with him on the trip. With Melliman now gone to Ely's command—

Commander Ely! He had to be sure to recommend to Tuuneo that Ely take Kuskuvyet's place. Frye would have preferred Ely all along, but there had been no way to encourage that choice before. Now Judoff and Kuskuvyet had opened a huge way with their insanity, and Frye was glad he was prepared to make the best of it.

But who would make the best out of what Fugisho had done to the Oinaise? That was worse insanity—far worse. It compromised not only everything the U.C.S. stood for, but also all their war efforts. The Oinaise only controlled four or five systems, but their influence as merchants was felt across both arms of the galaxy. An unjustified attack on them might unite all the neutrals against the U.C.S.

That could mean disaster. There was no way the U.C.S. could win a war against the whole galaxy—no way at all.

*   *   *

"How do I look?" Dawson asked, standing at attention in front of Pajandcan's desk.

"Like you're wearing someone else's uniform," she answered with a smile. "But I think we can get someone to fix it."

"That bad, huh?" Dawson looked down at the dark green trousers with their red pinstripes, then flopped one arm in the solid green tunic. "It is a little baggy."

"Gives you growing room. Quarter Admirals have a habit of getting fat at their desks."

"*Acting* Quarter Admirals stay lean," Dawson said with a tight-lipped smile. "Fear does that to them."

Pajandcan knew he was only half-joking. "You have to have faith," she said. "Matthew is better prepared for defense than I ever imagined it could be. The battle group will be assembled in a few days, and Admiral Gilbert will be coming out to—"

"Gilbert's coming here?"

"Not exactly." Pajandcan was surprised by the intensity of his reaction. "Why, do you know him?"

"That old bear was the one who negotiated the treaty when Gyle came to terms with Sondak."

She chuckled at his description of Gilbert. "He can be rather fierce when he wants to be, but underneath that exterior, there's an extremely compassionate man."

"Sounds like you know him yourself." Dawson said as he sat down opposite her.

"I served under him." And loved him, she thought.

"But why is he coming here? I thought you were going to be in command of the battle group."

"I am. He's going to coordinate assembly and dispersal, and—" She paused and looked at Dawson, wondering if he would understand what this meant. "—and command the reserve force."

"Reserves? How can you afford a reserve force? You told me

Sondak was almost gutting the fleets to put this battle group together. What is the reserve going to be made of?"

"A launchship. A cruiser. Two hundred short-range attack ships. It's all in here," she said, handing him a thin black folder. "Gilbert's reserve will be on nonrevertor status. Do you know what that means?"

Dawson looked puzzled. "No."

"It means his one launchship is barely spaceworthy. It is capable of putting almost two hundred short-range attackers into space, but incapable of retrieving them."

"So what happens to them? Will you pick them up?"

The grim idea did not sit well with her, but Pajandcan understood her old friend's thinking as if it were her own. "If he has to launch them," she said slowly, "that will mean that my battle group is in serious trouble. There probably won't be anyone to pick them up."

"A suicide force? That's crazy!"

She waited a moment before responding, not wanting to give her own feelings away. "Perhaps. Perhaps. But Admiral Gilbert believes we have to make our stand here and give ourselves every possible chance for victory. I think he's right."

Dawson leaned forward. "Your words say you do . . . but I suspect you have your own reservations about this."

"It's a big risk for high stakes. I'd be stupid not to have some reservations about it."

With a sudden laugh, Dawson relaxed in his chair. "I guess you would, Admiral. So who makes the decision about launching the reserve?"

"I do." A grim smile invaded her face. "If I can. If not, Gilbert will make the decision based on the battle reports."

"You're going to tell your commanding officer when to launch his reserve? That seems like a strange chain of command."

"Gilbert told me once that war demands pragmatism, not rules of order. Seems to me that you of all people should agree with that idea. Didn't you—"

"Damned by my past," Dawson said with a mock-sad shake of his head. "Look at me—an acting quarter admiral in my old enemy's military, watching my own tactics in someone else's plan. Sometimes I wonder how it all actually happened."

Pajandcan had decided that his negative humor was just

Dawson's way of dealing with the tension, but she was never quite sure how to respond to it. "You got too good at what you were doing. People who get that good tend to get caught in strange situations."

"That's me," he said with another shake of his head. "Too good for my own good. Any other surprises in this folder?"

"You tell me," she said, pulling an identical folder from her drawer. "I want to go over this with you section by section, point by point if necessary."

"Like reading the condemned man the menu for his last meal."

"At least the condemned man knows what he's getting. You only get to read the appetizers."

Dawson laughed loudly. "One for you, Admiral. Maybe I'll ask the Ukes for a description of the main course."

Pajandcan allowed herself a quiet chuckle, but it died in her throat. As she opened the folder she said, "Let's start with the list of your key officers."

*   *   *

Fire, ignited by the Isthians after Leri's kidnapping, burned on the fringes of Cloise's atmosphere.

Oxygen freed from carbon dioxide fed the slowly growing flames. Heat and the Isthian catalysts freed more oxygen. The fire grew to a rippling sheet of orange that spouted dark yellow flares as impurities in the methane were oxidized.

When the first crewman on one of the collectors saw it, he did a double take. Then he hit the alarm.

All systems went on automatic. Emergency circuits closed. Spring-loaded vents slammed shut. Motors whined shrilly in protest as the collector shut itself off. The half-full tanker severed its connections to the collector with a violent shake and started drifting slowly away.

A flaring explosion of gas caught the second collector's huge suction tube and blew it asunder. A tiny oxygen line fed the creeping line of flame that ate into the control module. A crewman panicked and uncoupled the module.

Five crewman died as the ruptured module fell like a slowly melting capsule into the flames of Cloise.

Deep in her closed mind Leri dreamed of fire.

The vision danced through shadow and light. Fire ate holes in the shadows. The holes grew and changed and became eyes—eyes that looked into an impossible future. The future burned.

Hot fluids drenched her body. Searing hands rubbed her flesh. Bright nightmares of pain exploded in her brain.

Voices screamed her name. "Leri! Leri! Leri!" they called in chorus.

The pain mounted. The fierce, awful rubbing tore at her nerves. In her vision the fires remained, burning brighter and hotter, stripping away the protection from her soul until she screamed in agony. The scream echoed back from the walls of her mind, trapped with her shriveling thoughts.

Cool shadows lifted her rigid form.

"Leri," a voice whispered. "Leri."

She knew that voice, had heard that tender whisper of love before. Desperately she clung to it, hoping, praying, begging that it would not go away.

"Leri," the voice whispered again.

It was Weecs. This was no dream. Weecs had come for her. Somehow Weecs had come for her. But Leri could not respond. She could not penetrate the heat-encrusted barriers around her mind and body.

"Leri, I love you. I am taking you home."

Weecs, she thought simply. Weecs.

Pain peeled back her consciousness and exposed the raw darkness of her mind. Weecs, she cried inside. Weecs.

The fires dimmed as she slipped into the darkness with his name floating above her agony.

No one aboard the collectors or the withdrawing tankers paid any attention to the Castorian ship until they received its emergency request for assistance. Then they were too busy to respond immediately and too involved with their own problems to be very concerned.

As quickly and unexplainedly as the fire started and spread, it cooled and died. By the time someone remembered the alien's request for help and passed it to the proper authorities, the Castorian ship was gone, and a tiny vessel was making its way unseen back to the surface of Cloise.

*　　*　　*

"You sure about this?" Rochmon asked.

"As sure as we are about anything," Bock said.

"And they transmitted it in the clear? Now what in blazes do you suppose that means?"

"It means," Bock said condescendingly, "that the Ukes have fouled up in the worst possible way."

"But Oina, for heaven's sake. Why would they attack Oina? It doesn't make any sense, Bock. They can't be that stupid. Where did we pick this up?" Rochmon couldn't believe that the Ukes would attack Oina—for any reason.

"Two of the CENFLEET monitors picked it up almost simultaneously. It's less than a day old, sir."

"You double-check them, Bock. I've got to tell Admiral Stonefield about this. But I want verification."

"As quick as we can."

Rochmon left her and went immediately to his office, his mind an agitation of improbabilities. When Stonefield's aide came on the viewscreen, Rochmon said, "I have to see the admiral, immediately."

"I'm sorry, sir, but the admiral cannot be disturbed for the rest of the day."

"Look, fleety, you tell the admiral I'm coming, and you make sure I get to see him, or you'll be standing watch on a space tug for the rest of your career. You got that?"

"But, sir,—"

"Don't 'but sir' me. Just tell the admiral I'm coming and that this is top priority. Understood?"

"Yessir," the aide said sharply, "but I cannot guarantee the commander he'll get his request."

"That's all right, fleety. I'll take care of the guarantees myself." Rochmon cut the connection with an admiring smile. Stonefield's aide was good. Have to mention that to the old man, he thought as he left Cryptography and headed for the J.C. Center.

By the time he arrived, the aide had done his duty and immediately ushered him into Stonefield's office. Rochmon was not surprised to find Admiral Gilbert and Avitor Hilldill there also. "Hate to bother you, sir," Rochmon said without waiting for the amenities, "but I've got some information that I thought I'd better tell you in person."

"Go ahead, Commander."

Rochmon didn't notice the cold look on Stonefield's face. "According to two interceptions made by CENFLEET monitors within the last standard day, the Ukes have attacked Oina."

"Impossible!"

"Are you sure?"

"No, and no," Rochmon said, responding to Hilldill and Stonefield. "Not impossible, sir. Highly improbable, but certainly not impossible. As for being sure, Admiral, we're trying to get verification now. But like I said, it was picked up by two separate monitors."

"And you are sure the code's correct?" Stonefield asked.

"It was broadcast in the clear."

"Then I believe it," Admiral Gilbert said, speaking for the first time. "What exactly did the message say, Hew?"

Rochmon pulled the small slip of paper from his pocket and read it. "Oina's defenses stronger than anticipated. Forced to withdraw. Awaiting further instructions." He handed it to Stonefield. "It's signed by Commander Fugisho."

"Thank you, Commander," Stonefield said. "Can you get verification?"

"I think so, sir."

"Good. Do it. And now, if you'll excuse us, we have a lot to do before Admiral Gilbert leaves."

"Yes, sir," Rochmon said with a polite salute.

He smiled at the aide as he left the office, but underneath the smile ran a swift current of concern. Somehow it didn't seem like they had responded properly to the message. They should have been angry, or upset, or happy, or something. But surely they weren't so caught up in the defense of Matthews that they failed to understand how important this was.

Rochmon shrugged. Gathering the information was his job. Using it was theirs. The best thing he could do was to make sure they got verification. Then maybe their reaction would change.

16

Lucky sat on the overstuffed basee with his feet barely touching the floor. His stomach and bowels were tight with too many courteous handsful of rich Oinaise food. His mind was bloated with contentment.

Since he had landed, the Oinaise had shuffled him around under the careful supervision of checkdroids from one official to another. None of the officials quite knew what to do with him, but each of them was gracious and hospitable to an extreme. Gradually he was lulled into an unnatural complacence—a careless acceptance of whatever happened. He had requested, and the officials had assured him that they would give him sufficient warning to get *Graycloud* into space if the Ukes returned. That was all Lucky cared about.

If the Ukes came back, he was going to fly for freedom. *Graycloud* was programmed to take bearings on the Spider Nebula and warp toward its center. Lucky wasn't going to worry about anything else until they exited the warp. Seemed like the only sane thing to do.

With a quiet sigh he lay back, took one of the dark, sweet candies from the bowl beside him, popped it into his mouth, and traced the finely intricate patterns painted in subdued colors on the vaulted ceiling. He did not know exactly what the sweet candies were, but he had become rather fond of them during his four days of doing the bureaucratic shuffle, and the checkdroids had been more than pleased to keep him well supplied with them. As the creamy confection melted slowly on his tongue, he wondered why he was giving up.

I'm not giving up, he thought in quick rebuttal, I'm just getting out of the way.

Running away is more like it.

Lucky sat up with an angry shake of his head. This same argument with himself had plagued him since he programmed *Graycloud* with the Spider Nebula coordinates. But now it was recurring more frequently, which didn't make sense because he was not running away from anything.

Except yourself and Marsha.

This is stupid, Lucky thought. There is absolutely no reason why I should talk to myself like this.

Yes, there is.

"Stop it," he said aloud. "Just stop it." He reached for another piece of candy just as a hand swept the bowl away from him, "Hey! That's mine!"

"No more, Captain Teeman. They are bad for you."

"Bad, sad—give them to me," he said. He stood up and faced the Oinaise, feeling rather foolish looking up into his huge face and demanding his candies. But he wanted them.

"I am sorry, Captain," Delightful Childe said as he put one hand on Lucky's shoulder and gently pushed him back down to the basee. "You will go through a withdrawal period of two days or so, and then you will be fine. Gorlet rarely has any serious side effects."

"Withdrawal? Who are you talking about? Me?" Lucky shook his head and suddenly recognized— "Delightful Childe? What are you doing here? I mean, I thought you had cargos to haul and everything like that." He tried to grab the bowl.

Delightful Childe gently blocked Lucky's arm then put the bowl of gorlet on a high shelf, well out of Lucky's reach. "The recent atrocity called me home. A more appropriate question might be, what are you doing here?"

"If you'll give me one of those, I'll tell you," Lucky said, looking up at the shelf and feeling suddenly prankish.

"I cannot, Captain. Humans are easily addicted to gorlet, never to any good end that I've noticed. Since I have been made responsible for you, you must resign yourself to no more of them." Delightful Childe wondered what he had done to deserve this stupid human whose eyes kept flicking up the wall—and what he had done to deserve the checkdroids who must have been the ones giving Lucky the gorlet.

"Then I won't tell you."

"Fine, Captain. We will talk about it again in two or three days when you have recovered."

"Recovered what?" Lucky shook his head. None of this made sense. Why wouldn't Delightful Childe give him the candy?

"Recovered from your addiction." Delightful Childe bared his teeth and clenched one hand firmly on Lucky's shoulder. "Do you not want some now? Would you not force me to give it to you if you could?"

"Yes!" Lucky shouted at that ugly face. He tried to throw himself sideways, but Delightful Childe's grip tightened painfully on his shoulder and held him fast. "Let me go!"

"Very well, Captain. Later you will beg for someone to hold you, anyone who can help you still the shaking your body will go through. I will be available then."

He released Lucky and plucked the bowl of gorlet off the shelf. Holding it high, away from Lucky's grasp, he left the room and closed the sliding door behind him. Poor man, he thought. Poor stupid human. But our fault—totally our fault. Someone should have been paying more attention to the checkdroids.

Lucky wasn't sure what had happened or why. He felt slightly dizzy and lay down on the soft cushions of the basee, but almost immediately sat up again and started searching through the tucks and folds of material that covered it. Maybe one of the candies had fallen from the bowl.

Nothing. "Nothing!" he said loudly. "He could have left me a couple of them. That wouldn't have been so bad, would it?"

No answer came from the silent walls. But one came from his head. You're addicted to that stuff, he thought.

"That's crazy! Who ever heard of getting addicted to something like that?" Suddenly he knew the answer and was angry. "Why did they give it to me then?" he shouted.

He ran to the door and tried to slide it open. When it wouldn't move, he pounded on it. "Childe! Delightful Childe! It isn't fair! They started it. Your people. They offered it to me."

A thin sheen of sweat covered his skin. He turned his back against the door and pressed as hard as he could. "Dammit, Childe! It isn't my fault! Don't do this to me. How was I supposed to know?"

His knees buckled gently as his back slid down the door in sudden despair. This is ridiculous, he thought, totally, utterly ridiculous. With arms wrapped tightly around his legs and his head on his knees, he thought, I'll just rest for a minute, just for a minute. Then I'll find a way out of here. Surely there has to be a way out of here, he thought as a tear rolled silently out of his eye. There must be a way out of here. There must be. The heavy hands of lethargy pressed him down into himself until he cried himself to sleep

When he awoke, his eyes refused to focus properly. His body shook uncontrollably. A helpless sense of fear filled his mind. Delightful Childe was holding and rocking him with gentle firmness.

"The worst is over, Captain. Your body will calm down in a few more hours, and in a day or two you will be fine," Delightful Childe said quietly as he began massaging Teeman's back to help relieve the shaking.

"Wh-wh-wh-why?" Lucky clenched his jaw to stop his teeth from chattering, but could not stop the awful shaking of his arms and legs or the twitching of his head.

"A mistake, Captain. Who gave you the gorlet?"

"Ch-ch—droids."

"As I thought. No one was monitoring them." Because there aren't enough of us left, Delightful Childe thought darkly. Beyond that thought was the vision of the female, Nindoah, he had made arrangements to mate with.

"Why?" Lucky asked again, barely managing to hold the word to one syllable.

"The atrocity. Your war," he said, working his fingers against Teeman's muscle spasms.

"N-n-not my war." Lucky fought to speak, afraid to let go of the conversation, afraid his body would shake him to death. "Y-y-y-yours now."

"No!" Delightful Childe regretted the anger in his response as soon as he made it. Captain Teeman shook harder than before. "No," he repeated calmly, his fingers urgently pressing the muscles to relax. "It is not our war. The attack on us was a mistake. The Ukes will not do it again."

"Fight . . . back."

"It is not our way."

"Have to . . . fight back." Lucky wanted to say more, wanted to demand that Delightful Childe agree with him, but now he knew suddenly that his bowels were about to give way. "Let me go," he said weakly.

Before Delightful Childe could respond it was too late. Lucky's bowels emptied uncontrollably. The stench made him dizzy . . . lost . . . dark . . . as he faded away under Delightful Childe's persistent massage.

*   *   *

"The commodity you wish me to handle for you?" The nameless alien broker asked in a voice without inflection.

"Information," Ayne Wallen said simply. He was as tired as miseryfolk, and more than a little afraid for his safety, but the more he had run from the fleeties, the more he had been channeled in this direction.

"Ah, information is a precious but difficult commodity to deal in. Exactly what kind of information do you have?"

As inexperienced as he was, Ayne knew better than to give his position away here. "Valuable information. Significant information for the U.C.S. military."

The alien cocked a hairless eyebrow. "Really, now? And where is this precious military information of yours?"

"In my head."

"Pardon?"

"In my head," Ayne said, giving the nameless broker a brief smile. "Is all in my head."

"My customers will not pay for your head," the broker answered. "They must see proof."

"Sondak will pay for my head." Ayne couldn't read any expression in the Oinaise's eyes, but he wasn't about to give up simply because the broker was uncooperative. He had traveled too far and risked too much. "I have answers, and Sondak knows it. If U.C.S. wants answers to Sondak weapons secret, they will pay for my head."

The broker bared his teeth. "Why shouldn't I just sell you to Sondak? They're much closer."

"Because U.C.S. will pay more," Ayne said quietly. He was prepared for the possibility of danger and let his hand slide down to the handle of the stunrod in his pants pocket, ready to fight his way out if necessary.

"No weapons," the broker said with a quick blink. "No violence, citizen Wallen. My question was meant in jest."

"Not taken in jest, nameless one." His hand trembled

against his leg. "You tell me if you have customer. You find me way off this planet. There are other brokers."

"None who will help you. You are, uh, warm property, as I believe you humans say—too dangerous for anyone but me."

Ayne tightened his fingers on the stunrod, unsure of what to say or what to do. "Fought my way to get here," he said finally. "Will fight again. Nothing too dangerous for the right price. Patros has other brokers."

The Oinaise snorted. "No brokers as good as I. But do not let me stop you. Go to Cavra. He will sell you to Sondak because his connections are poor and he is lazy. Go to the scoundrel Beliss'hatot. She might get you off planet, but then she, too, would sell you back to Sondak. Like most Castorians, she has no scruples when dealing with others not of her own race." He joined the tips of his fourteen fingers and slid his hands around his yellowed poboscis as though thinking.

Ayne had no response. He had been warned about Beliss'hatot, but he had never heard of the other broker and did not want to suffer again through the difficulties he had encountered finding this nameless one.

"No, citizen Wallen," the Oinaise said finally, "there are no other brokers on all of Patros you wish to deal with. But please," he added with a wave of his hand toward the door, "feel free to discover that for yourself."

With a distressed sigh Ayne stared straight at the broker and said, "Conditions must be established. Guarantees must be made if I am to deal with you."

"Conditions are simple. Guarantees are not. But first tell me, citizen Wallen, what exactly do you expect to receive for your, uh, shall we say, contribution to a bargain with the Ukas?"

"Freedom in exchange for information—important scientific information. We be knowing much that U.C.S. can use."

"Yet still no proof of that. No, do not protest. I can understand your need for secrecy. However, I would look extremely foolish if I were to approach my contacts and tell them that I had a human scientist who previously worked for Sondak—"

"Drautzlab. Worked for Drautzlab." For the first time Ayne thought he saw true interest on the Oinaise's face.

"Drautzlab, was it? Hmmm, that does make it a bit more interesting." The broker paused. "But even so, the fact that you claim to be a scientist and claim to have worked for Drautzlab gives me little to bargain with. I must have something substantial to offer. Surely you understand that."

Ayne did understand, but he did not know how much he could or should tell this alien. Were his degrees from the Kobler Institute important to them? Or his work with Heller on neutronic spacetime contractions? Even his work at Drautzlab wouldn't mean much, because no one outside of Sondak had probably ever heard of the Ultimate Weapon. Even if they had, they certainly could not understand its true implications. Yet he knew he would have to give this broker more information in order to get the U.C.S. to pay attention.

"Yes," he said slowly. "I understand. Tell your contact to pass this on to authorities in U.C.S. Tell him to pass it to physicist, one who understands Guntteray's theories. You know Guntteray?"

"The privilege has not been mine. Does he live on Patros?"

"Guntteray is dead," Ayne said disgustedly. "Question is, do you know theories?"

The broker bared his teeth again. "No, I am afraid that my experience has brought me into limited contact with the universe of science. Are they important?"

Ayne sighed. "No. Are not important for you. Is important only that information go to someone who knows Guntteray's theories. You can guarantee that?"

"As I told you, guarantees are difficult. My agents, however, are adept at finding and maintaining the proper contacts, and I am sure we can pass your information on to someone with a scientific background. Does that satisfy you?"

"Still need guarantees," Ayen said stubbornly.

The broker snorted and mumbled something in a foreign language. Then he said, "I can offer you safe lodging, food, credits, women, alcohol—satisfaction of many vices—and a promise that I will do my best to accommodate you, citizen Wallen. That is all that is within my power. And that I do at great risk to myself with little promise that I will be repaid."

Ayne hesitated. The fleeties were sure to have followed him to Elliscity, and he had no idea where else he could go. "Your name," he said. "Tell your name, and I will agree. Do not like dealing with person with no name."

"No one knows my name," the broker said simply, "but you may call me Xindella."

"But that is name—"

"Of my business, and the street where I live, and many other things. It is also the only name by which I am known on this planet. If that will not suffice, I have nothing further—"

"Will suffice. You will put this in writing?"

Xindella laughed, or snorted in an approximation of a laugh. Ayne couldn't tell which.

"In writing? You want a contract for our illegal enterprise? I am afraid, citizen Wallen, that you have lingered too long in the laboratories of science. In my business there are no contracts. There are agreements, verbal agreements, honored because each side has something the other wants. You want to give your precious information to the Ukas. I want to make a profit helping you do that. If the Ukas want what you know badly enough, I get to make my profit. That is the only kind of agreement there ever has been or ever will be."

"Only kind?" Ayne knew now that he would accept whatever Xindella had to offer. He was too tired from running and hiding to go on, and he had paid the last of his credits to get him this far. He had no choice.

"The only kind." Xindella gave him a curious look. "Suppose, however, that I hire you, pay you a wage to work for me while we are attempting to make the proper contacts and strike a bargain with the Ukas. I could give you a contract for that. Would that please you?"

"Work for you?" Ayne shook his head. "Do not understand. What work would I do for you?"

"Oh," Xindella said with a hint of amusement, "I have many people on my payrolls who do many different things. Right now I need someone to work on my personal spacecraft, someone who understands Gouldrive. Could you do that?"

"Mechanic's work? You ask me to do mechanic's work? I am scientist." Ayne was insulted. He had worked his way through school as a mechanic, but he had no desire to do such demeaning labor again.

"But scientists without jobs cannot be choosy, citizen Wallen, especially scientists on the run. Do you understand Gouldrive?"

"Yes," he said reluctantly. "Is simple drive for faster-than-light travel developed by Gould for pioneer ships and freighters. Odd to have such a powerful drive on—"

"Can you fix one?"

"Is broken? We be knowing how to fix with proper tools and parts. But still is mechanic's work."

"But you would agree to work for me in that capacity, to fix my Gouldrive in exchange for my efforts on your behalf?"

Ayne knew he shouldn't say yes, knew that there was more to Xindella than he could possibly guess. But he had no one else to turn to. He had already killed two fleeties and stolen four vehicles. He had cheated an innocent traveler out of her credits, and fought off more than one ruffian who would have parted him from those same credits. At least working for Xindella would be more honorable work, however demeaning it was to his dignity.

"Will fix Gouldrive. Will work for you. Must trust you, but do not like it."

"That is your prerogative for the moment. The time will come, citizen Wallen, when you will have to trust me, so save what little trust you have until then. You will need it."

With a slight sigh Ayne felt a little of his tension drain away. For some reason he was sure he had managed to do the right thing. "Now what?" he asked.

"Ah, first I have some chores to attend to, some people to contact who will take care of you. So for a short while I will have to leave you alone here. But let me offer you some food." He opened a small door in the wall behind him and pulled out a shiny crystal tray.

Ayne's mouth immediately started to water, and he realized how long it had been since he had eaten.

Xindella put a tray on the desk between them and pointed to a small dish. "These are dried meats of various kinds, most tasty when eaten with the shollo."

The word didn't make any sense to Ayne, but he knew the decanter contained something to drink, and he had to restrain himself from reaching for it immediately.

"These you most certainly want to try," Xindella said, indicating a polished gold cup filled with small, dark brown balls. "They are sweet and delicious, the perfect food when you are tired and hungry. These are gorlet."

17

Mica hung weightless, staring through the *McQuay*'s viewport as the words of Admiral Stonefield's message came back to her. She knew the other ships in the nonrevertor force were too far away to be seen, but she hoped for a glimpse of them, as though that might reassure her and erase Stonefield's message.

Be cautious. When the traitor reveals his presence, you must be prepared to act. Trust no one.

The last part bothered her most. She longed to go immediately to her father and tell him . . . tell him what? Tell him that her duties as honor trustee had been expanded to include him? Tell him that she was the Joint Chiefs' official spy aboard his beaconship? Tell him that . . . There was nothing she could tell him.

Matthews Star burned brightly a quarter of a parsec away on the upper edge of the port. Half a parsec beyond that, Admiral Pajandcan's defense fleet was assembled and waiting—the only Sondak force between Matthews System and the cluster of stars near galaxy's center that marked U.C.S. space. Mica wished there were something between her and the duty Stonefield had imposed on her. But more than that she wished there was someone she could confide in.

It was almost a relief when the gravity warning sounded and forced her to do something. But just as she reached the deck that would be down when the gravity came on, she heard her name.

"Captain Gilbert. Captain Gilbert. Report to Battle Center in zero-five minutes. Captain Gilbert, report to Battle Center."

Mica braced herself against a bulkhead as the gravity was

initiated, then immediately began climbing up to the Battle Center. Could the attack have started? she wondered. No, there would have been a call to stations if it had. This must be something else.

"Captain Gilbert reporting," she said as she stepped into the anteroom of the Battle Center.

"The Admiral wants you. Inside," the young duty officer at the desk said with a glance at her and a jerk of his thumb over his shoulder.

"Thanks," Mica said, giving him a salute he didn't deserve as she stepped past his desk through the doorway.

"Ah, Mica, good," Admiral Gilbert said as soon as his daughter was announced by the door guard. "Here's something we need you to evaluate."

"A message?" she asked as she took the paper he handed her.

"Part of one. What can you make of it?"

Mica read the fragment slowly and carefully. Then she read it again. "Wasn't Ushogi a famous Uke admiral?"

"Yes."

"Then I'd guess that they've named a fleet after him. That would fit their culture, I think. 'Ushogi and Shakav dispatched' must mean that they have two fleets on the way as Cryptography guessed." Mica swallowed hard. "How old is this message?"

Gilbert turned to his aide with a raised eyebrow.

"A realtime day, sir," the aide said, "maybe less. It's hard to tell."

"If it's much more than that, Lieutenant, the Ukes could be down Pajandcan's throat any time now."

"Yes, ma'am, I know that. But there's no way we can guess more accurately."

Mica knew better than anyone else how right he was, and she could tell he was feeling the pressure. "I understand, Lieutenant."

"I think you'd better tell Pajandcan and Dawson," Gilbert said quietly to his daughter. "Then send a message to Rochmon, and tell him it is time to intensify all his intercept actions in this sector as we discussed."

"But, Father, uh, sir," Mica said, "if we send a message to Rochmon—no matter how well we code it—don't we run the risk of the Ukes knowing that—"

"It does not matter, Mica. If this is another of Charltos's operations—and there's no reason to believe otherwise—then the Ukes already know we're waiting for them. What they don't know is how strong our force is, or how much we're prepared to sacrifice. Your message to Rochmon will not tell them anything they don't already know, so get to it."

"Aye-aye, sir," she said with a quick salute. Suddenly she felt an urgency that swept everything else aside. It was almost as though she could sense the Ukes moving through space toward Matthews system, dodging and hiding, thinking they had all the advantages. They probably do, she thought as she composed the messages for Pajandcan, Dawson, and Rochmon. They probably do.

* * *

An hour after the Ushogi Fleet broke from subspace in the Hiifi system, Frye Charltos sat alone in his command cabin cursing silently as Bridgeforce's priority messages reeled off his microspooler. Judoff had withdrawn from Bridgeforce and taken not only her trained dog, Kuskuvyet, but also eighty militia ships and their crews.

What angered Frye the most was that she had every legal right to act as she had. The militia ships were what remained from her father's old pirating days and were technically only on loan to Bridgeforce. Furthermore, there was no way to force her to remain a member of Bridgeforce.

Frye wouldn't miss Judoff or Kuskuvyet in the least. But he had counted on those ships. They were supposed to be guarding the base of Shakav Fleet's cone of attack. Now Commander Ely would have to use some of his own precious ships to guard the base of his formation.

Adding Judoff's desertion to Commander Fugisho's attack on the Oina system made Frye very uneasy about what could happen behind them as they attacked the Matthews system.

With a quick shake of his head he dropped that worry. Admiral Tuuneo was quite capable of contending with Judoff and Fugisho. His priorities lay ahead of him, and—

"Shuttle approaching, sir," a brusque voice said, interrupting his thought.

"Identification and mission?" Frye asked.

"Replacement Corps with additional officers and technicians as expected, sir. Also the civilian you were looking for, one Marsha L. C. Yednoshpfa."

Frye's heart jumped. Lisa Cay! She made it! "What's the

E.T.A. on that shuttle?" he asked, his voice barely under control.

"Estimated time of arrival one-four-four minutes, sir."

"Very good. Notify me when they dock. And have Yednoshpfa sent directly to my cabin."

"As you will, sir,"

Suddenly Frye felt better. He leaned back, clasped his hands behind his head, and allowed himself a smile. Lisa Cay was going to be with him, and regardless of how irrational his thoughts about her were, he knew that everything would be easier with her at his side. Hadn't she come through Decie only knew what to get to him? A daughter with that much determination would make the best AOCO he could possibly have.

A slight flicker of regret came with the thought of AOCOs. He wondered how Melliman was doing under Ely—and wondered if he had truly done the right thing. The regret was shaded by a wisp of anger. It isn't fair to feel this way about her, he thought, but no one promised me life would be fair.

"Now I'd better check the rest of the reports before Lisa Cay gets here," he said aloud.

Three hours later as he cleared his last response through the microspooler, someone knocked outside. He crossed the cabin in three quick strides and slid the door back. For the briefest moment he saw Vinita in Lisa Cay's face. Then he opened his arms, and she stepped into them with a fierceness that surprised him.

"It's been a long time," she said quietly as she tightened her arms around him and pressed her head against his shoulder.

"Too long."

"How is Mother?" She felt him stiffen and pulled her head back to look at him. "Father? Is she . . .?" The look on his face gave her the answer. Guilt and sorrow washed through her and spilled in quick tears down her face. "When? How?" she stammered as he pulled her into the cabin and shut the door.

"She was sick for a long time," Frye said quietly as he led her to a chair. "The end was quick and painless." The look on Lisa Cay's face tightened a hard knot inside him. He pulled a chair up to hers, sat facing her, and took her hands in his. A cold, closed fist gripped his chest. That angered him. He had hoped, had expected, had believed Lisa Cay would open the warmth inside him again.

"Tell me about it," she said softly.

"She was sick. The doctors said it was incurable. She died in my arms. There's nothing else to tell."

Marsha Lisa Cay heard something she couldn't identify in her father's voice, an echo from the time and distance which had separated them. "Father . . . if I had been there," she said as she freed one of her hands and wiped the tears from her eyes, "if I had known that she was sick, I—"

"There was no way you could know," he said, releasing her other hand and unconsciously folding his own hands together. "You were . . . Decie only knows where, and there was no way—"

"There was the message drop."

He felt himself clenching his fingers and looked at her with an anger that opposed his deepest wishes. Frye forced his hands to relax and leaned back in his chair. "I tried that, Lisa Cay. You never answered."

"I go by Marsha, now. And I checked the message drop regularly," she said, fending off the tone of accusation she heard in his voice. "There was never a message from you." Now she heard the accusation in her own voice.

"It doesn't matter," Frye said firmly. "It's over now, part of the past. I'm just glad you are here."

"Somehow I have a hard time believing that."

"Please, Lisa Cay—"

"Marsha."

"All right, then, Marsha. Your mother always liked that name, too. . . . Marsha, try to believe that I am very, very pleased to have you here with me."

As steadily as she could, she looked him straight in the eye while her mind seethed with images of the day she had left home. No matter what he said, she doubted his words. Even when he had made her promise on that day of departure that she would return if they needed her, she never believed that he really wanted her to stay. Her disbelief had driven her away in the first place, yet she had hoped that it would change, that she would be able to believe what he said. Now she knew it hadn't. "Why?"

Frye looked at her and realized that he was actually facing a woman he barely knew. "Why what?"

"Why are you pleased to have me here?"

"Because I need your help. I want you to be my Aide-of-

Commander." He had not meant to spring that idea on her so quickly, but—

"Your AOCO? Me? Why?" Regardless of the other emotions whirling around inside her, she was flattered that he wanted her for that.

"I just think we would make a good team—the best team I can imagine," Frye said, pushing aside a brief image of Melliman.

Marsha hesitated. There was something else there, some other emotion lurking just behind his words. "Just like you and Mother in the old days?" she asked suddenly.

Her comment startled him. Was that what he wanted? "I, uh, I don't know." He looked down at his hands and tried to sort his thoughts, but the pressure of her presence after all these years slowed his mind. "Look, Lisa, uh, Marsha, I don't know if that's it at all. I hadn't even thought about that." As he looked up at her and read the sadness in her eyes, he wished this meeting had gone differently—much differently. "But I do know that I want you here—for whatever reasons."

For a long moment Marsha stared at him and waited, hoping he would say why, holding her response as she had held it years before in anticipation of the words he could never say to her, the words she needed most to hear. Finally she couldn't stand the silence or his gaze any longer and looked away. "Mother was the only one, wasn't she?" she asked softly.

Frye shook his head slightly. Her question didn't make any sense. "What do you mean?"

"She was the only person you ever loved—I mean, really loved in your whole life."

"Now listen, Marsha. You have—"

"No, Father, you listen." Something snapped quietly inside her, and she knew she had to have the answer. "I'll work for you," she said firmly, "and I'll be your AOCO if that's what you want. But we have to clear this away. Did you ever love anyone except Mother? . . . Like me? . . . Did you love me?"

The intensity of her question lowered a dark curtain in his heart, but against that colorless backdrop, it was easy to be honest with her. "No," he said softly. "You're right. She was the only one—ever. I tried to love you, but that's just not the same thing . . . is it?"

His words relieved her even as they disappointed her. "No, Father, it isn't the same. But I'm glad you tried." Tears spilled slowly from the corners of her eyes—not for the love she had never had from her father, but for the love she had given up to get to him. Somewhere out in the galaxy was Lucky Teeman, a man who loved her without question.

"Did you mean what you said, about being my AOCO?"

"Yes," she said as she wiped away her tears. "I'm here. I'll serve you and the U.C.S. as best I can until this war is over, or until you don't need me any more."

"Good," he said with a smile that felt awkward on his face. "I'm glad. I really am."

*   *   *

Admiral Pajandcan acknowledged Gilbert's message and notified him that she was moving her fleet into its initial defense position. Then she called Dawson to wish him luck before giving the final movement order.

"Worried, Admiral?" Dawson's fuzzy image asked from her screen.

"Not me. You're the one who'd better be worried. Even if we find the Ukes, you're probably going to take a beating."

"Maybe so. We found another of those Uke missiles. Same results as before. It self-destructed well before we could get to it. That makes four altogether."

"I just hope you have enough time to find the rest of them."

"I have enough methane for my fighters. But can you and Admiral Gilbert give us the time? What are you going to do on short fuel rations?"

"The best I can, Dawson—just like everyone else, the best I can. That's all any of us can do. If we're careful, the fuel we have will get us through."

"Well . . . break an arm, Admiral."

"What?"

"I said, break an arm. That means I hope it works out all right for you."

"That's an odd way of wishing someone good luck."

"Odd or not, it's my best for—"

A burst of static from the short-range transceiver cut him off. "If you can hear me, Dawson, you break an arm, too," Pajandcan said. She shut down her transceiver and rejected the idea of sending the same message to Gilbert. I'd give a broken arm to win this one, she thought . . . an arm and a leg, too.

She ordered her fleet to move, then with a sudden smile she loaded her transceiver with three words and sent them in a burst toward Gilbert's nonrevertors. Let them figure it out, she thought. It will give them something to do to break the monotony of waiting.

*   *   *

Mica read the first message with a faintly puzzled look in her eyes and a bare echo of understanding. "Of course," she said as a small grin crept across her lips. "It means good luck. It has to." For a moment she marveled at the perversity of the human spirit expressing positive wishes in negative form. But she knew her father of all people would understand that, so she printed out a hard copy of the message and sent it up to him. Maybe he would grin, too.

The second message was from Rochmon, and Mica caught herself unexpectedly wishing she could talk directly to him. Why, she could not be sure, but she knew Rochmon fulfilled a need for her, a need for confidence that no one else quite seemed to satisfy.

The message looked routine, another report that the Ukes had definitely divided into two fleets, both heading in the general direction of Matthews system. On second reading she decided it wasn't routine at all. Hidden between the words was something else, an implication that Mica might have missed had she not read it again.

"Smaller of the two fleets commanded by Ely, one of their lesser known commanders," the message stated.

If Commander Ely controlled one fleet and Commander Charltos controlled the main fleet, what had happened to Marshall Judoff and Commander Kuskuvyet? Cryptography had been sure that one of those two would be in command of at least part of the Uke attack force. Could there be a third fleet they knew nothing about? Mica decided that her father needed this information as quickly as possible and carried it herself.

"And you think it's important," he said minutes later, after hearing her out.

"I do."

"Then why didn't Rochmon say what he meant?"

"Afraid of interception? I don't know, sir. But I am sure that he meant for me to catch it. Ely is not a lesser known commander. We can assume—if our intelligence is right—that he is politically less powerful than Judoff. But he rose through the ranks during the last war, and militarily he certainly knows what he's doing."

"And what do you think that means, Mica?"

"I think it means we're up against a tougher opponent than we thought we would be. If Ely is in command of the second fleet and leads an attack on the polar systems as we suspect, then I think it means we're in trouble."

Josiah Gilbert wrinkled his brow in concentration and absently rubbed a thumb along his chin. "There's no way Polar Fleet can stop a concentrated attack. We're not even sure we can stop one here. But suppose this is only the feint—suppose Charltos is leading the attack on the polar systems and—no."

He paused and looked slowly around at his officers and men. "No," he said again. "Tell Rochmon to alert POLFLEET Command and wish them luck. We're sticking with our plan. If Charltos is out there, he wants this system, and we have to keep him from getting it—at all costs."

18

"He's where?"

"On Patros—at least that's what Sci-Sec believes. They followed him there, but they cannot be sure he remains on that planet."

"Pardon my asking, sir," Sjean said quietly, "but if Scientific Security knows where Ayne is, why should we care?"

Caugust leaned forward and braced his elbows on his desk. "Because he is a security risk—one we can ill afford—and Sci-Sec wants to know how much of a risk he is so that they can—"

"But, sir—"

"Let me finish, Sjean. Sci-Sec would like to follow him rather than try to capture him if—and it's a big if—if he is not too much of a threat. I told them you'd have to answer that question, which is why I want you to talk to Inspector Janette as soon as she arrives."

Sjean was frustrated by this whole conversation. "And just how am I supposed to determine the risk factors, sir? What am I supposed to tell this Inspector Janette? That Ayne Wallen discovered the equations for reciprocal action at a distance? We don't even understand how valuable they are yet, and there's no guarantee this first series of tests will tell us. How can we determine how much his knowledge of them threatens us?"

"I don't know, Sjean. But if you cannot determine the risk factors, no one can."

He leaned back with a smile that surprised her, but before she could say anything his intercom buzzer went off.

"Inspector Janette from Scientific Security to see you, Dr. Drautz."

"Send her in."

They both rose as the door opened and were surprised to find themselves facing a tiny, beautiful woman with long blond hair. She wore a shimmering black suit that clung to her diminutive figure and made her look even smaller than she really was.

"Inspector Janette? I'm Caugust Drautz." His voice betrayed his surprise at her appearance. "This is one of my chief scientists, Dr. Sjean Birkie."

"Pleased to meet you both," Janette said in a quietly lilting voice as she crossed the room gracefully and gave them each a slight bow.

"As we are to meet you." Sjean couldn't identify the subtle accents in Janette's voice, but she was immediately intrigued by them and the woman herself.

"Please, be seated," Caugust said with a gentle wave toward the chairs opposite his desk, "and tell us how you think we can be of assistance to Scientific Security."

"If you do not mind," Janette said, "I would rather sit facing the door—an old habit of mine, no longer necessary, but one difficult to break."

"Then by all means, take my chair." Caugust moved away from his desk, and Janette slipped past him and sat easily in his large, overstuffed chair.

For the briefest moment Sjean thought the tiny inspector looked silly in a chair meant for someone much larger. But as she settled herself opposite Janette, her opinion changed. The woman's size meant nothing. She dominated the chair and the desk with a sense of sureness that Sjean could only admire and envy.

"I thank you both for agreeing to this meeting," Janette said as Caugust sat beside Sjean, "and I want you to know that your information—however slight it may seem to you—will be of much help to us."

"Perhaps if you could tell us exactly what you want to know, we could better assist you," Caugust said as he readjusted his bulky frame in his chair.

"That is difficult," Janette said, turning her gaze and slight smile from Caugust to Sjean, "but the most difficult part is yours. You must tell me enough so that Sci-Sec understands what Wallen knows without telling us so much that any of our agents could pose a security risk themselves."

"He discovered these equations?"

"Yes," Sjean said, annoyed by Janette's interruption.

"So much the worse. Please continue, Doctor."

"For us," she said, "they have only opened a highly promising channel toward practical applications. If they are correct, of course—and so far we have no reason to believe they are not— then they could guide us directly to the most devastating weapon the galaxy—"

"No!" Janette said sharply. "Do not tell me about your Ultimate Weapon. I already know more about that than I want to."

"But how then—"

"What do you—"

A wave of Janette's hand cut them off. "I am sorry. I do not mean to be rude to either of you. However, for the moment all I need to know is if Wallen's knowledge could assist the Ukes or anyone else in making a weapon such as ours. If we need more detailed information later, we know—"

"But we do not have a weapon," Caugust said, "nor are we sure we will have one. We are barely ready to begin our first basic tests."

Silence held the room for an endless moment as they waited for Inspector Janette to respond. Finally she leaned back into the folds of the chair with a grim smile that Sjean thought looked foreign on her pretty face.

"You will. You will. That is your job. My job is to ensure that the Ukes do not have one also."

Sjean understood the upcoming tests better than anyone, and she was worried that their outcome would be disappointing. How then, she wondered as she stared at this strange woman, can Janette seem so sure of her conclusions? And why, in the name of anything logical, do I believe her?

*   *   *

Leri's recovery was painful and slow, but Ranas insisted that she fulfill her duties as proctor. What bothered her was that he expected her to fulfill those duties cheerfully—yet he offered little or no sympathy for her pain and discomfort. But the worst thing was that when she complained, he belittled how she felt.

Finally she could stand his self-centered slithering around her no longer and sent him away with the guplings. Better to suffer alone where she could hiss and scream at the empty walls. At least then she didn't have to suffer the pain in silence or feel guilty about expressing it.

After Weecs rescued her from Exeter's ship, he had turned her over to the Isthians and stayed away from her. When she finally spoke to him, he refused to come to her, claiming that to do so would only threaten her position. "When you are well," he had said, "we will meet on neutral ground."

Now that she had banished Ranas, Leri wanted Weecs with her all the more, but understood his reluctance and honored it. She turned instead to the Confidantes.

"The rumors say other planets and systems have been attacked by the humans," she said quietly. The Confidante as usual made no statement, but as Leri stared at its great, grey bulk and waited for its question, she waited in vain. "The Council has demanded my recommendation. I have chosen isolation and will tell them so."

"Is that wise?" the Confidante asked.

"It is our only hope. Otherwise Sondak will suck our atmosphere dry and the Central Systems will try to find us and destroy Sondak's source of methane."

"How will you isolate us?"

"With the fires, if necessary."

"Would that not kill many of your kind?"

"And yours too," Leri said angrily, "but better to die that way than to have Cloise ravaged by the humans."

"Does Cloise belong to you alone? Are not others to be considered?"

"We will accept all advice from the others," Leri said, knowing that the Isthians, like the Confidantes, had refused any direct participation in making decisions for their planet. "Will you give us counsel?"

"Could you not join with those from the planets which have been attacked by the humans?"

Leri was shocked by the suggestion. "Shall we join with the soulless?"

"Would you choose to die alone?"

"We only have rumors," she said, hoping the Confidante would choose another direction. She should have known better.

"Cannot rumors be traced? Is there not strength in numbers—even with those you consider soulless?"

"They do not know the Elett. How can they have souls?"

"Can you know another's soul?" the Confidante asked sarcastically. "Can you slither in their life?"

"But an alliance—" Leri shuddered and a rasping pain grated through her. Suddenly she thought of the vision that had haunted her, and how she had seen a strange path through the mists of trouble, a path that would lead her people to a safer life. Just as suddenly she knew the Confidante was right.

Perhaps someone should seek the Oinaise and try to verify the rumors. If they proved true, then . . . then perhaps an alliance with the soulless ones . . . She shuddered painfully again. The idea still stuck in her gills.

As though sensing Leri's resistance, the Confidante said, "The false way is the safest way for everyone."

It was the first time Leri had ever heard a Confidante make a direct statement. The double shock of that and a possible alliance with the soulless Oinaise left her with no alternative but to withdraw. "I thank you, Confidante," she said in a shaky voice. "By the grace of the Elett I beg your leave."

"Will you go in peace?"

"If the Elett grant it."

"Will you take the one you love?"

"If such can be," she said thinking first of Ranas and then of Weecs. With no further word she slithered out into the darkness, her mind troubled, but her heart filled with a strange, inexplicable contentment.

*   *   *

Despite the many weeks he had spent living without the gorlet, Lucky still felt an occasional craving for it. So one day when Delightful Childe sent for him, Lucky asked if he could have just a taste of gorlet.

The Oinaise glowered at him. "One bite will addict you again," he said sternly. "Do you wish to repeat the suffering you went through before?"

Lucky smiled. "No, I don't," he said slowly. "But if your people have anything that tastes like gorlet at all, I wouldn't mind eating a sample or two."

"There are substitutes, but I doubt you would find them palatable. However," he said, holding up a seven-fingered hand, "I will see that you have the opportunity to taste them."

"Thanks."

"No thanks are needed. What is ours is, within limits, yours.

But now we must discuss the more serious parts of your future. What will you choose to do with your life from now on, Captain Teeman?"

Lucky had been expecting that question or one like it, and he had been hiding from it. When the Ukes failed to renew their attack on Oina, he had allowed himself to relax in the comfort of Delightful Childe's hospitality, content to enjoy the small pleasures of each day. He had thought as little as possible about the future—or the past.

"I don't know, Delightful Childe," he said finally. "I can hardly go back to lightspeed freighting while this war is going on without taking—"

"Why? Are you afraid?"

"You're damn right I'm afraid." That wasn't true, and Lucky heard the lack of sincerity in his voice.

Delightful Childe snorted. "I do not believe you. You are not the type of human who fears such annoyances. It is the mate you lost that holds you from action. Such attachment is pure foolishness for one like you."

"What would you know about it?" This time the emotion in his voice was anger, and the anger was real.

"Ah, so you think I cannot understand your species, or know how you tie yourselves so irrationally to one mate?" Delightful Childe bared his yellow teeth and brought the tips of his fingers together under his chin to form a spreading fan. "Do you think that because I am different? Or do you think that because you believe me to be stupid?"

Unfortunately, Lucky could not gauge Delightful Childe's emotions well enough to tell if the Oinaise was really angry or just teasing him. "I, uh . . ."

"Well? Which is it?"

"Neither one, dammit," he blurted. "How I feel about Marsha is none of your business."

"It is if we are to join into business together."

Lucky was stunned. "What did you say?" he asked quickly, afraid that he might have misunderstood.

"I said, my friend, that if we are to become partners, then everything about you becomes my business—just as everything about me becomes yours."

"But . . . I mean, are you serious?" Suddenly Lucky had a glimpse of a future with promise. "Do you really want us to form a partnership?"

"Was not that your suggestion originally?"

"Yes, but I didn't really think you would want to. I was just looking for—"

"If I did not want such a partnership, I would never have mentioned it to you." He lowered his hands from his chin and held them out in front of him. "The questions before us are whether or not *you* want it, and whether or not *you* are ready to ply your trade as a freighter again."

"Of course I am. I just never—"

"You are not afraid?"

"No. I only said that to—"

"Good. Then perhaps we should discuss—"

"Look, Delightful Childe," Lucky said with a grin that suddenly seemed plastered to his face, "if we're going to be partners, you're going to have to learn—"

"Is there still some question about it?"

"No. But I'd like to be able to finish a sentence with you once in a while."

Delightful Childe snorted. "Is that the condition you were about to put on this partnership?"

"Well . . . yes. I mean, it just seems to me that partners ought to listen to each other."

"But I do listen to the important things you say, Partner Teeman. What more do you want of me?"

Lucky still couldn't get the grin off his face and realized that partnership with Delightful Childe might not only be profitable, but also frustrating in an oddly humorous way. "Nothing, partner," he said finally.

"Excellent. Let us go eat, and I will outline the plan I have in mind for us."

"Uh, just one more thing," Lucky said. "Why do you want this partnership?"

"That is a simple question, yet one so complex I am not sure you would understand."

"Try me." For the first time since Lucky had known him, Delightful Childe looked uncomfortable.

"I have chosen to remain here and mate," he said slowly, "and that requires my physical presence for approximately one standard year until the child is born."

"And you need me to work the business while you're tied up."

"Your choice of words is most appropriate, Partner Teeman,

for I will be umbilically tied to my offspring. You are also partially correct in assuming I want you to 'work the business' as you said, but I do hope our association would well outlast my familial obligations."

Lucky brightened. "You're talking long-term, right?"

"For as long as we are both satisfied with the arrangements," Delightful Childe said. "Come, let us go eat."

As they walked side by side toward the dining room, Lucky was so filled with the possibilities that might spring from this relationship that he almost missed what Delightful Childe was saying about their first job.

". . . relatively simple, actually, if my cousin is to be believed. He has some goods and a passenger to be transported from Patros to an old friend of his in the U.C.S."

Ushogi Fleet and Shakav Fleet were ready to move away from the Hiifi system on schedule, but thanks to Judoff, they would each have fewer ships than Frye had originally intended for this plan. After the first leg of the journey, the task force would split, and Ely would take Shakav Fleet toward the south galactic pole to attack Sondak's fringe systems in that sector. From then on, in order to maintain absolute security, they would not communicate either with each other, or with Bridgeforce.

The plan was for Sondak to accept Ely's line of attack as his main one, but Frye knew better than to count on that deception. Besides, he thought, if the timing is right, it won't matter. All Shakav Fleet has to do is slow Sondak's reactions long enough for us to take control of Matthews system.

Or destroy it.

Of the twenty manned neutronic missiles he had sent into the Matthews system, fifteen had sent check-blips on the last status update. He did not know, nor was he concerned about what had happened to the others. If only six of them survived until he needed them, that would be sufficient. Three of the missiles exploding low over each of Reckynop's poles would start the ice caps melting and flood Sondak's two main spaceports.

If he could send five or six missiles to each pole, the destruction would happen faster, and if he had the twenty extra missiles that had been originally promised, and then withdrawn, that would have eased his worry. But his planning experts had assured him that three missiles to each pole would render Sondak's spaceports inoperable. That was all Frye cared about. If the U.C.S. could not control Reckynop, then they would deny it to Sondak as well.

Yet Frye deeply hoped that destruction would not be necessary. He wanted the whole of Matthews system, including Reckynop—wanted it as the forward base from which he could pound Sondak into submission. From there he could harass Roberg and cripple Sondak's logistical support. From there he could send missions into the heart of Sondak itself, perhaps even to its ruling planet Nordeen.

Deep strikes against Nordeen would be very costly in lives and ships when balanced against the limited physical damage they could do, but the psychological damage to Sondak's morale would be immense. For that he was willing to pay dearly. In fact, his officers were about to learn how much he was willing to pay to defeat their enemy.

With a sigh he turned on his lapelcom. "AOCO," he asked firmly, "are my officers gathered?"

"Yes, sir," Marsha answered from her small cabin next to his. "They're waiting in the commander's conference now."

"Very good. Tell them I will be there in five minutes."

"Yes, sir."

"Oh, and AOCO, I want you to sit in on the meeting with me. It's time you met the people under my command."

"Yes, sir," she said with hopeful hesitance. "Are you going to tell them?"

"Tell them what, AOCO?" There was a long pause before she answered him.

"That I'm your daughter . . . sir."

Frye had wondered about that himself and was surprised to realize that he had already made his decision. Yet, he did not want to hurt Marsha's feelings. There was already too much distance between them. "Do you think I should?"

In the next room Marsha's face fell slightly but she held her voice in check, refusing to let him hear her disappointment. "Only if *you* think so, sir."

"Well, we'll see then . . . if it's appropriate. Five minutes, AOCO."

As Marsha walked down the short hallway to the commander's conference she allowed herself a brief moment of regret. Then she shook it off. She had come as she had promised, and she had promised to stay. She would serve her father and serve him well, and if after it was over he still could not express his feelings about her, then she could leave knowing the fault was not hers. With her head held high she entered the commander's conference to make her announcement.

Frye sat at his desk remembering Marsha as a little girl and how she had come to him for advice rather than to Vinita. Even when she could barely talk, she had sought his counsel and had listened with a child's intensity to what he had to say. He blinked quickly and took a deep breath at the memory of Vinita.

Yet as he exhaled and shook off that vision, he thought of his own childhood—a childhood filled with stories about the golden age of culture in the U.C.S. and how that culture had been destroyed by the invasion of people from what later became known as Sondak.

His paternal grandfather, ed'Laitin Charltos, had always been the one Frye had gone to for counsel. Grandfather ed'Laitin had been imprisoned for most of his life on Roberg for the crime of patriotism, and released only when he was too old and sick to do much more than come home and die. But the old man had not been too weak to pass his hatred of Sondak on to Frye.

After his grandfather died and Frye grew older, he learned more and more about the real atrocities and sacrilege Sondak had committed in the name of peace and harmony. The hatred planted in the boy became a permanent part of the man.

When young Junior Commander Charltos came home from the last war against Sondak, he was bitter and determined. The U.C.S. would not lose the next war. He had sworn that to himself on his grandfather's memory. As he rose to meet his officers, he hoped they would understand his determination and make it their own.

"Commander Ely. Gentlemen," he said as he entered the conference room, "I am pleased to see you all here." A quick survey of the room revealed Melliman sitting with Ely's staff. Frye quickly shifted his gaze from her before their eyes could meet. "This room contains the top three hundred officers in our fleet, and what we are about to do will demand the most excellent efforts from each and every one of you." He paused without a smile and watched the smiles fade from their faces in response.

"Our initial strikes wounded the enemy. Now our task will

be far more difficult and costly. We must gain the planetholds we need to cripple Sondak once and for all."

Marsha watched him with pride from her position at the side of the dais as the room erupted in grim-faced applause. There was no doubt in her mind that her father could lead these people and the U.C.S. to victory.

* * *

General Mari glared at Stonefield. "And I still say we have to reinforce the polar systems. If the Ukes gain planetholds beyond Ca-Ryn and Umboolu, POLFLEET will never be able to hold them away from Sutton. After that we'll be scrambling to save twenty systems instead of five."

Stonefield remained impassive.

"I agree," Avitor Hilldill said quietly, "but I think it is too late to do anything."

"Are you giving up?" Mari asked in dismay.

"Certainly not, Fortuno."

Mari flinched at the familiar form of address, but he immediately forgave his old friend. "Then what—"

"We must divert planetary troops to Sutton, Bakke, Yaffee, Satterfield, and Wallbank."

"Make the Ukes fight on every planet?" Stonefield asked.

"Yes, sir. They'll need bases on those planets—safe bases they can use to support attacks against the central sectors. If we cannot defend the systems themselves, at least we can make them pay in blood for every planet they try to control on the ground. I move that we double the garrisons and equipment on the planets I mentioned and all others in the polar sector where we possibly can."

"And where will we get these planetary troops?" Admiral Eresser asked. Her voice was laden with disapproval.

"From the conscription—led by trained cadre, of course."

"Green troops? Surely we cannot—"

"They're the only ones we have for such an operation. Our cadres are already spread too thinly. Or am I wrong, General Mari? Do we have experienced reserves we could commit to an operation of this size?"

"Barely four legions from the inactive reserve that were recalled last month are currently equipped and ready," Mari said firmly. He had rejected a similar idea because of the lives it would cost, and he shuddered to think what would happen

with untested troops and out of shape veterans against a Uke
invasion force. But now, now with Hilldill supporting the
idea—

"I second the motion," Admiral Lindshaw said.

"Discussion?" Stonefield asked.

The discussion went on for hours, but in the end Sondak's
Joint Chiefs voted in favor of the motion and put General Mari
in charge of the operation. It gave him no pleasure to know
that he was about to commit tens of thousands of men and
women to certain death if the Ukes attacked. Yet he knew that
their stand could prove to be a vital contribution to Sondak's
defense.

They would be trained and led by the best people under his
command. If they failed in their mission, it would be noted
that the decision to use such an inherently weak force be-
longed to the Joint Chiefs. But if they succeeded, General Fortuno Mari's name would go down in the annals of military
history as one of Sondak's best. He might even get to become
chairman of the Joint Chiefs. No one could ask for more than
that in his career.

*   *   *

Admiral Pajandcan spread the defense fleet and sent out the
first patrol wave of fifty Long Range Reconaissance Ships. She
had little belief that the LRRS would find the Ukes in the
depths of space. But those small lightspeed ships crammed full
of detection devices were the only insurance she had beyond
the subspace monitors. Their highly skilled three-member
crews had the cocky assurance of elitists that even her stern
send-off did not seem to dampen.

Perhaps that is what we need, she thought as she cleared the
acknowledgement of their departure from her report screen.
Perhaps we need more people with that kind of assurance.
"And perhaps I need it," she added aloud. "Maybe I should
take my lesson from them and Dawson."

Dawson. The thought of what he and Reckynop would be up
against if the Ukes got past her sent a quick chill down her
spine. Then she smiled grimly. Cold chills were hardly the way
to start a campaign of self-assurance. No, Dawson would do the
best he could with what he had, and probably better than anyone else could with the same resources. Her job was to make
sure his resources weren't strained beyond his abilities to use
them.

She leaned back and wearily rubbed her eyes. Now's the time to get some rest, she told herself. "Torgy," she said into the intercom, "I'm going to catch forty. Don't interrupt me unless there's an absolute need. Is that understood?"

"Yes, ma'am," his disembodied voice said from the speaker, "but before you do, ma'am, you might want to switch on your screen and take a look at this stuff Subspace is sending up."

His suggestion snapped her alert, and she had her screen on before he finished speaking. "Any comment with this?" she asked as a series of sine wave graphs flicked across her screen at three-second intervals.

"No, ma'am, not yet."

"What do you make of them, Torgy?"

"Hard to tell. Captain Nickerson is standing by. Shall I have him come up?"

"You'd better."

Minutes later Nickerson entered her office wearing an odd smile and carrying a thick folder. "Top of the watch, Admiral," he said after she returned his salute.

"If you say so, Nick. Now what have we got here?"

"A better scan than we hoped for, I think. I ran some selected hard copies for you," he said, handing her the folder.

She took it and flipped it open immediately. The form of the first graph looked familiar to her, but she knew better than to try to interpret it. Nickerson moved around her desk and stood beside her.

"See this spike," he said, putting his thick forefinger in the middle of the graph. "That's the Ukes heading this way."

Pajandcan was used to his dramatic statements and waited for him to continue.

"Of course they're still pretty close to home, and it's hard to get any definite vectors at this distance, but I'll tell you what, Admiral, that's a damn big fleet they've put together."

"Sit down, Nick," Pajandcan said with an easy smile and a wave to the chair across from her, "and tell me how much of this we can actually depend on."

"All of it," Nickerson said, moving back around the desk. "You can depend on all of it."

"So when will they be here?"

Nickerson started. "Ma'am?"

"I said, when will they be here, Nick? If I'm going to depend on all this, I need to know when they'll be here."

"Uh, that's not exactly what I meant, Admiral."

"No, I suspect it isn't. So try it again." She shut the folder and tapped it repeatedly. "How much of this information is actually worth something to us here and now?" She stared him directly in the eyes, and he looked hurt.

"Why, all of it, Admiral. Every bit of it. Those charts give us background radiation, consistency patterns, normal fluctuations, and the general location of the Uke fleet."

Pajandcan smiled. "How general? Within a tachymeter? Two? Five? Ten?"

"More like twenty-five," he said without looking at her.

"Come on, Nick. Give me something to work with." When she saw the deflated look on his face she understood why. "You're proud of this information, aren't you?"

"Yes, ma'am."

"And you wanted to share it with me, right?"

"Yes, ma'am," he repeated with a slight smile.

"And I ruined it for you. No," she said holding up her hand and waving off his protest, "I know what I did. But listen to me, Nick. We're sitting here trying to catch tidfish with a net that wouldn't hold a Reckynopian goliathshark. I appreciate your net and what you're trying to do with it, but until you can close it up a little, it's not going to do us much good."

Suddenly he looked at her, and his face brightened. "I understand, Admiral. I just thought you might—but never mind that. There is something toward the back of the folder," he said taking it and flipping it over, "something which just hit me." He turned quickly through the back pages until he gave a satisfied grunt and pulled out a folded blue sheet. After opening it, he stared at it for a minute until Pajandcan cleared her throat.

"Oh, sorry, Admiral. I just wanted to be sure I was right. Look at this," he said as he turned the sheet around and laid it on the desk in front of her.

Pajandcan immediately recognized a computer-produced set of star maps—six of them that all looked identical under her quick glance. "So?" she asked, looking up into Nickerson's grinning face. "Are you going to let me in on the secret?"

"It's dumb, Admiral. It's so dumb I can't believe we didn't think of it."

"Spit it out, Nick. What's dumb?"

"Admiral, those maps were sent in by the six major subspace

monitors. Except for some basically insignificant differences in angles and one other thing, they're almost exactly alike."

"And the other thing?" Pajandcan was becoming impatient, but she could tell Nickerson was working out the solution as he explained it to her.

"The other thing is that there ought to be a trail in front of all that star clutter—a detectable neutron trail on those maps from a Uke fleet that big. We ought to be able to see where they came from."

Pajandcan was one jump ahead of him now. "And tell where they're going," she said triumphantly. "Maybe," she added with less enthusiasm.

"It's better than what we have so far, Admiral. It'll take some fancy enhancement, ma'am, but I'll bet we can dig that trail out for you."

"Then what are you still doing in my office?" she asked as she rose to her feet. "Let's get to work." As much as she wanted to believe that Nickerson was right, and as much as she hoped he was, Pajandcan wondered if they really could get enough information in time to do the defense forces any good.

Well, she thought as she followed Nickerson down the companionway toward the subspace monitoring section, at least this beats sitting around waiting for the Ukes to arrive.

"Is important information," he said sullenly. The image on the screen was faded orange and fuzzy, but Ayne Wallen could at least tell that he was talking to a female human being. An old one, he thought derisively, not pretty like Sjean Birkie. "Is most important information," he repeated.

"We heard you the first time," the female said in thickly accented gentongue that was muted by the subspace transmission. "However, you will have to be more specific than that. And you will have to hurry. This is a narrow communications window, and we are rapidly losing it."

"Has to do with Sondak's biggest weapon," Ayne lied. He wasn't about to tell them that the weapon did not exist yet except in his mind. After weeks of working on Xindella's defective Gouldrive, bruising his hands and his head, and cursing anyone and everyone within thinking distance, he was less willing than ever to give up any information he did not have to.

The female made a rude sound. "We are not interested."

"Have to be interested!" Ayne screamed suddenly. "Will cost you war if not interested. Sondak will blow you to—"

Xindella's rough hand choked him off.

"Pardons a thousand, friend Judoff," Xindella said as he held Ayne by the neck away from the screen and sat in his place. "My client is irritated and frightened, as any man carrying such valuable secrets would naturally be. But I do ask you reconsider your interest. As I told you before, I have already—at great expense to myself, I might add—obtained secure transportation for this client in anticipation of your interest."

"I do not care about your client or your costs," Judoff said in a voice that was developing a scratchy subspace echo.

"Ah," Xindella sighed, "then I shall have to sell him back to Sondak." He tightened his grip on Ayne's neck as the gasping human tried to jerk away from him.

"Sondak would buy him?"

"But, of course, my old friend. I thought I had made that clear. Now I see you are fading. Perhaps I can find something else you are interested in at a future date."

"Squeeeeeezzk send der idiot heerumph . . ." the fading image on the screen said before its voice broke into static.

"Do you think that means she wants you?" Xindella asked, relaxing his grip on Ayne's neck and letting the human drop to the floor.

Ayne could only rub his bruised throat and make rough rasping noises as he glared at Xindella and tried to take a full breath. He would kill Xindella. Someday, somehow, if there was ever a chance, he would kill that despicable alien.

"Yes, I agree," Xindella said smoothly. "I do believe she wants me to send you. And that means she is willing to meet our price." He looked down at Ayne. "But that means, of course, that you will have to refrain from following that vicious impulse I see in your eyes, Employee Wallen. Otherwise I would have to sell you at a discount to Judoff as damaged merchandise. And of course, you would have to absorb the discount from your share of this venture. You wouldn't want to do that, would you?"

The no barely grated from Ayne's throat.

"Good. Now I believe you still have some work to finish on my Gouldrive."

Ayne staggered to his feet without quite comprehending the swirl of anger and hate in his heart. He swallowed painfully. "Stick Gouldrive in ear . . . and out other . . . alien dung," he rasped. As he steadied himself, he flicked his eyes around the room in search of a weapon.

Xindella snorted with bared teeth, and the sound rang painfully in Ayne's ears.

"Fix it, fool," Xindella said finally, "Or you will get no more gorlet. Then in the midst of your withdrawal, I will break your bones one by one until only your head will be working properly when you get to the U.C.S."

The thought of no more gorlet frightened Ayne more than any threat to his body. Without responding he turned and left the office. He wanted to turn back and say something, anything, but he knew he was addicted to the gorlet—knew he couldn't live without it. Xindella had withdrawn it from him for a day just to prove the addiction. But if it wasn't for gorlet, he thought as he walked slowly through the labyrinth back to Xindella's ship, I would kill him. I would. I would. I would kill him.

*　　*　　*

Rochmon turned his back as the latest ephemera faded away in a whisper of faint odor, and caught himself thinking about Mica Gilbert. It wasn't the first time. She had haunted his erotic dreams more and more since she had gone out with her father to help defend Matthews system. Yet those thoughts about her always made him angry—always pushed forward in his thoughts with hints of shame and recrimination.

"There is no time for this," he said quietly as he got out of the bed and stripped off the disposable sheets. He wadded them up and shoved them violently into the incinerator shute. And you have no right, he reminded himself. But as he stepped into the shower and tuned it to high intensity vibrations, he could not get Mica off his mind.

Love had only been a word with very limited meaning for so many years that even when he dared think that he loved Mica Gilbert, he immediately rejected that idea. He did not know how to love anything except his job. Cryptography was the only thing in life that mattered to him. Somewhere deep inside he doubted his capacity to truly love another human being. Two failed marriages and three bitter children should be evidence enough of that for any man.

The only person I ever loved, he thought as he roughly soaped his lean body, wasn't a person at all. Even after all these years, he flushed with a slight grin at the thought of the alien Brede and the incredible lust she had aroused in him. No, that wasn't love—a perverse, tender, consuming fascination for the alien, yes, but not love. Love was just a word he could no longer define.

Rochmon rinsed himself thoroughly and turned off the shower. As he dried himself and walked into the bedroom, he suddenly realized that something different had happened to him with the last ephemera. Always before he had let his mind float when he had intercourse with an ephemera, and always before his mind had floated sooner or later to Brede. But last night, somewhere on the brink of orgasm, Mica's image had taken Brede's place. She had moved into his active fantasy.

With a shiver he wrapped the damp towel around himself and opened his closet. Why? Why was he so obsessed with Mica? Why couldn't he push her out of his dreams? Why was she spoiling his one acceptable relief mechanism?

"Spoiling?" he asked aloud as he pulled on his uniform. What was she spoiling? And why was he trying to shift the blame to her? She was innocent. He was the one who had dragged her rudely into his lust.

On the way to headquarters, his mind played with questions about Mica, and how he felt about her, and the ever recurring question of why this was happening to him. It was only when Bock greeted him at the door of his office that he managed to put the questions aside for the moment.

"Perfect timing," Bock said with a grim smile as she handed Rochmon a single sheet of paper stamped Ultra Secret.

"What do you mean?" he asked. As soon as he read the brief message and noted its reception time he understood. "There's no source code on here."

"It's a background interception. One of Pajandcan's LRRSs picked it up. She forwarded it through Mungtinez Relay. Probably didn't even know what it was."

"Damn," Rochmon said softly as he read the traitor's message again. Then he looked up at Bock. "What do you think?"

"Seems obvious, doesn't it? A traitor in Matthews system has access to subspace transmitting equipment."

"But this isn't enough. It tells us someone is sending defense information to the Ukes, but not what they sent or who sent it. Dammit, Bock, what are we supposed to do with this?"

"Dump it on Captain Gilbert. She's the honor trustee."

"What about Admiral Dawson?"

"Suppose he is the traitor?"

Rochmon had considered that. Dawson's past certainly made his allegiances subject to question. "All right," he said reluctantly. "Code it and send it to Mica with appropriate notations. But send a separate message to Admiral Dawson telling him he has a security leak. If he is the traitor, that might slow him down. If he isn't, then he can tighten his own operation. Either way, we don't have anything to lose."

Bock looked at him with an cruel curl in the corners of her mouth. "Well?" he said, "you think there's something wrong with that approach?"

"No. Not at all," she said, the curl turning into a smile of private amusement. "I just wonder what your little captain will do with this information."

No matter how long he had worked with Bock, Rochmon was still capable of being startled by her. "What do you mean, 'my little captain'?"

"Just what I said." Bock picked up the message and turning away from him.

"Hold it, Bock." Rochmon was surprised by the anger in his voice. "Sit down," he said when she turned around with deep wrinkles marking the smile still on her face.

"Something else, Commander?" she asked sarcastically.

"Yes, Bock," he said in a tightly controlled voice. "Apparently I have failed to make myself clear on this point with you, so perhaps this is the appropriate time to do so."

"Spit it out, Commander." Her smile disappeared. "Tell me not to make snide remarks about your precious little Captain Gilbert and then let me go back to work."

"I'll do better than that, Bock," he said with sudden inspiration. "You keep your personal comments to yourself in the future or I'll get you called back to active duty, then bust you to lieutenant for insubordination."

"You wouldn't dare, Commander."

"Try me, Bock. Just try me. You think because you're still a civilian that you can say what you damn well please. You keep doing that, and I'll remind you there's a war going on. You'll find you're not a civilian any more, and you'll have me and every senior officer in this headquarters censoring your words." He paused with pleasure as the look of belief crept onto her face. "Do I make myself clear?"

"Clear as steaming piss, Commander."

"Good. Now you can get back to work." Rochmon held his grin back until she left his office and shut the door. But as quickly as the grin came, it faded.

Bock's comments shouldn't have aroused that anger in him. After all these years he had gotten used to her sarcasm and innuendos about others and had tolerated her remarks about himself because she always made them directly to his face. It was only Bock's references to Mica that irritated him, and that told him something he didn't want to face. Whatever the center of his feelings for Mica were, they were deeper and more complicated than Rochmon wanted to admit. The only thing he allowed to the surface was an irrational desire to have her back from Matthews system and away from danger.

* * *

Pilot Da B'Barbara felt his usual rush of pleasure as Long Range Reconnaissance Ship One-Zero-Two entered subspace for the third time. They were within seven seconds of the original schedule, and that pleased him also.

"Da, I've got an echo," Louise said from the ops position behind him.

"What kind of echo?"

"Double one," she answered after a long pause. "Neutron clouds splitting in quadrant four, bearing two-seven-seven."

"Sounds like what we've been looking for. Kimkey, notify headquarters and tell the admiral we will break schedule."

"Da?"

"What, Louise?"

"It's fading, Da—fading fast."

"What do you mean it's fading?" He didn't want to lose this one. If it was the Ukes, he wanted to be the one to discover them. "Can't you pull it back?"

"I'm trying," Louise said curtly. She wanted to find the Ukes as much as Da did, but getting angry wasn't going to help her do it.

"Kimkey, send the message anyway." Da stared at the blank vista through the viewport. "Come on, Louise," he said finally. "Find those damn Ukes."

"Shut up, Da," Louise said as she searched for the echo with minute adjustments of her detection gear. The problem was one of range. If she searched too short or too deep, she might as well not search at all. This new detection gear was supposed to overcome that problem, but adjustments at faster than light speed were delicate at best, and impossible at worst. There were just too many variables to account for.

"Message sent," Kimkey said in their earphones.

"It's gone, Da. We have to go back."

"Back to where?"

"Where I found them the first time."

"But, Louise, that will take at least an hour. They could have gotten away by then."

"Maybe so. But if you want them, Da, that's our best chance. All I'm doing now is guessing. Take us back as close as you can to our original heading in normal space and go for it."

"You sure, Louise? I mean, couldn't we—"

"You're wasting time."

Da shook his head sadly. "Right. Kimkey, alert HQ to what we're doing."

"Will do," Kimkey responded.

It took the better part of an hour and a half with all the ship's dampers working at redline temperatures for B'Barbara to bring One-Zero-Two almost back to the entry point in normal space. "Ready, Louise?"

"Ready as we're going to get."

"Subspace in twenty-seven seconds," Da said calmly.

Only the sound of breathing came through their earphones as they waited for the slow seconds to tick away. "Five, four, three, two, ONE!" Da said.

Louise stared at her screens, praying for the echo to reappear. "There it is! There it is! Same quadrant. Split farther apart now." She fine-tuned her instruments and gave him the readings. "First bearing two-seven-five. Second bearing two-eight-one. Those are the Uke fleets, Da. They have to— Damn! I'm losing them again!"

"Kimkey—"

"Already started, Da."

"They're gone," Louise said quietly. "Why can't we hold them longer?"

"I don't know, lady," Da said with a smile of triumph, "but at least we got the admiral some information to work with. Think we should go back for another try?"

"Absolutely. Ought to see if I can figure a better angle for us on this run, though."

"Better figure a long range one, 'cause if we try to do this loop as fast as we did the last one, we won't have any dampers left to stop us."

"How much time?" Louise asked.

Da looked at his equipment monitors and the smile of triumph faded slowly from his face. "Four hours. Maybe five. And that's the best we can do."

"Damn." Louise shook her head. "Damn, damn, damn."

Then she clamped her jaws and set to work on the calculations. With some good numbers and a little luck, they would find the Ukes one more time. There were only eighty-million people on Reckynop——and Admiral Pajandcan and all of Sondak depending on them.

The switch closed.

The two tiny lead spheres in the giant crucibles at opposite ends of the test chamber exploded almost simultaneously. The crucibles shattered in the beginning of a chain reaction.

Thick chunks of metal slammed against the shockproof walls. Burning gobs of safety glass arced in fiery trails across the chamber. Plastic and wire vaporized.

With slow grotesque movements equipment collapsed into smoldering, molten heaps as the helite crystals over the observation cameras cracked in fine weblike patterns that distorted the view.

In the security bunker Sjean turned to Caugust with an embarrassed grin on her face. "Did I tell you I wasn't sure how much force we would get?"

"You certainly did," he said, still staring at the fuzzy picture on the observation screen. "How soon do you think it will be safe go in there?"

She glanced at the temperature and radiation monitors, then up at the screen. "An hour or two at most. The vaporized material will condense out of the air fairly quickly, but it will take awhile longer for the system to cool off the debris. Say, three hours—just to be safe."

"Doesn't look like we'll salvage much." Caugust shook his head and let out a long breath. "Do you know what you did, Sjean? I mean, do you really understand it?"

For a moment she wasn't sure what he meant. After a long, deliberate pause she took a chance at giving him the answer he was looking for. "No, I don't. I know what was supposed to happen, but not what did. Given the display we just saw and the mess it made of the equipment, I doubt if we will know for some time either."

"You're missing the point."

"Pardon?"

"You proved the equations, Sjean. You made the numbers work on reality. You made the weapon!"

"No, not a weapon. We made some test equipment that destroyed itself. I don't see how that is much of an accomplishment."

"Sjean," he said with a smile filling his face, "the numbers worked. You made them work. You proved reciprocal action at a distance. Wallen's equations are valid."

His words finally hit the center of her mind. She had been so concerned about monitoring the experiment, so startled by the ferocity of the demonstration, that the realization of what had actually happened had not struck home. "They did work," she said softly. "They really worked."

"And you made them," he said, putting his burly arm around her shoulders.

"With a good team behind me," she whispered. "They worked."

"When can we begin phase two?"

Sjean pulled herself away from Caugust and sat heavily in her chair, her fingertips pressed against her temples. "I don't know," she said, looking at him finally. "It will take some time to evaluate the data we captured here. A month, maybe two or three before we can construct the equipment for something bigger." It all seemed so immense a project that she was not quite sure where to start. "I don't know, Caugust," she said, hearing the fatigue in her voice. "I just don't know."

He patted her shoulder. "You get some rest. Tomorrow we'll talk about it some more. In the meantime I have to contact Sci-Sec and tell Inspector Janette. If you can build a weapon around Wallen's equations, so can he."

* * *

"So when have the Gilberts ever gone strictly by the book?" Mica asked. "Did you always go by the book when you thought something was wrong?"

Gilbert smiled at his daughter. "Not according to my superiors, I didn't. But this case is a little different. I am your superior."

"And you're going to make me follow the rules?" Mica couldn't believe it.

He paused before he answered. "No. If you think it's important enough, go ahead and tell me."

Mica swallowed hard. "Before you even got back to Nordeen, Admiral Stonefield made me an honor trustee," she said, looking her father squarely in the eyes.

"I am aware of that."

"I know you are. But did you also know that I am supposed to watch you just like I watch everyone else?"

"Of course."

She released her tension in a long sigh. "You don't know how much better that makes me feel. I've wanted to come tell you so much it hurt."

"Is that what this is all about?" Gilbert was slightly surprised that Mica was so concerned about it. Perhaps it was just her lack of experience.

She looked up at the overhead then back at him. "No, there's more to it than that. There's a spy—a traitor—both in our security set-up. Someone's been sending defense status information about Reckynop and Matthews system to the Ukes—someone with classified information."

"That doesn't surprise me. There are thousands of people in the system with access to that information, and millions more with eyes and ears who can—"

"But how many of them have access to subspace transmission equipment? How many of them could be sending—"

"More than we'll ever know," Gilbert said with a grim smile.

Mica paused and looked at him questioningly. "If I wasn't your daughter, I'd say you were acting far too calmly about something this serious."

"If you weren't my daughter, we wouldn't be having this discussion. But if for some reason I were discussing this with some other junior officer in your position, I would tell that officer that security is both fundamentally important and fundamentally impossible in wartime. Then I would press that officer to get to the point of this discussion."

"If I knew the point, I'd tell you," she said quickly. No matter how she sorted this problem, she wasn't sure where to begin. That was why she had come to him now. "Commander Rochmon sent me a copy of a message—an intercept from one of Pajandcan's Long Range Recon Ships. From the notations that came with it, I'd guess that Bock forwarded it to—"

"Bock?"

"His civilian cryptography chief—a strange woman, but a brilliant one. Anyway, I'd say she forwarded the message. And that's what bothers me."

"That she sent it? Surely Rochmon has more important—"

"No, not that she sent it, but her notations with it. Something about them hits me the wrong way."

"What she said, or how she said it?"

"That's it!" Mica looked at her father with a sudden grin. "That's it, Dad. It's not what she said, at least not exactly, but she didn't say it right . . . almost as though . . ."

"As though what, Mica?"

Her grin turned quickly to a frown when she realized where her thoughts were leading her. "I'm afraid to think it, much less say it to anyone."

"Then let me second-guess you for a moment. Could what she said have been intended for more than one recipient?"

"Yes," Mica said slowly, "but who?"

"The Ukes?"

She shook her head. "I can't believe that. Bock's the one who broke the Uke code in the first place."

"So?" Despite the seriousness of their discussion, Gilbert enjoyed watching her dig into this problem—and he enjoyed helping her with it.

"So why would she break the Ukes code then turn around and send them information? It doesn't make any sense."

"Maybe it doesn't make any sense because you haven't considered all the possibilities. Did she break the code alone?"

"No. She and the lead team—"

"Then how do you know that the team wasn't on the verge of a breakthrough, and she just let it happen?"

"I don't, but—"

"That's right. You don't. You don't know anything for sure. All you have is a set of possible theories. Now you have a new theory to work with."

"I still can't believe it. Rochmon says she's the best cryptographer we have—maybe the best he's ever seen."

"If she was working for the Ukes, it would seem to me—"

"Suppose she's not working for the Ukes?" Mica said suddenly.

Gilbert gave her a small smile. "Yes, suppose she's working for someone else. That's possible, too, isn't it?"

Mica leaned back in her chair with sudden fatigue. "A wise man I know once said that anything in the universe is possible, but that probability was a totally different matter."

"Then maybe you ought to be asking yourself what the probabilities are, and how you can determine them."

"You've told me that before, too."

"Indeed I have."

With a slow gathering of resolve she stood up. "Thanks, Dad. I think I know what to do now."

"Want to share it with me?"

"Not yet. I have to get it straight in my head first. But if I figure it out before the Ukes get here, I want to talk to you about it before I do anything."

"By all means," he said with a proud smile. "Didn't that wise man also say never to attack a problem on an empty stomach?"

"You did." Mica didn't want to eat, but she knew he would insist. "Shall we eat?"

As she followed him out of his office toward the mess, her mind churned with ideas and notions that refused to stay still long enough for her to examine them. Maybe eating was a good idea after all.

"Still nothing further on the Uke fleets?" Gilbert asked.

"No," she answered. He already knew that, but she was glad for the change of subject. "Pajandcan is working on it from two angles, the subspace monitors and the LRRS reports, but no further contact since that LRRS spotted them moving. All we really know is that the Ukes are on their way."

*   *   *

"I still don't understand why you want me to go to Cloise," Lucky said. There was something more going on than Delightful Childe had admitted to him. "What's in it for us?"

"Ah, yes, our profit motive, as you like to call it. That, my dear partner, depends upon what you accomplish there. This Proctor Geril demands a personal conference with one of our representatives. And since you can, shall we say, move more easily through Sondak, it falls on you to do the negotiating."

"Yeah, but even if they grant us the methane franchise,

what's going to keep Sondak from setting the price they want to pay, or just flat taking it from us?"

"Proctor Geril said that Sondak had, uh—burned its fingers; to use her words—trying to take the methane by force and would be most happy to pay whatever price we set."

"Doesn't sound like Sondak to me. Anyway, what about that cargo and passenger run from Patros to the U.C.S.? How are you going to handle that one?"

"By ignoring it for the moment. My cousin has exhibited his usual reluctance to offer sufficient advance recompense for such a hazardous task. Until such time as he is ready to pay, we will let him sit on his cargo and defer his profit."

The more time he spent with Delightful Childe, the more Lucky liked him. Sometimes he seemed almost human—especially when it came to the way he made business decisions. "What if your cousin comes around?"

"Comes around? Ah, I see. You mean, what if he agrees to our terms? Well, then you can fulfill that contract after you leave Cloise." Delightful Childe watched his partner's reaction and saw the displeasure in his face. "Something bothers you?"

"No . . . I guess not. I just wish you weren't going to be tied down here. Suppose I get into trouble?"

"There are always risks. We will do what we can to assist and protect you. I have already explained—"

"I know that." Lucky frowned. "I'd just feel more comfortable if . . ." He let the sentence trail off.

"Yes. I think I understand. You will feel vulnerable conducting these transactions, and wish for some greater assurances from me. Is that not so?"

"Something like that."

"We have already armed your *Graycloud*. Is that not sufficient? Is there something else we could do?"

"Yes," Lucky said with sudden inspiration. "Make me a citizen of Oina."

"Impossible!" Delightful Childe snorted. Business was important, but such a request was not only impossible, it was intolerable.

"Why? You've registered *Graycloud* to Oina. Why can't you register me, too?"

"Never! No. Absolutely not. Impossible. No alien has ever become a citizen of Oina!"

"There's a first time for everything," Lucky said with a determined smile. "If this trip to Cloise is so damned important to you and your people, and if you want me to risk my neck in the partnership while you screw around for a year, then maybe you'd better find a way to make it possible."

Delightful Childe understood Lucky's logic, but the very idea was repugnant. Still, he was asking a great deal of a mere human. Perhaps there was a way . . . "Suppose we offered you, uh, a form of conditional citizenship? Suppose—"

"Conditional on what?"

"Suppose," Delightful Childe continued, ignoring the interruption, "that we made you a *citizen inreprus.*"

"What the tensheiss does that mean?"

"It means, my agitated partner, that as a representative of Oina, you would be a citizen in *fact* if not in duties and obligations. We could probably give you documents asserting that, of course, and—"

"You'd damn well better give me documents. Wouldn't be any good to me otherwise."

"True. True." Delightful Childe stroked his proboscis. "Very well, we will give you the necessary documents. I will have to twist some noses, but it will be done. However, you will have to agree to certain, uh, limitations."

"Like what?" Lucky tried not to let his pleasure show. Whatever the limitations, Oinaise citizenship had potentials he was only beginning to understand.

"Formalities, really," Delightful Childe said, "like agreeing not to endanger our neutrality, and promising to relinquish your citizenship upon demand when you are no longer representing this planet."

"Sounds easy enough to me," Lucky said.

"Do not be so sure, nor so eager, Lucky. You will carry a grave responsibility in this matter—to us, and to yourself."

"I'll worry about the responsibility." A sense of triumph broke the smile free on his face. "You just get me that citizenship. Then we'll really be in business."

"And you will leave immediately for Cloise?"

"Of course." His smile broadened. "And don't worry. I'll do my best not to shame you or Oina."

22

Marsha watched the fine lines streak across the remote sensorscreen—lines representing the paths of the tiny search ships as they disappeared from sight. "How long will it be now?" she asked quietly.

"Thirty-five hours until we leave subspace," Frye said. "As soon as the search ships locate Sondak's defense fleet, we will launch our attack."

With a gentle shudder Marsha turned to face her father. "We're going to take a lot of casualties, aren't we?"

"What makes you ask that?" Like many of her questions, this one angered and annoyed him—not so much the question itself, but the accusatory tone in her voice when she asked it. Possible casualties were none of her business.

She heard the edge of anger, but refused to back away from it. "Because I don't see how we can avoid them. And I'm still not sure why the Matthews system is so important."

"In Decie's name, Marsha! Haven't you been listening to me? Matthews system is midway between us and Sondak. Whoever controls Matthews controls a hundred-thousand tachymeters in every direction. If you're so concerned about casualties, think about all the people in the U.C.S. who won't have to suffer under Sondak attacks once we control Matthews."

She sensed something deeper under his anger—something coldly separate from any concern about future lives that might be spared. With a quick blink she reminded herself of the thing that had always been the hardest to face as she grew up. Her father was first and foremost a military man. Maybe that was why he hadn't acknowledged her to his officers. Everything else in his life competed for secondary priority.

"I understand your strategy," she said carefully, "but I do not understand your callousness about casualties."

Frye looked at her sternly. *Maybe I should have kept Melliman after all,* he thought. *There is so much stubbornness in Marsha that I had forgotten. Or never accepted.*

"Be reasonable, Marsha. Wars create casualties. Men and women die in battle. That's a fact, not callousness. A commander's job is to obtain his objectives with a minimum loss of life . . . but he cannot—ever—let fear of casualties dominate his thinking."

"I didn't mean that you should—"

"I don't care what you meant."

His sharp rebuttal didn't surprise her. She had been pushing him for a reaction since their reunion. What she needed was some evidence from him that would help justify her decision to leave Lucky to come here. Instead, the things he said and did made him seem more and more like a stranger than the father she thought she remembered.

"Did you ever care what I meant?"

"We're not going to get into that again, Marsha. I don't have the time, or the inclination—or the energy—for that kind of dead-end conversation. If you want to help me, then bite your tongue and suck in your self-pity. If you don't . . ."

When he didn't finish his statement Marsha thought again of Lucky and the terrible moments when she had watched *Graycloud* rise from Alexvieux into space without her. "Do you know what my partner said right before I left him on Alexvieux? He told me to tell you that he hated you."

"Because I wouldn't let a Sondak space-tramper like him come with you," Frye said flatly.

"No. . . . I thought that then, too. But I was wrong. Now I think he said it because my obligation to you was stronger than my love for him. And he's not a space-tramper."

"You loved him?" Frye was genuinely surprised. She had said so little about that time—

"Yes, I love him . . . maybe more now than when I was with him. Then I didn't know what I had. Now I do."

"So you're sorry you came to me." Even though he knew he was right, Frye regretted the words as soon as he said them.

The last thing he wanted to do was alienate her any more than he already had.

"I didn't say that."

"No, but you meant it."

"You've never known what I meant," she said as she stood up and walked to the door. Quiet tears edged into the corners of her eyes, and she did not want him to see them. "Unless you need me, sir, I'm going to my quarters."

"Very well, Marsha." He returned her silent salute with ambivalent emotions, unsure of what to let himself feel.

After she shut the door he turned immediately and activated the holospan galactic map of the space surrounding Matthews system. Somewhere in the void around that system Sondak's forces were waiting for them. For the hundredth time he asked himself what he would do if he were commanding those forces.

As he considered all the possibilities again, thoughts about Marsha and what she had said slipped without notice into the dark emptiness under his heart.

* * *

Fatigue had joined LRRS One-Zero-Two as an unseen member of the crew who altered their judgments and slowed their reflexes.

When Louise picked up a strange echo, she should have recognized it as a black hole. But she wasn't looking for a black hole, she was looking for the Ukes. Without thinking she gave the heading of the unidentified echo to Da B'Barbara. He made a quick course correction and told Kimkey to report that they had located the Uke fleet.

"But, Da," Louise protested, "we can't be sure of that." She stared at the echo reading and knew there was something familiar about it—something important.

"You just get their range," Da said. He wasn't going to be cheated out of this chance again.

Minutes later Louise realized what she had found. "Da!" she screamed. "Turn away!"

Her warning was too late. LRRS One-Zero-Two slipped over the event horizon of an uncharted black hole and disappeared forever.

The crew of LRRS Ninety-Three picked up a true echo, locked onto it, and recorded nine minutes of valuable data before the echo faded. They, too, reported having located the Uke fleet.

When Admiral Pajandcan received the conflicting reports, she shook her head. "What in the blue novas is going on out there, Nick? Are the Ukes coming at us from two directions?"

Nickerson looked up at her with tired red eyes. "Beats me, Admiral. Neither one of those reports fits this." He handed her his latest computer chart drawn from the subspace monitors' data.

"Why not three directions?" she asked suddenly.

"Do they have the forces for that?"

"Who in blazes knows?" She looked at the LRRS reports again, searching for anything that would give her the information she needed. "Look at this," she said finally. "If we put Ninety-Three's reports aside for the moment, and just look at your data and One-Oh-Two's, does it make any more sense to you?"

After carefully comparing the two, Nickerson said, "Well, given the angles and One-Oh-Two's speed, plus the time adjustment factors, I guess you could say these aren't far apart. But—"

"I know," Pajandcan said as she snatched the papers from his hand. "I know. They're not close enough to bet this fleet on. But dammit, Nick, we've got to bet on something. I'm going to send out another wave of LRRS."

"We only have forty left, Admiral."

"Don't you think I know that? We'll send twenty out and call the others back. They've been out there too long already. If they continue searching as they return, that will give us a cone grid." She paused, staring at nothing, thinking of those fifty little ships and their crews like tidfish searching the ocean for a school of goliathsharks. "I want to find those Ukes, Nickerson. I want to find them now."

* * *

"A human?" Leri asked. "Why are they sending a human?"

"They did not say, Proctor," the Isthian answered from his suckling position on her neck.

He sucked hard, and Leri was glad. It was difficult for her to concentrate in the middle of an exchange, but it would have been harder if this one were less aggressive. Still, Leri resented the distraction. Normally, exchanges provided the time for her to relax and meditate, to appreciate the music she loved while the Isthian renewed her antibodies and took its nourishment from her blood.

But these were not normal times. Cloise had suffered under the burning and would probably suffer more. Her vision of the future had been distorted somehow, and no amount of meditative coaxing seemed capable of calling it back.

"I taste your unhappiness," the Isthian said through a slurping of its lips.

"My apologies, tender one."

"No apologies necessary, Proctor. We all taste the bitterness of these days in one way or another. I seek no other for exchange."

His reassurance relieved her slightly. "May the Elett bless you," she whispered.

"And may you share my blessing," he replied before he resumed suckling the fat nipple on her neck.

Leri concentrated on the sensation, seeking the tranquillity that might let her think more clearly. Yet every time she felt herself slide toward contentment, the thought of humans intruded. Thus she was surprised to hear the Isthian speak to her.

"You slept well, Proctor."

"I slept?" She did not believe it until she realized how rested she felt.

"I helped you," he said calmly, "but now I must go."

"May your blessings double, tender one."

"By the grace of the Elett," he said before scuttling off her back and disappearing behind her.

One day, she thought, I will look upon an Isthian and know my benefactor. That might make up for having to look at a stupid human sent to represent the soulless Oinaise.

* * *

Dawson allowed himself a grin as he watched the eighth missile explode in a brief flash. They were getting better, his hunter crews, a damn sight better at finding the Uke neutronics. For some reason the Ukes had not shielded their weapons properly, and as faint as their radiation emissions were, they were strong enough to give away their locations. "Wish we knew how many more there are," he said aloud.

"Would be nice, sir," the tech beside him said. "But you can bet on at least one more."

"Why?"

"One of the civies, the *Anned,* just picked up a reading."

"A good one?" He was pleased that the civilians had finally found one. It reminded him of their defense of Granser's planet.

"Looks like it, sir. They're closing on the target with two of our ships in support."

"Put it on general broadcast," Dawson said, "and tell them to be careful."

"Aye, sir."

Dawson looked at the faint starfield on the viewscreen with its superimposed grid and found a green civilian blip and two blue military blips closing on the telltale orange blip of the Uke neutronic device.

After twenty minutes watching and listening to the communications between the ships, Dawson sensed something was wrong, "Mr. Edwards," he said into the transceiver, "how close are you to the target?"

"Just reached the safety point, sir," the civilian answered thirty seconds later.

"We're stopping, too, Admiral," the leader of the military ships said. "It ought to blow in a second."

But it didn't. The orange blip pulsed steadily in the center of a triangle formed by the three ships. The tension mounted in the communications room as everyone waited for the explosion.

"Lieutenant Welch here, sir," a voice finally said from the speakers. "Request permission to close with the target."

"Negative, Lieutenant," Dawson said automatically. "That thing could blow any second."

"But the readings are different on this one, sir. Electronic emissions are lower. Power source appears unstable. I think it's malfunctioning, sir."

"All the more reason to wait. Maintain your distance, Lieutenant. You, too, Mr. Edwards."

"Aye, sir."

"Yes, sir," came the overlapping responses.

Dawson was intrigued with the possibility of capturing one of these devices, but he wasn't about to risk losing a crew and a ship to do it. Still . . . "Lieutenant Welch, lock your weapons on the target to fire automatically if it moves. Then continue monitoring and inform me of any noticeable change in its status. Is that understood?"

"Affirmative, Admiral . . . Weapons locked . . . Will continue monitoring and keep you posted as instructed."

"Mr. Edwards, you may withdraw the *Anned* and resume your search pattern."

Edwards answered after a longer than usual pause. "It's our find, sir. We'd like to stay."

Dawson smiled. "As you will, Mr. Edwards. But at the first sign of movement, you get the hell out of there."

"Yes, sir."

After three hours of intermittent reports of steadily declining electronic emission from the Uke missile, Dawson made his decision. "Lieutenant Welch, do you still wish to close with the target?"

"Affirmative, sir."

"What about your crew?"

"Only me and Longpat, sir. We're ready when you say so."

Dawson listened to the background static for a long minute. "Very well, Lieutenant, close slowly and carefully to within ten kilometers. And give us a continuing report as you go. If its power increases in the slightest, I want you gone on full thrust. You got that?"

"Initiating closing action now, sir. No change in electronic emissions. Target remains steady. Radiation constant. Three hundred kilometers and closing. . . ."

Dawson listened for twenty minutes with growing anxiety, expecting to lose the target and Welch any second.

Finally Welch said, "Ten kilometers and holding, sir. Pictures on their way."

Dawson shifted his eyes to the video screen and for the first time saw one of the Uke devices. It was shaped like a sphere with a long, pointed projection sticking out tangentially from its axis. "I want views from all sides, Lieutenant," Dawson said clamly. "Then I want you to return to the safety point and destroy it."

"But, sir . . . we could get a tow on it."

"Negative on the tow. You have ten minutes to get your pictures and begin your return, Lieutenant, or you'll spend the rest of this war dirtside." Dawson was surprised at the fierceness with which he spoke until he realized both his fists were clenched with tension. He relaxed only slightly when the angle of the picture started shifting.

"Aye, sir," Welch said, "circling target."

Dawson could not relax until Lieutenant Welch had his ship back behind the safety point. When the two military ships fired on the Uke missile, its neutronics were detonated in another of the familiar flashes. Nine, Dawson thought, nine down, but how many to go?

23

"They're coming in, sir!" Mica said as she hurried into the Battle Center. "The Ukes are on their way! Pajandcan's LRRS picked them up in subspace about eighty thousand tachymeters out."

Gilbert frowned. "Eighty thousand tachymeters? I would have expected them to be much closer by now."

"She said the subspace monitors confirm it." Mica was still excited, but by now she understood her father's caution. If the Ukes actually were closer—

"How many LRRS picked them up?"

"Just one, sir, but like I said, the subspace monitors—"

"One isn't enough, Mica. Let me see." He took her printouts and compared them with the projections on the holospan map in front of him. "Plot these," he said to the map operator.

By the time the new projections came up, the deck officers were crowding around the map, and Gilbert frowned again. Turning to Mica he said, "Tell Pajandcan she needs at least two and preferably three more confirmed echo sightings before she moves to engage them."

Mica saw the differences on the map, but did not share his concern about the LRRS sightings. "Yes, sir," she said, "but may I ask a question, sir?"

"Certainly, Captain."

His tone told her to be careful, yet she felt the question had to be asked. "Sir, what if these are true sightings? Won't she be wasting valuable time?"

"That she will. But what if they're not true sightings? She

might be maneuvering to engage an enemy who's not there.
Now pass that message."

"Yessir."

"And Mica?"

"Sir?"

"Alert our fleet to this possibility."

"Will do, sir. Anything else?"

"No. That will be all for now—except that I think it's time for
you to shift your operation here. On the double." He turned
back to the problems at hand without acknowledging her salute. It seemed like only a minute later that she was back,
flushed with excitement.

"Three more confirmed sightings," she said triumphantly as
she handed a new printout to the map operator.

When the new coordinates appeared on the map, they were
totally off line from the first set. "What's this?" Gilbert asked,
"a two-pronged attack? Extend the projections."

Pale orange lines extended from the pulsing coordinates
across the sphere.

"I don't like that one damn bit. It doesn't make any sense,"
Gilbert said to the officers crowding around the map. "If the
first sighting was valid, they're going to have to do a radical
maneuver to get anywhere close to us at that speed. If the
second sighting is valid—"

"The first one could be heading for Roberg, sir," one of the
deck officers volunteered.

"Damn! You're right, Lieutenant. You're absolutely right.
Mica, send Roberg a Fleet Order for Full Alert. Then notify
Nordeen and HOMFLEET Command."

Mica moved over to the communications console to send the
messages, but listened as her father continued.

"If one of the Uke fleets is trying to bypass us, there's no way
we can stop them." He paused and looked at his officers as
though waiting for a response.

"Lieutenant Joygee," he said to the officer who had suggested that Roberg might be a Uke objective, "I need a volun-
teer. Not you," he said holding up his hand, "but the best
flying officer we've got."

"That would be Flight Leader Donna, sir. She's aces above
everyone else."

"Good. Get her up here, on the double. And tell the flight
deck to prepare to launch the *Reed*."

"The *Reed*, sir? Isn't that—"

"My command corvette," Gilbert finished for him. "Yes, it is, Joygee, and she's the fastest ship we have. Now get to it."

"Gentlemen," he said after Lieutenant Joygee left, "I propose we send Flight Leader Donna out in the *Reed* to intercept and confirm this bypass line of attack. She won't be able to do much more than confirm, but at least Roberg will have additional information if that's the Uke strategy. Any suggestions or comments you would like to offer?"

When there were none, he sent them back to their duties and stared at the map with a growing feeling of desperation. If the Ukes were trying an end run on Roberg, all his assumptions would be proven wrong—and at a cost he did not want to consider.

* * *

Frye cursed silently. In another fifteen hours Ushogi Fleet would return to normal space and the attack on Matthews system would begin. But according to the report on his microspooler, only ten of his secret missiles had reported from Matthews on the last status check. Somehow Sondak was eliminating his final line of attack.

That he had four missiles to spare gave him little comfort. He wanted more than enough to wreak havoc on Matthews if necessary, and the margin was becoming too thin. Yet he was stuck with the plan he had initiated, and there was nothing he could do now to improve the situation.

In a few hours Ely would strike the first of the polar systems with Shakav Fleet in an attempt to draw Sondak's forces there. If Frye was going to take advantage of that, he could do no more than proceed on schedule and pray for the best.

"But only ten missiles," he said quietly.

"You called, sir?" Marsha asked from the next room.

Frye had forgotten that his lapelcom was still on. "No, AOCO. I was just thinking out loud. Sorry. I'm going to take a short nap. Wake me in three hours."

"How about five, sir. You really need some rest."

"Three will do, AOCO." He turned off his lapelcom and moved from his desk to his bunk. As he stretched out, he wondered what Sondak's commanders were doing at this moment and if they would be as determined in their defense as he was in the attack.

The latest intelligence reports were fragmentary and vague

about the strength of the fleet Sondak had managed to assemble for the defense of Matthews. Those same reports indicated Admiral Gilbert would be commanding that defense, but Frye seriously doubted that. Sondak's bureaucratic military wasn't about to put an old war dog like Gilbert in a defensive command. They would be saving him for some big offensive. No, he would probably be opposed by some junior admiral he had never heard of.

That was a shame. He wouldn't mind going up against Gilbert and thrashing that old heretic. He wouldn't mind that at all.

*　　*　　*

"And I'm telling you, Admiral, that we made a mistake. LRRS Ninety-Three was right. I don't know what One-Oh-Two picked up, but it wasn't the Uke fleet."

"Then what was it? And why haven't we heard from One-Oh-Two? They picked up something, Nick."

"Yes, ma'am, they did. But it wasn't the Ukes. I'm sure of it. There's only one Uke fleet, and it's headed in this direction. I'd bet my life on it."

"You'd be betting all our lives." Pajandcan paused. "Somewhere out there we lost seven LRRS, six of them in the same search quadrant—and one of them said it picked up a Uke fleet. But you want me to ignore that. Am I right?" She smiled when Nickerson shook his head in frustration.

"No. But I am saying that *all* the indications now are that whatever One-Oh-Two picked up was not the main Uke fleet. The data is overwhelming on the other sightings."

"I think you're right, Nick, but I wanted to know how sure you were. How far out do you project them now?"

Nickerson looked at the latest printout. "Fifty tachymeters at the farthest. Probably inside that."

"Then the question becomes one of guessing where they'll hit normal space." Pajandcan said quietly. "I want a projection of the total area of normal space they could operate from if they leave subspace from their present course. And I want it fast."

"Can do, Admiral. Give me two hours."

"Maximum," she said quickly. "The sooner the better. We've got to move this fleet into position as soon as possible, so don't take any more time than you have to."

*　　*　　*

General Mari had made the decision to arrive with the first contingent of fresh troops to arrive on Sutton Six in order to make an on-the-spot assessment of the situation.

His only concession to personal comfort on the trip had been to bring his pikean mistress, Giselda, with him. But rather than sending her back to Nordeen after they had arrived, he had decided to take her planetside. For all her stupidity, and occasional insolence, she catered to his sexual desires and made life slightly more acceptable for him.

Now he regretted his decision. The main garrison in Esqueleada where he would establish his temporary headquarters was dominated by pikean troops who had hooted and whistled as she emerged from his staff skimmer.

Worse than that, the planetary commander was a pikean.

Pikeans, he thought derisively. How am I supposed to defend a planet with pikeans? With a sigh he left his quarters and headed for the Situation Room. Maybe Sutton could only be the buffer against the Ukes. Maybe he would have to set his hardest line of defense on Bakke.

He locked his jaw with a quick shake of his head. No. Pikeans or not, they were Planetary Troops and he would demand their best. Fight to the death. Those would be his standing orders for every legion on every planet. No quarter asked, none given. No surrender. If the Ukes wanted the planets in these systems, they would have to pay for them.

"Welcome, General," the tall, pale pikean captain said as Mari entered the foyer of the Situation Room. "General Porras is waiting for you inside."

Mari returned the captain's salute without answering and marched through the door.

"Ah, General Mari. I am General Porras. You may not remember me, but I met you once before on—"

"Nice to see you, Porras," Mari lied as he accepted the other's handshake. "It was on DeBrin, wasn't it? Your legion was losing a training exercise against Colonel Ozznich."

"Your memory is too good, General," Porras said with a broad smile on his pale face. "But then, you must also remember that we were outnumbered three to one."

"I remember you held the high ground," Mari said "and you lost it." The disappearance of Porras's smile satisfied him momentarily. "However, that was a training exercise in the past.

Now you are about to engage in the real thing—but the Ukes will hold the high ground."

"We are well aware of that, sir. This arrived from POLFLEET moments before you did. I've deployed our fighters."

Mari took the message and read it quickly. "How many?"

"A little under three hundred waiting off the second moon, sir. Our cruisers and destroyers are holding behind the first moon with another hundred reserve fighters."

"How's your fuel supply?"

"Most of the ships have about forty hours of methane."

"They'll kill us," Mari said softly. "If POLFLEET is right, the Ukes have a force that will chew up your fighters in the first skirmish."

"Maybe so, sir, but with the reinforcements you brought—"

"Dammit, Porras! What the hell's the matter with you? Those reinforcements are still being shuttled planetside. Our destroyer escort is preparing to leave at any minute and—"

A loud siren interrupted him.

For a long moment he stared at Porras as the siren faded and rose again. "Where's the communications room?" he asked finally.

"Through here," Porras said, leading the way.

"We've got them on the scope," a tech said as the two generals entered the room. "They're coming around Dimdim and—damn, sir!"

They both stepped behind the tech and stared at the scope. From behind the solid shadow of Sutton's eighth planet came a Uke force that looked like a swarm of starving locusts.

"Orders!" Mari barked with a twisting knot in his stomach. "To all units: No surrender! We fight to the death!"

Rochmon stood with Admiral Stonefield and Avitor Hilldill as the latest reports from Gilbert and Pajandcan came in by way of Mungtinez Relay.

"Roberg!" Stonefield whistled softly when he read Gilbert's Fleet Alert. "How soon before we can get a com-window to Roberg?"

"Eleven days, two hours," Rochmon said after glancing at the sychronization readouts, "but I don't think Commander Charltos is going to—"

"Well, Hilldill?" Stonefield asked, ignoring Rochmon's comment. "Can your Flight Corps there defend Roberg? Because if they can't . . ."

"Depends on the odds, sir. I told you that after General Mari left. Roberg has most of the best forces we have left. If they can't do it, no one can. But they took quite a beating, and if they're outnumbered—"

"I know. I know. None of us can do much when we're outnumbered." Stonefield took a deep breath. "That's what's wrong with this damn system of ours," he said quietly. "We train people to believe they can be defeated just because the odds are against them."

"Sir," Rochmon said slowly, "seems to me we're overlooking something." He did not want to anger Stonefield, but the admiral seemed to have missed the point.

"What's that, Commander?"

Despite his sense of caution, Rochmon was neither afraid of the old man, nor of speaking his mind. "Well, sir, we don't know for sure that the Ukes are headed for Roberg. Admiral

Gilbert makes it clear that he is operating on an assumption. However, now that we have bolstered the Flight Corps at Roberg, couldn't we use some of them to reinforce POL-FLEET?"

"And strip Roberg's defenses?"

"That is insane," Hilldill added.

"You'd better stick to cryptography, Commander, and leave the tactics to us. Send this to Roberg by relay. Tell them they are on their own and will have to hold out as long as they can."

"Yes, sir," Rochmon heard no real censure in Stonefield's voice, and after a moment's hesitation, he decided it was better to press his point than to miss the opportunity. "But suppose Roberg isn't attacked? I mean, suppose that turns out to be a false alarm?"

"You heard me, Commander," Stonefield said, "Avitor Hilldill and I will be in the Command Center. Pipe all further communications of note in there."

"Yes, sir," Rochmon said again as they left the Situation Room. "You bet, sir," he whispered to himself.

Damn admirals and generals thought they knew everything. But they didn't know Charltos. He wasn't about to risk an attack on Roberg until he had secured Matthews. Even the Efcorps had been able to figure that out. For a bunch of snoopy civilians, Rochmon thought, they had done a better job of assessing the overall strategic situation than Stonefield.

"Sutton window in ten minutes," the tech said. "Stand by for incoming reports."

Mari's landing reports, Rochmon thought. Ought to pipe them in to Stonefield and put him to sleep. No one could write as boring a report as Mari.

*　　*　　*

Lucky read the operating monitors with growing concern. *Graycloud*'s engine was running hotter than normal subspace temperatures, and even though the increase wasn't serious yet, Lucky wasn't interested in taking any chances.

"You ever tinker with a Gouldrive?" he asked Morning Song.

"No," the Oinaise replied. "I am a chemical analyst, not a mechanic or a physicist."

"I know what you are. I just thought maybe—"

"There is no need for rudeness, Captain Teeman. When my

father directed me to join you, he said you were an exceptional human. I doubted that at the time, and your present attitude makes me question his assessment."

"You're a touchy bastard," Lucky said with a smile, "but I apologize anyway. My concern is for our mission and the fact that the Gouldrive is running hot. I know how to fix minor things on the drive and do the usual maintenance—even centered the damn thing once. But if this heat buildup is serious, I just wanted to know if you could help."

"I appreciate your concern, Captain Teeman, and your apology is accepted. What recourse do we have if this is indeed a critical malfunction?"

Lucky liked Delightful Childe's son better when he was being practical and put his xenoapathy aside. "We would have to find the closest system where we could get it checked—and fixed if necessary."

"Where would that be?"

The genuine interest he heard in Morning Song's voice made Lucky feel better. At least his Oinaise companion was beginning to appreciate the situation. "Let's see," he said as he keyed in a navigation library search and waited for the readout. "From the looks of it, the closest one would be the Matthews system. That's one of Sondak's outpost systems and about two days away at this speed."

"Perhaps we should notify my father."

"Your father's busy making babies." Lucky meant that as a joke, but he didn't think Morning Song appreciated his attempt at humor. "Anyway, no sense in worrying him unless we actually have to break off our route. In the meantime, we'll just watch the drive carefully and see what happens."

* * *

Only half of the sophisticated sensors on the launchship *McQuay* had been repaired before it was called back into service, but one set which was working picked up the faint searchscan that its operators immediately identified as a typical Uke frequency. They traced its brief course across the static on their screens, then reported it to the Battle Center.

"Sir," Mica said, "I think the Ukes may have spotted us. The sensor team picked up a searchscan."

"Do they still have it?"

"Negative, sir. Whoever it was popped back into subspace."

"Notify the fleet and tell Pajandcan that we're moving to our secondary position in thirty minutes."

"Yes, sir." Mica quickly relayed his instructions, then paused as several new reports came over her earphones. "The *Reed* is beginning its second warp, Admiral. No contact with—" She stopped talking and listened in dismay to the voice in her earphone. Without waiting to hear all of it, she switched it to the overhead speakers.

"—attack fleet size. Sutton already under fire. Repeat. Sutton under fire. All forces are engaged. General Mari requests all available—"

A ferocious burst of static held the Battle Center in suspense for a long ten seconds.

"—broken through . . . estimates full scale landing within five hours . . . help beyond the reserves . . . standing orders to fight to the death. No surrender. Repezzzzz—"

The voice trailed off through the static. After a long moment of listening to the insane crackle, Mica switched off the speakers. Silence held the *McQuay*'s Battle Center as still as a funeral service.

"Back to your stations," Admiral Gilbert said finally. "The most we can do is pray for them." He said his own quick prayer as he tried to visualize what Sutton must be going through. Those were his people under fire. A momentary pang of guilt for not being with them jabbed at his thoughts. Then it disappeared in a deeper concern.

How many Uke fleets were there? One attacking the polar systems, one headed for Roberg, and one for Matthews? Three fleets? It didn't seem possible they could have amassed that many ships. But if they had, which was the main fleet?

Or were they of equal strength? If that was the case, they would probably sweep through the first group of polar systems without effort. POLFLEET was stretched like a highly permeable membrane across its quadrant of responsibility. That mismatched set of ships and men he had so lovingly commanded might be able to conduct a harassing action. But in no case could POLFLEET confront a full-scale Uke battle fleet directly.

If he had guessed wrong, if Matthews was not the primary target, he and his advice would be responsible for millions of deaths in open space and half-a-set of systems—deaths of friends and colleagues, people he had come to know and love during his years of isolated command. Yet beyond that grief, it could mean a military setback from which Sondak might never recover.

Gilbert had to believe he had guessed right. There would be time enough later for second-guessing himself and the Joint Chiefs. Time enough if we make it through this, he thought.

"Admiral Pajandcan's moving her fleet, sir." Mica could see the concentration in her father's brow, and knew he was thinking about POLFLEET as well as Sutton.

"Did she receive the Sutton transmission?"

"Yes, sir. She said the Ukes will have to fight like hell to beat General Mari at anything."

* * *

"Sighting of Sondak's defense fleet confirmed," Marsha said. "They're laying back on the fringe of the system."

Frye allowed himself a brief smile. "Doesn't sound like they're too eager to fight, does it AOCO?"

"No, sir . . . unless it's a trap of some kind."

"Good thought, Marsha. But I don't think we need to worry much about a trap. Intelligence says that at the very best they can only have five launchships against our twelve. Combined with what we know about their methane shortage, I'd say they're just waiting for us to come within striking range. Anyway, in a few hours we will know for sure."

"Are you surprised that Shakav Fleet hasn't drawn them off?"

"No. But I will be surprised if that action doesn't draw off any reinforcements they might be expecting."

"Pardon me for interrupting, Commander," the officer-of-the-bridge said, "but we believe we're being followed."

"Followed? By whom, Lieutenant?"

"Don't know for sure, sir, but we're picking up some standard Sondak-type navigation signals from about half-a-day behind us."

Frye laughed. "That has to be normal traffic, Lieutenant. No Sondak warship is going to be sending navsignals if they're following us."

"Could be, sir. We're breaking down the inherent I.D.—ah," he said, taking a small slip of paper from one of the crew, "here it is. Oinaise registered freighter, number four-four-seven-alpha-two-two-nine-three, name *Graycloud*."

Marsha gasped.

"What's the matter?" Frye was startled by the expression on her face. When she didn't answer, he repeated his question.

"That's my ship—I mean, our ship—Lucky's ship."

Frye looked at her with surprise and empathy. Then he turned away. "Warn them off, Lieutenant. Send them a message to stay well away from Matthews system. Now!"

"I, uh, sir, uh—" Marsha stammered.

"No," Frye said. "I don't want to talk about it."

Marsha lowered her eyes from his stern look and listened as the lieutenant sent the message. Tears rolled down her cheeks.

25

"We're taking a big chance, Nick," Pajandcan said as the first wave of long-range fighters left her six launchships.

"If they don't come out there," Nickerson said, jabbing the printout with a slender finger, "or damn close to it, Admiral, they're going to sub right past us."

"Maybe that's what they plan. After the way they hit Sutton, how can we be sure what they'll do next?"

"An admiral once told me that nothing is sure in war."

"Don't quote me, Nick. Not at a time like this. We've got over two hundred people in those fighters, and if the Ukes don't follow your scheduled escape from subspace, we could damn well lose all of them."

"They will," Nickerson said. "They have to. It's the most advantageous place to strike Matthews from."

"Give or take a hundred thousand kilometers."

"Yes, ma'am. We're monitoring them as closely as we can, and in an hour or so, we'll know if we're right or not."

Pajandcan had a vision of the Uke fleet bursting from subspace like an opening umbrella with her fighters caught directly in front of them.

* * *

Pandemonium reigned in Sutton system.

Most of the remnants of the defense squadron in space were doing their best to follow General Mari's standing order. One by one they were being isolated and destroyed. The smaller of the two troopships had managed to completely discharge its cargo before being blown in half by Uke missiles. The other crashed to the surface of the planet still carrying one and a half legions—three thousand Planetary Troops who would never raise a weapon in Sondak's defense.

General Mari retreated to what passed for a secure command bunker just outside of Esqueleada, only to discover that half the pikean troops were in revolt, sabotaging equipment and stealing supplies. Much to Mari's amazement, General Porras took swift action, and within hours, the mutinous troops had been captured, dispersed, or killed.

But during that time, the first of the Uke landingships had started disgorging battle contingents around the city, and reports began coming in that the Ukes were armed with portable artillery.

Mari didn't believe that. Yet the continued reports, even from his reserve legions which had faced combat in the last war, made him realize that no matter what he did, Sutton was going to suffer terrible losses before succumbing. His choice was clear. Rescind the standing order, or live with all those deaths on his conscience.

Without hesitation he made his decision. "General Porras, I want the standing order repeated every hour on the hour on every command frequency we use. No surrender. Let's show these Ukes what we're made of."

"Yes, sir!" Porras said. "They'll pay in blood for this one, sir."

And so will we, Mari thought. And so will we.

*   *   *

"We're in trouble," Lucky said quietly.

"How so, Captain Teeman?"

"Because that disturbance we picked up is a Uke war fleet, and they're telling us to get the tensheiss out of here."

"Perhaps we should obey them."

"Sure. And burn out the Gouldrive in the process. How would you like to die of old age with me while we limp through normal space toward the next closest planet?"

Morning Song made a fluttering noise through his proboscis. "My father would send someone to rescue us."

Lucky shook his head. "You just don't understand, do you? Our subspace transmitter operates off the Gouldrive. If it goes, so do our communications. By the time a message got to Oina, your great-great-nieces and nephews would be receiving it."

"Then send the message now."

"That's what I'm about to do," Lucky said. "Then we're

going to see if we can find somewhere near Matthews where we can exit subspace without getting caught in the battle."

* * *

"Three minutes till normal space," the officer-of-the-bridge announced. "First attack flights prepared to launch."

Frye sat in the center of the bridge, watching and listening as the crew of *Hondono* went through their final exit checks. In a few minutes nine attack flights would be spewing from his launchships——six flights toward Matthews, and three flights toward Sondak's defense fleet. In less than an hour the enemy would be fully engaged in battle.

Externally he was calm. Internally the growing anticipation had drawn him tighter than guy wire. This would be his third triumph of the war. His second was already being well carried out by Shakav Fleet's capture of Sutton. The resistance there had been minimal in space—as he had predicted. Despite the fact that Ely's latest update reported heavy fighting on the planet, Frye was sure that he, too, would quickly come to an end.

"Exit . . . NOW!" a voice said.

For a long second Frye stared at the screens as the image of normal space resolved into a clear view. "Begin launch," he ordered. "All ships away."

Marsha stood at her station behind her father and observed the launching of a thousand and eighty light attack ships from the bellies of the launchers. It was a magnificent sight that caused a swell of pride in her breast. Without realizing it, she joined in the cheers of the crew as the attackers disappeared from the screens on their way to strike Matthews.

"ATTENTION! Attention!" A loud voice broke through the fading cheers. "Possible enemy ships, quadrants two and three closing at point-seven-eight."

"Sound General Quarters!" Frye shouted. "Alert all ships!" How in Decie's name had the damned Sondaks guessed where he would be? "Deploy fighter cover!"

"Estimate enemy force at one hundred . . . type Messerole-Class long-range fighters."

Frye released part of his tension. One hundred Sondak fighters would be no match for his own. But Messerole-Class fighters? They must have come from Matthews itself, rather than from the defense fleet. Otherwise, how could they have enough fuel to return to their launchships?

He turned back to the screens and watched as the tiny specks representing the enemy approached in a well-disciplined formation. As the minutes went by and the specks grew larger, he had to admire the courage of those crews who must surely have understood that they were flying to their deaths.

"Incoming missiles!"

Frye could not see what the sensors had picked up, but he did not doubt the information. Already the first of his defense fighters had engaged the pitifully small enemy force.

A faint tremor shook the *Hondono*. With a grim smile Frye forced himself back into the cushions of his chair. The battle had begun.

*   *   *

"Contact! Contact!" the voice screamed over the speakers. "Eight . . . nine . . . maybe ten launchships. Bandits coming your way!"

"Prepare to launch the second wave," Pajandcan said quickly. "I want all ships away in fifteen minutes."

"But, Admiral!"

"Shut up, Nick. It's hit them now or get our butts blown from space. Take your pick." When he didn't say anything, she tried to smile at him. "It's our only choice, Nick. Now notify Admiral Gilbert that we've made contact."

"Going in! For Sondak and glory," a young pilot shouted.

"Look out! Look out! Fire from the—"

The scratchy transmissions mixed and overlapped through the speakers in the terrible excitement of the moment.

"Fighters are out! Spread! Spread!"

"Missiles away," a calmer voice said. "That's for Roberg."

"Turn that down," Pajandcan ordered. "Ops? I want status on the second wave launch."

"Ready in nine minutes, ma'am."

"Launch when ready." After the terrible monotony of waiting, Pajandcan suddenly felt as exhilarated as a young girl in love. These were the moments she had been waiting for. She only wished she could be piloting one of those fighters herself.

*   *   *

Dawson sat patiently and waited as the Uke ships streamed in toward Reckynop. His defenses were set, but if he acted too soon, he would give them away. The best he could hope for was that the Ukes would think the planet was an easy target and get careless. If they did, he had a surprise for them.

Reckynop was ringed with a thousand empty ships—freighters, personal craft, space tugs—every ship he could commandeer that was capable of being remotely controlled. These ships would lock their hodge-podge of lasers and limited missiles on any approaching ship not broadcasting the proper radio frequency and would fire at that target until it or they were destroyed.

The radios were the secret, the same secret he had used to identify friendly forces during the defense of Granser's planet. Admiral Y'Ott hadn't figured it out then, and he hoped the Ukes wouldn't figure it out now. And while they were coping with the remote targets, his personally formed defense force would move in behind them and try to get close enough to use their antique laser cannons and microbeam blasters.

It was a desperate gamble, but it only had to work long enough for Pajandcan and Gilbert to strike back for him. Yet deep inside, Dawson already mourned the loss of lives they would all suffer.

26

"Trailers report an estimated three hundred light enemy ships approaching on our last position, Admiral."

"Good," Gilbert said with a smile. "Tell the trailers to observe and report from the safest distance."

"What will the Ukes do when they don't find us?" Mica asked.

"Keep looking. At least that's what I hope they'll do. Are the interceptors ready?"

"We've confirmed Pajandcan's coordinates. They're prepared to launch at your word, sir."

Gilbert stepped over to the transceiver. "Attention all interceptor crews," he said calmly, "this is Admiral Gilbert. You know what your job is. Pound the Ukes with all you've got. But remember to leave yourself enough fuel to point your way back to Reckynop. We'll do everything we can to pick you up." He paused for a moment and then said, "Good luck, and good hunting. Commence launch."

The partially repaired *McQuay* shuddered in response to the launch of its interceptors. When they were all well away, he returned to the transceiver. "Attention all commanders. Prepare to execute Operation Matthews Return."

Her father had explained the plan to her, but until this moment she had not really understood what was going to happen. The tactics of it had eluded her before. Now she saw that the Uke ships looking for them in their previous position would be caught between the nonrevertor force and Reckynop.

"New trailer report, sir. Enemy ships have split on orbital courses. . . . One trailer's lost, sir."

"Execute!" Gilbert said harshly into the transceiver.

Mica flinched. For the first time she was truly frightened. They were going to engage the Ukes in a battle to the death.

*   *   *

"Find them," Frye said. "They can't have moved far since that first sighting. Find them and destroy them." He waited impatiently for the normally delayed response.

"Sir . . . I've divided my group in an orbital search."

"Idiot!" Frye screamed. "Pull them back together again. If they catch you like that, you won't stand a chance." Again he waited—this time even longer before Group Leader Weavening responded. *Hondondo* trembled as another missile from Sondak's suicidal attackers found its target.

"Found them . . . sir . . . Pulling my forces . . . In Decie's name, Commander! We have—"

The speaker went silent. Seconds later, a barely audible voice came across. "Heavy resistance. Hundreds of ships. Concentrated fire. Losing—"

Again the speaker went silent.

"Who was that?" Frye demanded.

"I don't know, sir. One of the Reckynop—"

"I know where! I want to know who! Doesn't anyone—"

"More enemy fighters, Commander! Same quadrant."

For the briefest instant, Frye felt disoriented. Where in the name of everything holy was Sondak sending all these fighters from? Then he caught himself.

"Prepare to launch the reserve," he said with great control.

"Against the fighters, sir?" Flight Leader Trukken asked.

"No. Against Reckynop. Can't your people handle a few more of theirs?"

"—closing fast," a faint voice on the speaker squawked. "We're taking hits and they're still out of range. Regrouping to burst formation in—" Static filled the air.

"There are hundreds more, sir. But we will handle them. Preparing to launch reserves."

"Damage report. The *Bolen* is out of action, sir."

Frye cursed. "Launch reserves."

"Yes, sir."

"—mander Charltos, we've broken through. Beginning missile runs on Reckynop. Enemy—" Another voice died in static.

"Reserves away."

"AOCO, I want damage reports from every ship in this fleet.

Trukken, I want to know what's going on around Reckynop, and I want to know *now*. Is that understood?"

"Yessir!"

Marsha sensed panic in her father, but immediately dismissed that thought. It is the battle and the tension, she thought as she took over the intership channel and started demanding the damage reports he wanted.

* * *

"Damn," Lucky whispered as they listened to the fragments of transmissions coming to them from Matthews system. "I'm glad we're not in the middle of all that."

"I share your sentiments totally. But I do not see how this action of yours is going to help us."

"You want to go busting in there? Well, neither do I. So we cruise for a while in normal space, then pop a short warp into Reckynop when things settle down a little."

"What if the Ukas win?" Morning Song asked.

"We don't have any choice, my friend. Your father said they couldn't get anyone here for a month. And what's this shortage of brolkers have to do with us?"

"Bolkers, Captain Teeman. Bolkers. They are, how shall I say this? They are what you might call servants, and it is they who provide the majority of our navigators. It is a rare ship that does not fly without a bolker. But their population, unfortunately, has failed to keep up with our need for them, so the bolker shortage—"

"I don't need a lesson on your society, just the facts. No bolkers, no rescue and repair mission."

"That is correct, Captain."

"Then why can't you understand what I'm doing?"

"Because, humans at their best are most difficult to understand, and I fear that the stress on you caused by the problems with the Gouldrive has kept you from being your best."

* * *

"Sutton's under heavy bombardment, Admiral. According to Mari, the Uke forces are landing by the thousands."

Stonefield frowned. "What about Roberg?"

"Their report just passed through relay. No signs of enemy activity." Vindication of his position gave Rochmon little pleasure. Despite the dry simplicity of Mari's reports, they smelled of death and blood.

"Well, Hilldill? What do you think? Should we try to send reinforcements to Bakke? Or do you think it is too early to make a decision?"

"It's still too early," Avitor Hilldill said firmly. "If we respond too quickly, we could be falling into a Uke trap."

"Begging the Avitor's pardon," Admiral Eresser said, "but I think you are most wrong. If we do not respond now, we could lose Bakke as well as Sutton. Then what's to keep them from moving on to Satterfield and Wallbank—or Yaffee?"

"The contingents of Planetary Troops are already—"

"I'm talking about space reinforcements," Eresser said with an uncharacteristic glare in her eyes. "I'm talking about putting some muscle behind POLFLEET."

"We understand your concern," Stonefield said, "but we cannot rush into this decision. The remainder of us will be here within a day, and I think this is a decision for the full Joint Chiefs."

"Then you ought to ask Mari, too. If he's still alive." She turned without waiting for a response and left the Command Center.

"There's another problem, sir," Rochmon said. "The Efcorps is screaming for more information, and I'm afraid its representatives are looking for someone with more authority than Captain Carpenter."

"Let the damn civilians look till they turn green. I have more important things to do than to brief them."

"I wasn't suggesting that you do it, sir, but I thought—"

"Admiral Lindshaw," Stonefield said suddenly. "That ought to satisfy them."

"Only for a while," Rochmon said. "The civies are getting hungry and mad. They seem to think it's their war, too."

"Commander . . ."

"I know, Admiral. You want me to watch my tongue."

"On the contrary," Stonefield said with a strange smile, "I want you to be the briefing officer for Efcorps."

"But, sir, I wouldn't—"

"That's an order, Commander. If you're so damned concerned about the civies, you talk to them."

"Aye, sir." As he returned to the Situation Room, Rochmon fought hard to suppress a grin. He would indeed talk to the Efcorps, and to representatives from the TriCameral and the

Combined Committees, but he did not think Stonefield would like what he was going to tell them. No, he wouldn't like it at all.

But then, people of Stonefield's rank seemed to have a natural prejudice against telling the truth to civilians. They didn't trust the common citizens much—nor did they give them credit for much intelligence. Rochmon wondered what it really must have been like when civilian leaders actually had control of the military. Those must have been great and wonderful times for civilians and military alike.

"First reports from Matthews are coming in, sir," a tech said, interrupting his thoughts. "All forces appear to have engaged the Ukes."

*   *   *

Missile after missile found its mark before the Ukes rallied and returned fire on Admiral Gilbert's nonrevertor force. At the front of the cone-shaped formation, *McQuay* took the brunt of the initial fire and rocked time and again as explosions ripped into its massive armor.

"Damage Control, sir," a sweaty young captain said as he stepped up to Gilbert. "We've lost three engines, sir, and had to shut down two others. Sections eighty-one through eighty-seven and both rear launch bays have been breached. We have—"

Another explosion shook the deck.

"Go on, Captain," Gilbert said grimly.

"We have moved the fire control line back to section seventy-nine, but I think we're going to lose her, sir."

"How soon, Captain?"

"Three hours at best, sir."

"Very good, Captain. Keep me posted. Mica!"

"Here, sir."

"Order shipout of all nonessential personnel. I want everyone not directly involved with fire, navigation, communications, or power off this ship in one hour. When that's done, inform the *Janet* that she will assist in the final evacuation. Now get to it."

The *McQuay* shuddered and bucked, knocking Mica to the deck. As she pulled herself back up she saw her father lying with a gash across his forehead. But even as she moved toward him, he waved her off. "Shipout, Mica," he said as someone helped him to a sitting position. "Clear this ship."

27

"Two more ships destroyed, Commander, launchship *Quesque* and heavy cruiser *Denora*. *Moro Ree* is still running on reduced power and out of action. Attack flights One through Six are returning for reload."

"How many fighters returning in those flights?"

"Latest count is . . . uh . . . three hundred-twelve, sir."

"Out of seven-twenty? Impossible! Get a recount!"

"That is a recount . . . sir."

Frye shook his head sadly. Four hundred ships? Lost so quickly? Five launchships crippled or destroyed? What had he done wrong?

"New enemy attackers approaching from quadrant seven, sir."

"Trukken? How many defenders do you have left?"

"Two hundred naggers and over ninety timinos of swarm flights. But some of them are coming in now for refueling and rearmament."

"Damn! Tech, what's the count on the new attackers?"

"Looks like about two hundred, sir."

"Trukken," Frye said without hesitation, "the naggers will have to hold while the swarm flights refuel. AOCO, order the fleet to close formation. And tell the returning timinos to split and reload aboard *Nesiniah*, *Hondono*, and *Poul*. I want *High Victory* and *Beamon* prepared to receive flights Seven, Eight, and Nine." Or what's left of them, he thought grimly.

"What about the *Lann*, sir?"

A sudden tremor passed through *Hondono* as it took a hit from the new attackers.

"That's our reserve, AOCO, and we—"

The deck dropped slightly then slammed against his feet. Only the combat straps kept him in his chair. "Close the formation!" he shouted. "Now!" In the back of his mind he knew he might have to use his secret missiles. He only hoped there were enough of them left to do the job.

*   *   *

Dawson was too busy to be relieved after the Ukes ceased their bombardment. As he marshaled the fragments of his forces to prepare for a second attack he was sure would come, he was interrupted by casualty reports, loss counts, damage assessments, and requests for instructions and orders from every part of his command.

"Admiral Gilbert for you, sir!" a voice rang through the babble in the Command Center.

Dawson made his way to the transceiver and was surprised to see Gilbert smiling at him. "Dawson here, sir."

"Well done," Gilbert's fuzzy voice said seconds later. "We are retreating to assist you."

"Where are they now, sir?"

"Their fighters are dispersed, at least momentarily, and ours are chasing them. We'll hold at position alpha-one to try to recover our ships as they come back in. Are you ready for a second attack?"

"Hell, no, Admiral. I lost two-thirds of my firepower, and seventy-five percent of my ships were either knocked out of action or destroyed in the first attack. We've got casualties we haven't even located yet, and—"

"The Ukes got the worst of it, Dawson. You did a fine job—a damn fine job. Anyway, we should be in position in approximately one-five-five minutes. We're a little crippled up, too, but we're on our way."

"Good, sir," Dawson said as he scribbled a note on the pad a captain held in front of him. He couldn't stop giving instructions just because he was talking to Gilbert. "How about Admiral Pajandcan?"

"She is still observing communications silence, and she has to pick up her fighters before she can move her fleet. If you—"

The transceiver went suddenly silent except for the ever-present buzz of static. Just as suddenly an unidentified voice blared through the speakers.

"The *McQuay* just blew! The *McQuay* just blew! Retreat to alpha-one. All ships! Retreat to alpha-one!"

*   *   *

"—weak resistance . . . halo defenses . . . like they're pulling in their fi—"

Even through the crackling static Pajandcan could tell that her pilots felt they were winning this part of the battle. If they could keep up the pressure—at least until the nonrevertors were in place—Reckynop might stand a chance of survival. But what about Gilbert? What had happened to him? The intensity of her concern surprised her.

"—aunchships heavily damaged . . . losing swarm fighters everywhere to . . . aking them in but not launching . . . close and attack! Close and attack!"

Pajandcan decided it was time to break communications silence. She needed to know if Gilbert was still alive. Before she could do anything, a new voice dominated the transceiver.

"Flight Leader Gamma to base! Attention, base! They're turning! They're turning! By damn, the bastards are going to run for it!"

Gamma's voice came in over the open fleet channel, loud and clear and sweet to Pajandcan's ears.

"Confirm that, Gamma," she said as she grabbed the mike.

"Confirmed, Admiral!" Gamma shouted long seconds later. "They're pulling in their fighters and turning away from Matthews and pointing toward home."

*   *   *

Frye stared blankly past the activity around him until his gaze narrowed and focused on the red panel that covered the controls to his final resource. He did not know how many of the massive neutronic devices remained in the Matthews system, but he was prepared to use them all.

Thousands, maybe millions of civilians would die, and Frye knew that once that would have mattered to him. Once his heart would have been wrenched by such a decision. Now there was nothing left of that softness that might have weakened him when he most needed to be strong.

Vinita was gone. Melliman was gone. Marsha was learning to hate him. He could see it in her eyes.

With a quiet sigh of relief Frye released his combat straps and stood up. He was bound to no one now. He was ready and free to devote all his energy to winning this war. Consequently, it was time to unleash the final destruction on Reckynop.

Marsha watched as her father walked calmly to the communications section, took out a small key, and unlocked a narrow red panel.

"May I ask what that is?"

"Yes. In case of defeat," he said, pointing to a small black switch, "flip this switch and Reckynop will become a water planet—of little use to anyone."

Before Marsha could say anything, he moved the switch with a fierceness that surprised her.

From that panel a coded message went out to the remaining neutronic missiles waiting in Matthews system.

*   *   *

At Drautzlab another reciprocal action experiment destroyed half a million credits worth of equipment, and Sjean wondered if they would ever be able to build something that really was a working weapon—much less the Ultimate Weapon.

The floodwaters on Reckynop had risen one hundred fifty meters in less than two days. Forty-nine major coastal cities and uncounted numbers of towns and villages, some as far as five hundred kilometers inland, had disappeared under the deluge. Millions of people had drowned, and millions more were stranded on eleven continents—isolated on high ground, surrounded by water they could not drink, and slowly starving to death.

Even with all the assistance the military could give them, the civil authorities knew that millions more would die before they could be rescued or assisted. Reports of rioting, looting, and mass hysteria were commonplace amid the frantic requests for assistance that overwhelmed every remnant of authority. Whole regions had no authority at all and were totally out of contact with the rest of the world. The grim truth was that Reckynop had barely survived the explosions above the poles—survived at a cost that would take decades to fully evaluate.

Mica sat in the grim meeting with her father and Admirals Dawson and Pajandcan in the temporary government headquarters on Reckynop high above the still-rising waters. It seemed more than a little incredible to her that they were all together.

"We thought we'd lost you then," Pajandcan said looking at Gilbert with more affection than she had felt for anyone in a long, long time.

"The *Janet* just hadn't gotten far enough away before we blew the *McQuay*. We lost half of our communications. But we

229

had to do it then. The Ukes were closing on her and it was *McQuay*'s chance to take some more of them with her into the void."

"Well, you sure scared the hell out of us, Admiral."

Gilbert smiled slightly, but there was no pleasure in his mind. Over twenty-one thousand defenders had died in the battle for Matthews system.

Dawson guessed that two of the Uke neutronic devices had exploded over the northern ice cap, and in addition to the flooding, there was a serious question about whether or not Reckynop's orbit had been altered.

"What about that civilian ship?" Pajandcan asked.

"An Oinaise freighter, piloted by one of our citizens, a *homo communis* named, uh, Benjamin Holybear Teeman. Had some problems with their Gouldrive and tried to come here for help," Dawson said. "We interrogated him and his Oinaise companion—politely, of course. Their story checks out and seems to be quite legitimate."

Gilbert sighed. "Give them what help you can, and get them out of here. And inform Oina. Let's avoid any diplomatic hassle with Oina if we can."

"Any further word from Sutton, sir?"

After a nod from her father, Mica answered Admiral Pajandcan's question. "The Ukes have control of the system, and about half of the major cities on Sutton itself." She paused at the thought of what that meant, but swallowed hard and continued, "But we're still getting reports of heavy resistance by our Planetary Troops and guerrilla action from them and the civies."

"Mari's standing order," Pajandcan said with a shake of her head. "He's a tough old dirtsider."

"We'd all better be as tough as Mari," Gilbert said. "We may have held Charltos out of Matthews, but we haven't even begun to fight the war. Unless I miss my guess, Charltos will attack us somewhere else as quickly as possible."

"A full-scale campaign through the Polar systems?"

"Quite likely, Dawson. Quite likely." Josiah Gilbert would have given almost anything he had at that moment to rush to assist POLFLEET and take some pressure off Mari and Sutton. However, he accepted the fact that there was almost nothing he could do in that direction until the Joint Chiefs could assess the damages from all the engagements. But he was determined to let them know that he wanted to go back to his old command.

The satisfaction of saving Matthews was grim in the face of the long struggle he was sure they all faced. Whatever joy he might have felt was destroyed by the terrible losses Reckynop had suffered. Yet Gilbert felt a sense of pride that could not be destroyed by the blood and death that surrounded him.

They had beaten the Ukes in their first major confrontation—outguessed them and beaten them in ship-to-ship battle. Whatever the cost, the victory itself would do more for Sondak's morale and long-term chances of success than any trillion credits worth of ships and missiles. Now if every citizen of Sondak could take that victory as inspiration, the federation's chances of holding its own in this war would be much improved.

*　　*　　*

"Unavoidably delayed by the hostilities? Is that all the reason the soulless Oinaise gives?"

"Yes, Proctor," Weecs said quietly. "We do know there was a major battle between Sondak and the Central Systems. But the message indicates that their delay is only temporary."

"It is just as well, my lover. The longer it takes them the better. I will soon be proud to bear your guplings."

"But so soon? I thought—"

"As soon as I could," Leri said, curling around him. "Let the humans kill each other, and let the Oinaise die without souls to carry them forward. All I want is you."

"You have me," he said, matching his body to hers. "But soon you will have to deal with the new agriculture chairman from Sondak and provide him with—"

"Hush. Do I have you now or not?" she asked as she curled her body more tightly around him.

"You have me for as long as you want me."

"Good," she whispered as she caught the scent of his growing desire for her. "Later you must send the Oinaise a message telling them we accept the delay."

*　　*　　*

Ayne Wallen stuffed one piece of gorlet into his mouth after another as Xindella talked to Judoff on the transceiver. Ayne's desperate hunger made it difficult to concentrate on what they were saying.

"Do I understand you correctly?" Xindella asked. "You want me to ship him to the Castorians on Juene?"

"That is correct."

"Such an operation would be even more expensive than we first discussed."

"Ten thousand credits in advance, and twenty more when he is delivered. Will that satisfy you?"

"Plus expenses," Xindella added.

There was a long pause. "Plus expenses," Judoff said finally. "How soon can we have him?"

"I do not know, my old friend, but assuredly in the very near future."

"One month, or the contract is void."

"As you wish . . . Marshall Judoff," Xindella said to the empty screen. "As you wish."

None of the conversation meant anything to Ayne. Nothing at all meant anything to him these days except the gorlet and his hate for Xindella.

Rochmon felt a tremendous sense of relief that stayed with him for days after he found out that Mica Gilbert was safe. He was careful not to analyze that feeling too much, but instead just allowed himself the pleasure of it. Despite all the terrible reports from Matthews and Sutton—despite the fact that it looked like it would take a long time for Sondak to respond with the kind of industrial output it would take to win the war—it was difficult for Rochmon to keep a slight smile off his face as he sat across from Admiral Stonefield.

"I just read Captain Gilbert's honor trustee report," Stonefield said solemnly, "and since part of it affects your headquarters, I think you should know what it contains before I take any action."

So that's what's bugging him, Rochmon thought. "Sir, I—"

"Please, Commander. I find this an onerous chore at best. Allow me to finish. Captain Gilbert, in a rather well-reasoned argument, suggests that your chief cryptographer's loyalty is subject to question."

Rochmon almost laughed. "Bock? I don't believe it, sir. Not for one minute."

"At this stage, Commander, it does not matter what you believe. What matters is that this Jecti-verdi-fiaad . . ."

"Call her Bock, sir. It's easier."

"Very well. What matters is that this Bock cannot be allowed to continue in her present position until we ascertain the validity of Captain Gilbert's assumptions."

"Guilty until proven innocent," Rochmon said sarcastically.

What in the blazing novas did Mica hope to accomplish by accusing Bock? It didn't make any sense.

"That's the law, Hew. You know that as well as I do."

Suddenly Rochmon's warm feelings for Mica were washed away in a cold wave of anger. Yet even as he rejected the very idea that Bock might be a traitor, he knew Mica would not have made her assumptions without evidence.

The conflict churned in his mind as Stonefield reviewed the security procedures they would have to follow . And in a quiet corner of his mind, a lonely voice screamed in frustration.

*   *   *

"But you abandoned them!" The tears ran freely down Marsha's face and she didn't care. "Wasn't there some way, any way we could have saved them?"

"No," Frye said coldly. The defeat angered him enough without having to put up with this whining from his own daughter. "In a situation like that you take what you can and retreat. If we had stayed, we would have lost ten times as many as we might have picked up."

"I'll bet Mother is turning over in her grave."

Frye's anger erupted into rage. "Shut up! Shut up! Just shut up and get out of here!"

Marsha was stunned into silent retreat. As she closed the door to his office, her tears flowed even faster. She had lost her mother without knowing why. She had lost Lucky because of a stupid promise—and somewhere, somehow, years before, she had lost her father. Whatever hope she might have had of getting him back was gone now.

After she left, Frye turned slowly back to his summary of the battle. As meticulously as he could, he had recorded the essential data for the Bridgeforce, but beyond the events and statistics lay a patch of space littered with the wasted lives of the people he had led to destruction.

Frye felt no sadness, no remorse, no sorrow for them—nor any need to feel such emotions. They had died in a good cause, as they had been willing to die.

But behind them lay the ghostly image of Vinita—an image colored by the sense of joy she had felt when he told her they would finally get their revenge. It was her image that hung in the back of his mind and forced him to reevaluate what had happened.

His most critical mistake had been in underestimating the

personnel and equipment costs. He would not make that mistake the next time.

The next time he would match Sondak body for body and ship for ship on every front. The next time he would be prepared to sacrifice whatever it took to overwhelm them. The next time he would carry Vinita's image with him as he led the U.C.S. to total victory.

Mel White

About the Author

WARREN NORWOOD is the author of the highly popular series, THE WINDHOVER TAPES, and also THE SEREN CENACLES, written with Ralph Mylius. He was a nominee for the John W. Campbell Award as one of the best new writers of 1982. With a delighted grin he told friends, "It was an honor to have been nominated, but it was perhaps an even more singular recognition of my writing ability to have placed last in the balloting behind *No Award*."

Warren is a Texan who recently moved to Willard, Missouri, where he says, "They have all four seasons—in order—something I always felt Texas was missing. But don't get me wrong. I love Texas and will always consider it home. However, I needed to get away for awhile so I could appreciate Texas more."

In addition to writing, Warren has a fanatical interest in photographing wildflowers and is—by his own definition—"a pseudo-botantist who knows just enough to bore the socks off anyone who shows the slightest interest in my photographs."

MIDWAY BETWEEN is the first book in his new series, THE DOUBLE SPIRAL WAR.

Coming in Spring 1985 . . .

THE DOUBLE-SPIRAL WAR
VOLUME TWO

POLAR
FLEET

By Warren Norwood

Having lost the offensive against the Matthews system, the UCS begins a war of attrition against Sondak. Meanwhile, the three major alien forces in the galaxy move toward a neutral alliance against the warring human factions . . . and a non-allied Oinaise broker holds the future in his hands when he comes into the possession of a prototype of the Ultimate Weapon.

Read POLAR FLEET, on sale in Spring, 1985 wherever Bantam paperbacks are sold.

OUT OF THIS WORLD!

That's the only way to describe Bantam's great series of science fiction classics. These space-age thrillers are filled with terror, fancy and adventure and written by America's most renowned writers of science fiction. Welcome to outer space and have a good trip!

THE EPIC CONCLUSION TO
THE MAJIPOOR TRILOGY

VALENTINE PONTIFEX

by Robert Silverberg

The majestic trilogy begun in LORD VALENTINE'S CASTLE and MAJIPOOR CHRONICLES concludes with this towering novel. Majipoor has seen unabated peace for fourteen thousand years. But now the native Metamorph race has unleashed a deadly plague on the planet and a war of revenge is begun. Aided by Hissune, the young man, now a brilliant military strategist, Lord Valentine must gather his forces in an attempt to save all the peoples of Majipoor.

An unforgettable end to a science fiction masterpiece.

Buy VALENTINE PONTIFEX, on sale October 15, 1984, and all the works of Robert Silverberg, available wherever Bantam paperbacks are sold or use the handy coupon below for ordering:

☐ LORD VALENTINE'S CASTLE (23063-8 • $3.50)
☐ MAJIPOOR CHRONICLES (22928-1 • $3.50)
☐ VALENTINE PONTIFEX (24494-9 • $3.95)
☐ LORD OF DARKNESS (24362-4 • $3.95)
☐ TOWER OF GLASS (23589-3 • $2.95)
☐ DOWNWARD TO THE EARTH (24043-9 • $2.50)
☐ DYING INSIDE (24018-8 • $2.50)
☐ BORN WITH THE DEAD (24103-6 • $2.75)

SPECIAL MONEY SAVING OFFER

Now you can have an up-to-date listing of Bantam's hundreds of titles plus take advantage of our unique and exciting bonus book offer. A special offer which gives you the opportunity to purchase a Bantam book for only 50¢. Here's how!

By ordering any five books at the regular price per order, you can also choose any other single book listed (up to a $4.95 value) for just 50¢. Some restrictions do apply, but for further details why not send for Bantam's listing of titles today!

Just send us your name and address plus 50¢ to defray the postage and handling costs.

BANTAM BOOKS, INC.
Dept. FC, 414 East Golf Road, Des Plaines, Ill 60016

Mr./Mrs./Miss/Ms. _____
(please print)

Address _____

City_____ State_____ Zip_____

FC—3/84